GETTING EVEN
WHAT GOES AROUND IN ALASKA
COMES AROUND IN FLORIDA

Ron Walden

Alaskan True to Life Crime Writer

ISBN 978-1-95-726324-3
eISBN: 978-1-5-726325-0
Library of Congress Catalog Card Number: 2017937566

Manufactured in the United States of America.

Dedicated

to

Betty

Acknowledgements

This book was written during a trying time in my life. I take this opportunity to thank all my loving family for the support they have given me. Without them I would still be in my dark place. I also thank all my wonderful coffee table friends for helping me keep my life together and maintain my sanity during this time. There is no way to thank you enough. May God bless each of you.

I thank the wonderful people of Homer, Alaska for allowing me to use your town as the setting for this new book.

A special thanks is given to Brad Gamble for allowing me to use his restaurant as one of the places mentioned in this book. I have been stopping at the Duncan House for many years and never been disappointed. Wonderful people and wonderful food.

Chapter 1

It had been an arduous flight across the United States from South Florida to Seattle. His Cessna 208 Caravan, had a cruise speed of 190 knots, indicated air speed, but flying west into the prevailing wind lowered the ground speed considerably. The Caravan is a large, single engine, turbo-prop, ten passenger aircraft. Galen Mason had bought this one new from Cessna about a year ago. It was equipped with all the latest electronic devices and navigation aids. Mason enjoyed flying it and had built up more than 200 hours in the plane since purchasing it in Wichita, Kansas. The plane was painted red over white with a black accent stripe, a full belly baggage pod in which Mason had installed a large fuel bladder to accommodate long range flights. Cessna had numbered the plane N2098P. Galen Mason was the only passenger/pilot aboard 98 Papa on a flight he had planned for nearly five years.

For ten years Galen had been the accountant for a small corporation in South Florida, Atlantic Bluefin Processors. In the beginning, he had ignored the fact that this small fish packing company could not possibly generate this kind of cash flow legitimately, but as time went on he accepted it as a fact of life for which he was being paid a great deal of money. He even accepted the fact that some of the cash he received was never recorded and he paid no taxes on those funds.

Over time Mason became one of the inner-circle among management personnel at Bluefin Processors. He became aware of the source of the ample cash flow for which he was responsible. The company fishing boats were doing well on the fishing grounds, but even better by meeting drug runners from Venezuela and Columbia on the open ocean. Drugs were being loaded into the fish holds where they were packed into fish carcasses and transported back into the U.S. and distributed from the South Florida fish packing plant.

The man in charge of the fish packing plant was a Cuban national, Orlando Perez. A short man with a heavy accent and a bad temper, Perez was a very good business manager and could have made a success of Bluefin Processors without the drug business, but the drug business was more lucrative than the fish sales. Once Perez found Galen Mason to be trusted with knowledge of the inner workings of the business he gave the accountant a great deal of responsibility and authority. Mason was tasked with transporting large sums of cash to nearby island nations for deposit in off-shore accounts. The company owned a small, twin engine Beechcraft for Mason to use when flying to the islands; avoiding customs officials and Coast Guard boats and landing at private airstrips on the islands.

Perez liked Mason, and on the anniversary of his fifth year awarded the bookkeeper a 100 percent increase in his wages. The size of the raise started him thinking he could get even more and began a systematic syphoning of one percent of all totals being deposited in island banks. He covered the losses by entering false expenses in his journals that has been accepted by his boss.

When his bank balances began to mount into astronomical figures he started devising a plan to exit his employment and disappear forever. Now, five years later, he was executing his plan. He knew it would be dangerous, and Perez would never let him leave alive so he had made a plan to make Perez believe he had died. It was risky, but it would work (he hoped).

He pointed the Cessna westward in a random path toward California, stopping twice to fuel up and be seen. His second fueling stop was in southern Colorado. Now it was time to begin his true route. His first layover was to be Santa Barbara, California where he needed to find a sign-making shop. He had used the Internet to find what he needed. He had talked with the shop owner and sent him designs of what he needed via the Internet. The shop owner said it would be ready when he arrived.

Mason overnighted in Santa Barbara and picked up his order early the next morning and returned to the airport transient parking area where his Caravan was parked. It was warm and there were few other people on the ramp. Mason took the vinyl lettering out of the bag along with a plastic spatula and a clean rag. Taking a stool from the baggage pod he was able to reach the rear of the fuselage and attach the signage over the last two numbers of his identification designation. It took less than an hour in the sunshine to change the aircraft designation from 89P to 87F. Once done he performed a preflight check and climbed aboard. When airborne he filed a flight plan to Seattle using his new numbers as identification. In Seattle, Boeing Field, he took on fuel and filled both his wing tanks and the fuel bladder in the baggage pod under the fuselage. He filed another flight plan to Ketchikan, Alaska and on to Seward, Alaska where he would spend the night.

From Seward Mason flew around the outer side of the Kenai Peninsula, avoiding any populated areas, and made his way to the island of Kodiak where he parked the airplane and checked into a nearby Best Western Hotel for the night. About midnight he walked to the airport in the dusky light. It was warmer than he had anticipated, making his task much easier than expected. It took him only twenty minutes to remove the plastic decals and return the aircraft number to its original designation. He doubted the tower would notice his reported number was different than the one on the fuselage. Once done with the removal he returned to the hotel.

He arose early the following morning, showered, shaved and walked to the dining room for a fantastic omelet and orange juice for breakfast. It was another bright and sunny day with scattered clouds above. He walked to the transient parking area to do a preflight check. Climbing into the pilot seat he sat, thinking about the day ahead. Today Galen Mason would die in an airplane crash.

"Here we go," he said to himself as he started the engine.

"Kodiak tower, Cessna 2087 Foxtrot in position for takeoff, northbound."

"Roger, 87 Foxtrot, no other local traffic at this time. Have a nice flight."

As he taxied onto the runway and lined up on the center line he became apprehensive. The success or failure of his whole plan would play out in the next hour. He added power to the jet engine and felt the plane surge forward rolling straight down the center of the wide runway. He was airborne and climbing, raising the flaps, reducing power and setting the prop for cruise. He climbed to 7,500 feet and leveled off, keeping away from the shore and following the shoreline toward Anchorage. Things went smoothly for nearly an hour. As he winged his way past Chinitna Bay he put his plan into motion.

"Anchorage Center, Cessna 2087 Foxtrot, I am having engine problem and . . . ing . . . titude . . . down. Losing control. I . . . ." He turned off the radio and transponder, diving the craft toward the water. At 50 feet he leveled off and turned southeast toward the town of Homer on the other side of Cook Inlet. Once half way across the Inlet he began to climb to 2,500 feet and leveled off.

There is no tower in Homer but he reported entering the airspace and his intentions to land there, but was using the designator 2098Papa. He had prearranged a hangar rental prior to setting off from Florida.

It was still early in the day when he finished backing the Caravan into the hangar and closed the door. He changed clothing while inside the hangar, now dressing in a flannel shirt and jeans. His first plan had been to buy hiking boots but changed his mind and opted for running shoes instead. He emerged from the hangar with a small pack on his back and a light jacket under his arm. He now had to find a place to live. His new name, Dan Hanson, was printed on a fake identification in his wallet. Next week he would need to apply for an Alaska Drivers License and Identification Card. Meanwhile he would try not to look like a tourist as he hiked along the path to the end of the Homer Spit and the Homer Boat Harbor.

Steve Meadows was communicating with 2087F when it issued the distress call. Steve had been an air traffic controller all his adult life. It was his career while he was in the military and he continued it with the FAA when he mustered out. In his career with the FAA he had handled hundreds of distress calls; most were inexperienced pilots unable to find the airport. Some were true emergencies and this call from 87F sounded like one of those. He notified his supervisor and called the Coast Guard to alert them to a possible search.

A Coast Guard C-130 was practicing instrument approaches at the Kenai Airport when they received the call. The crew immediately turned the Hercules toward the area of Chinitna Bay about 125 miles southwest of Kenai. Within minutes they were searching the area where Air Traffic Control said they had lost contact with the airplane.

"ATC, Coast Guard Rescue. Do you have a description of the missing aircraft?"

"Affirmative, Rescue. Our records indicate the aircraft is a Cessna 208, red over white, en route from Kodiak to Anchorage. The last transmission we had indicated he was having some sort of mechanical trouble and his radio transmission was broken up. We had him directly in front of Chinitna Bay when his transponder went off the air. This usually means he is in the water. The records indicate the owner is from Santa Barbara, California. Our records indicate he is a high time pilot with an instrument rating and Air Transport Rating."

"Thank you, Center. We are in the area and searching."

The Coast Guard pilot descended to 1,000 feet where the observers inside the rescue plane could see any debris floating in the water. A search grid was established and the crew scanned the surface for any sign of the missing aircraft. The days were long now and the search could go on for another several hours without losing daylight.

Just over an hour later they were joined in the search by a National Guard Rescue helicopter. The two pilots were in constant contact with each other. The search went on until dusk, and the Blackhawk helicopter returned to Anchorage low on fuel. The C-130 continued to search until they, too, were forced to return to Kodiak for fuel and await daylight to continue.

Chapter 2

Dan Hanson had spent the night in the hangar, sleeping on a cot he had brought with him in the airplane. He was awakened early by the sound of an airplane taxiing past his hangar on its way to the runway with a payload of sightseers. The café at the airport looked clean and had a good crowd each time he had walked passed it so he decided to eat breakfast there.

He sat alone at a small table when a tall, thin, acne-faced, young man wearing an apron tied around his waist came to take his order. The young waiter dropped a menu on the table.

"Want some coffee?" he asked politely.

"Yes, and a small orange juice, please," Hanson replied, scanning the menu.

Moments later the young man returned with a steaming mug of coffee and a frosty glass of orange juice. "Is that you in the hangar on the far end? The one with the Caravan inside?" he asked.

Dan Hanson was concerned with the question and sipped the steaming coffee before answering. "Yes, I'm thinking about starting a small business here in Homer. I have never been to Alaska before and picked Homer because I don't want to live in another large city."

"Homer is a good place to live. I was born here. My dad owns the café. What kind of business are you looking to start?" asked The lad. "A flying business with the Caravan?"

Hanson chuckled, "No, I'm not a commercial operator, just a private pilot." He sipped his coffee again. "I thought I might start some kind of consulting business. You know, helping people invest for retirement and helping businesses increase profits through better business practices." Dan now tried the orange juice, it was fresh-squeezed and delicious. "It's what I do for a living."

"Not many folks around here have a lot of cash to invest, but most of the businesses could use some help with management, including my dad."

The young man took a pad from his apron and smiled, "Can I get you some breakfast?"

"Yes, you can. I'm famished. Give me the hamburger steak, three eggs, hash-browns and whole wheat toast."

"Coming right up," said the lad as he turned and walked away.

Hanson was perusing a newspaper he had taken from an empty table when the boy returned with his order.

"Have you heard there is an airplane missing on the other side of the Inlet?"

"No. What happened?" asked Dan in a curious tone.

"I don't know for sure, but one of the FAA guys from the other side of the runway said the Coast Guard searched half the night and were out early this morning looking for an airplane supposedly down in the Inlet near Chinitna Bay. The last he had heard they were still looking, but hadn't found any debris or anything. I guess the National Guard helicopter was out there, too."

"That's too bad. I hope they find them and everyone is OK."

"Me, too," said the young waiter, "Can I get you anything else right now?"

"No, thank you. This will be fine. It looks wonderful."

There had been no news of the missing plane in the paper he had read, but personal messenger in the form of a high school age waiter had delivered the news he was looking for.

When Dan had finished his breakfast the boy returned and asked, "How was it? Did you get enough?"

"Plenty thank you." Dan wiped the remains of his breakfast from his chin and hands, and asked, "Is there somewhere nearby to rent a car?"

"Dad has an old truck he loans to pilots sometimes. I'll ask him to come out and talk to you about it. He has one more order to finish and he'll come see you." The boy gathered the plates and glasses and returned to the kitchen.

Minutes later a middle-aged man wearing another soiled apron around his waist came to the table. He wiped his hands on a towel hanging from his shoulder and stuck out his hand.

"Hi there, I'm Bill Peyton. I own the café. My son said you were looking for a car."

Shaking the cook's hand he replied, "Dan Hanson. I just got to town yesterday and I would like to rent a car for a few days. I am going to look for office space here in town. If I find it I will also have to find a place to live and buy a car. But, my first order of business is to find a suitable office space for my consulting business. You wouldn't happen to know of one, would you?"

"Most of the office space in Homer is old and kind of dingy, but Anatoly Rivkin just built a small row of offices just past the Carrs Store on the other side of the lake. You can't miss it. Just follow the road through the signal light and it will be on the right just past the bank and the supermarket. As to using my old truck, it's right by the front door, the old Chevy. No charge, just fill the tank when you bring it back."

"Thank you Bill, that is very kind of you."

"Us pilots have to stick together, right?" Bill Peyton dropped a set of keys on the table and walked back toward the kitchen.

"If all the people in Homer are as friendly as Bill Peyton and his son I'm going to like it here," thought Hanson. He inspected the old pickup and found it to be in good shape. He started the truck and followed the directions he had been given to the new suite of offices on the main drive into town. The building was almost new with two of the six offices rented and new signs in the window. One was a tax accountant, the other a real estate office. It was early and nothing was open, but Dan peered through the window of one of the empty offices. It looked to be adequate for his needs. The small sign in the lower corner of the front window gave a phone number for Anatoly Rivkin. Checking the time Dan decided to wait an hour before making the call.

He used the time to drive around the town and acquaint himself with the area. Most of the town was old, but neatly kept. He was unable to separate the residents from the tourists as they walked on the streets. For a small town, there were a large number of people out walking in the morning sunshine. Hanson had a good feeling about the town and thought his decision to pick Homer as his new home was a good choice.

In the center of town he decided to take a tour of the East End Road instead of returning directly to the route he had just taken into town. A city map he had seen indicated there was another route back to the airport and he wanted to explore it. This route was lined with beautiful homes on the ocean bluff side of the road and boat storage yards on the other side for nearly the entire length of the drive back to the airport café. He drove the truck to his hangar and went inside to call Anatoly Rivkin and inquire about the office space. Rivkin agreed to meet him at the building in a half hour.

Rivkin appeared to be about 70 years old and walked with a cane. He smoked a pipe and carried a perpetual smile. "I'm Anatoly. Are you Mr. Hanson?"

"Yes sir," Dan held out his hand to shake with Rivkin. "Call me Dan."

Taking a large string of keys from his pocket he unlocked one of the office doors. "Come inside, Mr. Hanson. Let's see if this will suit your needs."

The space was larger than Dan had expected. There was an ample waiting room where a receptionist or secretary could be accommodated. Down a short hallway there was a restroom and a small lunch room with a sink, refrigerator, a small table and four chairs. The lighting was ample and modern. Across the hallway was a large open office with no furnishings.

"I will rent this space to you, with or without furnishings. I find most folks have their own ideas about how they want the office to look. Their own personality, if you will."

"I think I would like to furnish it myself, thank you Mr. Rivkin. What is the rate for this unit?"

The price was agreed upon and Rivkin was paid in cash for a six month lease, including utilities. Anatoly was happy and said he would bring the lease agreement and a receipt to the office within two days.

"Is there somewhere to buy office equipment and furnishings here in Homer?" asked Dan. "And I will need to buy a vehicle, new I think."

"We have an office supply store here, but they will probably have to order what you need in the way of furniture. If you want to buy a new car you will have to go to Kenai or Soldotna, about 90 miles north." I am going to Soldotna this afternoon if you want to ride up there with me," informed Anatoly.

"Thank you, I would like that. I will be at the hangar on the airport grounds and here is my cell phone number." Dan gave the older man his card.

"I'll be there around one o'clock. I have a two-thirty p.m. doctor appointment in Soldotna." Anatoly reached into his windbreaker pocket and came out with a set of keys for the office door. "You will be needing these," he said.

On the ride to Soldotna Dan learned Anatoly had been a commercial fisherman and was injured when equipment on his boat failed and a steel rod struck him on his left hip. It took him more than a year to walk again. Because of his injuries, he was forced to stop commercial fishing. He sued the manufacturer of the broken hydraulic equipment and was awarded a large settlement. He used part of the settlement money to build the office building as an income.

Interestingly, Anatoly had not asked about Dan's past or what kind of business he was to open. Anatoly dropped him at the Chrysler dealership in Soldotna where he purchased a new Jeep Cherokee, dark green and well equipped. For being an SUV the new vehicle was rather plush. It had all the electronic devises available and Dan used the ninety mile drive to familiarize himself with the operation of most of the gadgets in the new car.

It was late afternoon when he returned to the hangar. He was exiting his new car when a small twin engine aircraft attempted to land on the main runway. Dan was watching with curiosity when something went horribly wrong with the landing. It hit the pavement hard and bounced back into the air, nose high. The pilot added full power attempting to regain control, but the plane stalled and rolled to the right. The nose went down as the right wing struck a runway light and the little twin began to cartwheel. Fuel began to spill from the broken wing, which was ignited by sparks from the skidding aircraft. The scene erupted into a flaming inferno.

Dan was shocked at what he had just witnessed. Jumping back into his new Jeep he sped to the scene, at least as close as the fireball would allow. He tried to approach the burning aircraft, but was turned back by the intense heat. As he stepped back, helpless, he heard the sirens of approaching fire and police. The firemen motioned for him to step away from the scene as they prepared to douse the flaming horror scene. When the flames had been controlled the rescue personnel hurried to extract the victims from the wreckage. Police asked Dan to stay back while the frantic rescue was progressing.

Standing near his new car he could see the victims as they were taken from the wreckage. There were four in all. Emergency medical personnel worked quickly to assess the injured. Dan heard one medic tell his captain there were one fatality and three severely burned victims. He also said the three survivors needed to be transported immediately to Anchorage for treatment.

Fire Department Captain Owen Sutton rubbed his chin saying, "I'll order a medevac flight from Kenai, but we need them quicker than that." He was picking up his radio to call dispatch when Dan interrupted.

"Captain, I think I can help you here. Give me one man to take the seats out of my Caravan and I'll fly these folks to Anchorage. We'll worry about cost and liability later."

"Where is your airplane?" asked the Captain.

"In a rented hangar; the last one at the end of the row. I can be ready to fly in five minutes if I can get someone to help me take the seats out of the plane."

Sutton thought about it for nearly a second before deciding. "Evans," he shouted to one of the firefighters, "go with this man and give him a hand. We'll get the patients ready to fly."

"Yes sir," came the quick reply. Evans took a seat in the Jeep and Dan quickly drove to the hangar. He opened the large overhead door and the two men entered to begin removing the seats from the cabin area, leaving three for firefighter/medics to strap into during takeoff and landing. Dan showed Evans how to operate the electric tow bar attached to the nose wheel of the plane. Once it was disconnected with the Caravan outside, Dan started the engine. Evans pushed the button to close the hangar door and climbed into the rear of the plane as Dan added power to taxi to the crash site on the runway.

Evans instructed the other medics to load the patients, on metal litters, into the plane. When done Evans and two other medics boarded to tend the victims.

Dan had no time to watch the medic do their work, but climbed to 2,500 feet and leveled off for the flight to Anchorage International Airport where Captain Sutton had ordered ambulances to be waiting.

Once he reported to Anchorage Traffic Control he was given a priority position for landing and taxiing to a commercial hangar on the east end of the runway. Medics wasted no time loading the burn victims and taking them to a hospital. Two of the medics stayed with the patients, but Evans made the return flight to Homer.

Chapter 3

Captain Sutton had been notified and was waiting at the hangar when Dan and firefighter Evans returned. The three men wrangled the big plane back into the hangar with the aid of the electric tow bar. Dan closed the door and the three men met in a corner of the hangar where there was a table and a small refrigerator filled with Cokes and 7-Up.

Sutton was the first to report when they sat down. "We lost one more at the hospital," he said solemnly, "but the other two are in fair condition and will be flown to Seattle to the burn center. We lost one, but you probably saved the lives of the other two. I would like to thank you for what you did, but I don't even know your name."

Putting out his hand to shake the hand of the captain, "I'm Dan Hanson."

"Pleased to meet you Dan, sorry we haven't met before. I'm Owen Sutton with the Homer fire department."

"Actually, I've only been in town a couple of days. I've rented an office space on the other side of the lake. I hope to start a consulting business. I was happy to be able to help out today. Sorry about the two you lost, tragic. I saw the whole thing happen. I was just coming back to the hangar and heard the plane coming in. I turned just in time to see the crash. I'm surprised anyone survived. You fellas didn't lose any time getting here. Good job."

"The FAA boys called it in and we were just finishing a training meeting when the call came. We were suited up and ready to go."

"You've seen my airplane, and if I can be of any use to you in the future, please keep me in mind. I want to be a part of this community and I'll help in any way I possibly can."

"I certainly will, Dan," said Captain Sutton. You sure earned your stripes today. The entire community of Homer owes you. I'll try to figure out some way to pay you for the trip."

"I was only too happy to help. Call on me anytime."

"I have talked with the FAA guys and they say the pilot is a tourist from Washington state and not familiar with our airport. They don't know for sure, but think he was tired from a long flight and just misjudged the landing. You saw the crash, it was horrific."

"I guess those things happen. I've never witnessed a plane crash before and I hope this is the last one I ever see. I feel sorry for those poor people."

"Well, I have to go home. My wife will be sending out a search party for me." The captain stood to leave when he turned to the other firefighter, "Come on Evans. I'll give you a ride to the station." Turning back to Dan before exiting he said, "Come by the station any time. I'll introduce you to the fire chief and the police chief. I think the NTSB crew will be here in the morning and will possibly want to get a statement from you." He waved as he went out the small door in the side of the hangar.

Dan spent the weekend becoming familiar with the Homer area. He walked into almost every shop on the Homer Spit, a lot of shops. It amazed him at the number of tourists in the shops buying t-shirts and souvenirs. Busy, too, were the flightseeing businesses as well as the charter fishing offices near the Homer Small Boat Harbor.

Hanson drove to the end of the East End Road more than twenty miles from the downtown area. Two small villages were located near the end of the road at the head of Kachemak Bay. Both settlements were occupied by, primarily Russian Orthodox members, one by new believers and one by old believers; a definite distinction in cultures.

He introduced himself to most of the storekeepers and business owners in the small downtown commercial district and made inquiries as to how to advertise for a receptionist for the office. Office furnishings had already been ordered and would begin to arrive on Monday afternoon. He was surprised at how many of the locals had heard about his mercy flight and thanked him for his community spirit. Dan Hanson was beginning to like the town of Homer.

On Monday morning, he opened the office and cleaned the office carpet with a small vacuum cleaner he had purchased along with other cleaning supplies for the office. He had almost finished the chore when a truck backed up to the front door. The young driver hopped out and asked if he had ordered two four-drawer file cabinets. Hanson said he had and helped the driver move the boxes into the office and remove the crates before sliding the cabinets into position against a wall that would be behind the receptionist's desk.

Minutes later the telephone installer came to put in the new phone system. Dan had just finished giving the phone man instructions when a tall, gorgeous, blond wearing a very short skirt came into the office.

"Hello, are you Mr. Hanson?" she asked politely.

"Yes, what can I do for you?"

"How do you do, my name is Alma Petersen. I was told by a business owner friend of mine you are looking for a receptionist for your new office. If that's true I would like to apply for the position."

"Have you ever managed an office in the past?"

"Yes, I have. I once managed an office for a computer company in Seattle. They were taken over by Microsoft. My services were no longer needed and I decided to change location. That was two years ago. I came to Homer and was hired by a real estate firm. There were five agents working out of the office, each had a secretary whom I had in my charge. I did all the office management and the court research."

"It sounds as if you have the kind of experience I need here, but I have to ask, why did you leave the real estate office?"

"The company manager and I had a disagreement about my duties. He thought full time employment meant day and night. I explained I only worked in the front office and went home alone at five. He decided he didn't need me any longer."

Dan liked her honesty and thought she warranted a further check. "Do you have a resume with you?" he asked.

She handed him a large manila envelope she had in her left hand. "If it makes any difference, I was given your name by Owen Sutton. He is a captain with the Homer Fire Department."

"Thank you, Ms. Petersen. Can you come back in the morning, say around ten? I'll look at your resume and determine if you're the one I am looking to hire for the office." Dan had been impressed with her honesty, which he needed to check out, and swayed in his thoughts by her appearance and demeanor. It would be difficult to ignore her beauty.

"I'll stop by in the morning, Mr. Hanson. Thank you for considering me. May I ask, what kind of consulting are you planning to do in this office?" She asked a very pertinent question.

"Of course. I plan to specialize in financial and business management consulting. We will determine how to make a business more successful and efficient. My field is accounting and business management. Homer is a small community, but I intend to acquire clients from all over the state of Alaska. I appreciate the honesty of your question and I assure you I have no interest in acquiring clients with doubtful practices. I want only reputable clients. I'll see you tomorrow. Thank you for coming in. If your resume checks out you will have saved me a great deal of interview time."

The phone installer finished with his installation, Dan signed the work order. The phone man was gathering the last of his tools to leave when Owen Sutton came into the office.

"Owen," greeted Dan, "good to have you drop by. I met a friend of yours this morning."

Sutton entered the office, looked around, noting there was nowhere to sit. He nodded, "That would be Alma Petersen. I've known her quite a while and she's a very nice person. She's not bad looking either. I thought you might want someone to dress up the office."

"I'll have to check out her resume, but she appears to be perfect for the position. I am curious about one thing, though."

"What would that be?"

"She didn't ask about salary," said Dan in a questioning tone. "Usually that's the first thing an applicant wants to know."

Sutton chuckled, "That would be Alma. I've known her since she came to Homer. She's pretty easy to notice. We needed a girl in the office when she came. It was advertised in the paper. She interviewed, but said it wasn't her kind of work. I knew the realty office was looking for an office manager and sent her to see Dalton Pence. He had a reputation with the ladies. He hired her and she worked for him for about a year and a half. One day she just quit. No one knew why, but I suspect Dalton was hitting on her." Sutton chuckled again, "I think she's a very smart lady. I checked out her resume when she applied at our office and it all looked good, but don't let me influence the issue. I just like the lady and admire her spunk."

As they talked, another van backed to the front door leading Dan to comment. "It looks like we may have a place to sit." Two young men came through the door and asked for Dan. They showed him an invoice and asked where he wanted the items.

Owen Sutton saw Dan was about to become busy and excused himself. "I'll call you later for lunch," he shouted as he left the new office.

As Sutton was exiting the office Dan called after him, "Hey, Owen, come back a second."

"Yeah, what is it, Dan?"

"I just wanted to ask if they found the missing airplane."

"It's funny you should ask. The answer is yes and no. I received the report this morning. They called off the search after two days with no results. The FAA checked out the numbers on the plane and found it was registered to a lawyer in Santa Barbara, California and that the plane is still parked at the airport. The FAA concluded it was all a hoax. See you later," he said, exiting for a second time.

It took nearly an hour to place the furniture properly in the two offices. The chair for the receptionist was identical to the one Dan had ordered for his own use. The offices were taking shape and once the supplies and desk items were delivered he could call this a place of business. With the phone system working it was possible to use his computer where he looked up the number for a sign company to order an appropriate identity for his front window.

While waiting for the last order of office supplies to be delivered he fired up his computer and began to research the companies listed on the resume submitted by Alma Petersen. The efficiency of the Microsoft office was amazing. Within minutes of contact he had a printout of, not only Alma's non-history at the company, but a complete work history and list of evaluations while employed by the former owner of the business. Her credentials not only checked out, but were much better than the sketchy history she had related.

Dan picked up the new phone and dialed the number listed on the cover of the resume. There was an answer on the second ring.

"Alma Petersen," was the pleasant greeting.

"Alma, this is Dan Hanson. I've checked out your resume and everything looks good to me. You also have a personal recommendation from Owen Sutton. I was wondering, how soon could you come to help set up the office?"

"I can come in this afternoon, if you need me." There was a smile in her voice.

"The final delivery of office supplies should be here early this afternoon. If you can come in around two we can discuss salary and hours as well as duties. You might want to wear some jeans or something for working in the office today. We don't have any clients coming in, therefore, you should dress to be comfortable while arranging the office."

Dan came back from lunch and was busy in his little back office when the sporty little red Toyota parked near the front door. She was wearing a cotton shirt, blue jeans and boots and carried a large leather purse, which she placed on the desktop of the new front office.

"I like the reports I had from your previous employers. I think you will make a very good office manager here. I can start you at $24.00 an hour, if that's satisfactory with you. I may be able to increase that amount depending on your skills and my ability to generate new business. Will that be enough to get you to come on board?" Later he would confirm her health insurance and vacations. She happily agreed to the terms and set about arranging the desk, chairs, cabinets and computer screens. The final delivery of pencils, staplers, file folders and other office minutia were signed for and left in the middle of the outer office floor for her to stow in their proper place. She was cheerful and efficient, making Dan feel he had made a good decision.

Chapter 4

It was late in the afternoon when a middle-aged man with a bald head and wearing plastic rim glasses entered the office. He was carrying a large envelope. The man stopped inside the door and looked around the new office.

"May I help you with something?" asked the new receptionist.

"Yes, I would like to see Mr. Dan Hanson, if he's in."

"May I tell him who is asking for him?"

"Lou Cantor, Homer City Manager," he replied.

Alma nodded and turned toward Dan's new office to inform him of his first visitor.

"Send him back, Alma."

She led him down the short hallway to the office at the rear of the rented unit. "Mr. Hanson, this is Mr. Cantor, Homer City Manager."

Cantor entered and shook the outstretched hand of Dan Hanson. "Have a seat, Mr. Cantor. We're only beginning to get the office set up and things are in some disarray. In fact you are on my list of things to do. I will have to come to city hall to apply for a business license."

"Ask the city clerk to bring you to my office and I'll be happy to assist you as much as possible, but that isn't the reason I'm here to see you today. I came to thank you for your assistance at the airport last Friday. Owen Sutton explained how you volunteered to fly the injured crash victims to Anchorage and probably saved two lives in the process. As the City representative I want to express my gratitude for your selfless act." Cantor held out the large manila envelope he had been carrying. "I have here a letter of appreciation from the City and a check for one thousand dollars to offset some of your expenses incurred by the flight. It may not cover all your costs, but it is all the City will recover from the insurance companies. The point is that we, the City of Homer, thank you for your quick actions in response to the crash. The two survivors have been flown to the burn center in Seattle and both are expected to live, thanks to you."

"I wasn't expecting compensation, Mr. Cantor, but I thank you and your city. If there is any way I can be of help to the City, please feel free to call on me. I want to be a part of this community." Dan took the letter from the envelope and read the short citation. "Thank you again for the kind words. I'll have this letter framed and hang it on my new office wall."

"Sutton said you weren't a commercial pilot and couldn't fly for a fee, but I hope I can convince you to acquire your commercial rating in case we have need of your services in the future. There are several commercial operators in the city, but this time of year they are usually booked up with their own business and not available in case of emergencies like the one on Friday."

"I'll consider it, Mr. Cantor. Thank you for the letter and the check. I am available for you any time and I'll consider getting my commercial ticket."

Lou Cantor had been gone from the office for about a half hour when Hanson called Alma Petersen to come to his office for a short conference. She came to the office carrying a steno pad and pen.

"Yes, Mr. Hanson, how can I help you?" she asked politely.

"I have been trying to make a list of things to do, some of which I'll put in your care. With no clients I guess I have too much time on my hands. I'm going to City Hall to apply for a business license. I would like you to call the sign company and see when they will be here to put the name on the window. People don't even know we exist at this point." Dan was trying to think of important items needing attention, but was having difficulty with the list.

Alma made a note on her pad. "Will there be anything else, Mr. Hanson?"

"Yes," he said, picking up the $1,000 check. "I want you to go to the bank down the street and open an office account. Buy a small cash box for the office and put a couple of hundred dollars in it. Bring me a signature card from the bank and we will both be able to sign checks. That way you will be able to pay office bills as they occur. Get a list of all large newspapers in the state and we'll compose an ad using the same logo we will display on the front window."

"The only daily local paper is the *Peninsula Clarion* from Kenai. The *Homer News* and *Tribune* are weekly. Do you want to place an ad in the Homer papers?" she asked.

"Yes, and if there is a local shoppers guide we should put an ad there also." He paused to think, wishing he could go flying and remembering he had not fueled his Caravan since the flight to Anchorage.

"I'll get started right away." She stood to leave, but turned to face him again. "You know, sir, it would be a nice afternoon to go halibut fishing, if you're interested."

Dan smiled, "You and I are going to get along just fine."

She smiled, "I have a friend who is a charter captain. I can call and see if he has an afternoon opening. Would you like me to ask him?"

Dan checked the time, thought for a second and said, "Yes, I'd like that."

Moments later she returned with a note: "Meet Captain David at the top of the K Dock ramp at one. He had a cancellation and you ride for free."

Again he checked the time. "That will be perfect. It gives me time to go to City Hall and apply for the business license and to call the fuel truck to fill the Caravan. I can change clothes at the hangar." He chuckled a little, "You know, sooner or later I'm going to have to find a place to live. I can't camp in the hangar forever, although it's not a bad place to live."

She laughed with him. "OK, Mr. Hanson, I'm off to do my business."

As he was leaving the office he reached for the light switch and turned to survey the new office. Alma had made it look very nice indeed. He locked the door behind him and headed toward the city offices. On the short drive he wondered how soon Orlando Perez would wait before mounting a search for him. He had covered his tracks pretty well, but Perez was resourceful and persistent. Someday he would look up and see one of Perez's goons; not a pleasant thought. An hour later he was signing the ticket for fuel and, with the aid of the fuel truck driver pushed the Cessna back into the hangar and closed the big door. He changed clothes and found a more suitable jacket for the boat trip. He stopped at the airport café for a bite of lunch. The same young man waited table.

"How's it goin'?" he asked.

"Pretty good. I'm getting settled into my new office. I've been busy." Dan liked the soft-spoken young man, leaving him a nice tip after lunch.

He found a place to park, not far from the K Dock ramp. Dan didn't know who he was meeting, but as he approached the ramp a nice looking young man waved at him and asked, "Are you Dan Hanson?"

"Alma told me you were coming. Come on we have some fish to catch."

Dan followed the young man to a very nice 37 foot, gleaming white, Carver Cruiser. On board were five other fishermen. Captain David gave his safety speech before starting the engines. It was a slow, no wake, cruise to the entry of the Homer Small Boat Harbor, but once in the open salt water David moved the throttles ahead to a comfortable speed for the trip to the fishing area. It took more than an hour to arrive, but on the way the fishermen had seen several whales and many sea otters and a variety of sea birds. Dan stayed inside the cabin during the ride, chatting with Captain David. It was a very relaxing way to spend the early afternoon. The captain followed the GPS course to a spot marked with an X on the electronic map. David maneuvered the boat to an exact spot and ordered the deck hand to drop the anchor.

Once the tide drew the boat tight on the anchor line the deck hand, Ralph, began to bait hooks and add huge weights to the lines. Captain David gave a short course in halibut fishing, how to drop the lines, how to jig the lines up and down, how to tell when you have a bite and how to reel up any fish you will catch. The fish may range from eight to ten pounds to more than three hundred pounds, although those huge barn door fish are rare these days.

Dan found that in spite of the three pound weight the hook did not descend straight down to the bottom, but drifted quite quickly out the back of the boat. The deck hand cautioned the fishermen about tangling their lines. Almost immediately one of the fishermen had a bite. Captain David gave him pointers as he reeled the fish up from the bottom. The fisherman said it felt like a whale. It ran out the line twice during the fight to the top. All the fishermen gathered on the left side of the deck to get a glimpse of the fish as it neared the surface.

Captain David reached for a gaff and ordered all the other fishermen out of the way in order for him to bring the fish on board. He also warned the fishermen about being injured by the flopping fish when it was inside the boat. David pulled the fifty pound fish over the side and onto the deck. The three pound weight was flying around dangerously. David caught it and handed it to the man holding the rod. Pictures were taken and bragging began. The fish was marked with a cut on the tail before being dropped into the fish hold in the center of the rear deck.

Now all the fishermen were excited and jigging their rods vigorously. Dan had never fished halibut but knew instantly he was going to be fishing them often. It was hard work, but it was also a great deal of fun. As fishermen will do, each conversed with the man next to him. "Where are you from? What kind of work do you do? Are you married?" and all manner of small talk.

The man next to Dan was from California fishing with his son. The son had just graduated from University of Southern California with a degree in electrical engineering and was promised a job with Boeing Aircraft in Renton, Washington.

The two men were making conversation when Dan had a bite. He fought the fish to the surface while David watched.

"It's only about twenty pounds, Dan. Do you want to keep it or try for a larger one?"

"Let's release it and try for something bigger."

"Good choice, Dan," said David, reaching over the side to release the fish. He re-baited the hook and slapped Dan on the shoulder. "OK, catch a big one."

The action continued all afternoon, The sun was warm and the water calm. The tide went slack and the boat swung around on the anchor line. As the tide began to pick up again the bite became insane. There were three fish on at the same time and the lines became crossed. The deckhand and David handed rods back and forth in an effort to untangle them. One fish was lost during the mess, but the fisherman could not retrieve his hook because it was still tangled with the other two fish. Finally one fish broke the surface and was gaffed by the deck hand. David untangled the two empty lines and the third fisherman began to pull his fish from the bottom of the ocean, 180 feet. In a few minutes a fish estimated at forty pounds came to the boat and was gaffed by David. The fish were marked and dropped into the hold.

Dan had watched the excitement, keeping his line well away from the fighting fish. Suddenly he had a hit. The line bent the rod severely and the drag, retarding the fish's run, began to jerk and sing.

"Keep the line tight, Dan. You've got a big one," yelled Captain David.

The fight lasted nearly twenty minutes. Dan reeled in the line, the fish took the line and after several minutes Dan began to make a little headway. Inch by inch he brought the fish to the top. When it was close enough to see how large a fish it really was David ordered everyone back from the rail. He reached for a long metal pole with a harpoon on the tip. "Dan, back up a little; keep the line tight. Ralph, catch the sinker." David stood at the ready with the harpoon raised over his head. The huge fish was on the surface, coming closer to the boat. When the timing seemed right David flung the shaft in the direction of the fish striking it behind the eye. He dropped the shaft and held the stout rope tied to the cable on the harpoon tip. Ralph handed the sinker to Dan and joined David on the rope. The two men heaved the huge fish to the deck, warning the other fishermen to stay back to prevent broken bones. The hook was removed and a metal fish bonker, looking like a small baseball bat, was used to render the fish immobile.

"Good job, Dan. We will hang the fish up at the dock for pictures. I'm guessing this one at about 120 pounds. He's not a world record, but a nice fish, nonetheless."

All the other fishermen congratulated him on his catch before going back to trying to catch one like it. An hour later the limits were reached and all the lines taken out of the water. Gear was stowed and the anchor pulled from the deep water. Once the anchor line was secured aboard and the deckhand safely on the rear deck David put power to the engines and headed back into Kachemak Bay.

At the dock the fish were taken to a rack where they were hung up and pictures taken. From there the fish were taken to a cleaning station where each fish was filleted and packaged. Dan told the manager of the fish cleaning station he wanted his fish packaged for freezing. He would come back later and pick it up.

It had been a good and relaxing day for Hanson. It had been a long time since he had enjoyed a carefree day such as this. He was exhausted and would sleep well tonight.

Chapter 5

Orlando Perez had sent men to Galen Mason's office to learn why he had not contacted the boss in more than a week. The underlings found the office locked, but in order. All the accounting logs were locked in the filing cabinets as they should have been. As near as the goons could tell nothing in the office was out of place or missing.

Perez was worried Mason had skipped out with his money. He called the bank on the island and was assured by a vice president that his last deposit was in the bank, the balance had not changed and his money was safe. Orlando Perez now began to worry about the safety of his accountant. His second in command was a man by the name of Chico Miranda. Chico was intelligent and patient. He wasn't a thug like most of the men working the drug side of his business. Chico understood the fishing industry as well as the drug trade. He understood finance and in fact was the operational head of the fishing business, Bluefin Seafoods, Incorporated.

"Chico, come to my office. We may have a problem."

Several minutes later Chico came into the boss's office and closed the door behind him. "What's the problem, Boss?" he asked.

"The accountant, Galen Mason, has gone missing. He made our last deposit as scheduled and no one has seen him since. His office looked like he just locked it for the night and went home. His house was locked up and his car parked in the garage. He just disappeared. I want you to find him. I need him."

"I'll try, Boss. Do you have any idea where to start looking?" asked Chico.

"Not really, but perhaps one of our competitors took him to get information about our other business. He's been with me for many years and I trust the guy. This is totally out of character for him. Try to track down his last movements and locate him. If our competition took him he may be dead.

I hope not. I want him back. See what you can do, Chico." Orlando Perez spoke with a worried scowl on his face.

Chico Miranda was in charge of the legitimate fish business and did the job well. Bluefin Seafoods made a lot of money as a public company. Bluefin's fishing boats were used to transport drugs from the high seas to Florida, but none of the boats were allowed to enter port with drugs on board. Illegal cargo was transferred to powerful speedboats for transport to backwater stations where it was processed and loaded on trucks for distribution. All this was done away from populated areas and prying eyes. Employees were paid well and disciplined severely when they chose to bend the given rules. Over the years he had ordered many rule breakers taken out on open Atlantic Ocean and dropped overboard, tied to heavy weights. He had chosen his enforcers well. They were ruthless and feared by everyone who worked for the illegal side of the business.

Chico called two of his enforcers to a meeting. Lenny Pierce was from New York and had worked for Chico since getting out of prison for armed robbery. His partner, a Cuban refugee, was a thug by the name of Juan Castillo. Lenny was a slightly built man with a bad temper while Juan was quiet. Casillo was about two inches short of six feet and weighed in at 230 pounds. Chico explained the few facts of the missing accountant to the men.

"We don't have any clue as to where he has gone. It's possible he was kidnapped by one of the other cartels, but we have no evidence of that. I want you two to drop everything else and track down Galen Mason. Here is a sheet of phone numbers for him, license plate numbers, keys to his office and a list of some of his known hangouts. The boss says this is important. Find him, and do it as quickly as possible. Any questions?"

"It's not much to go on, Chico, but we'll see what we can come up with." Without further conversation the two left the office.

Juan was in the passenger seat reading the list of addresses and phone numbers he had been given. "Hey, Lenny, I have an idea. Drive out to the airport. Let's check the hangar to see if the plane is in there. Maybe he just went flying and never came back. I ain't never seen the bookkeeper drink, but maybe he just went somewhere and got drunk."

"Good idea, Juan," said Lenny. "I'm surprised you thought of it." Lenny took the next left turn and headed to the airport where the small two engine plane was kept.

As they sped east toward the airstrip Juan began to dial numbers from the list on his lap. Each number he called went to an automated voice mail. The list was long and his cell phone was beginning to get hot from the intense use. When Lenny drove through the automated gate onto the airport apron Juan closed his phone and began to search the ring of keys for the one needed to open the door of the hangar. There were no windows in the hangar.

"Try the side door, Juan. If it's unlocked just push it open and step back. I don't want you to get shot. I can't lift your fat butt to get you back in the car." Lenny liked chiding Juan about his weight. Juan gave his partner a dirty look and tried the door knob. It was locked. He found the proper key and opened the door, stepping back and allowing Lenny to enter the dark hangar, gun in hand. Lenny searched the darkness for movement while Juan found the light switch. Both men now had their guns out, searching the large hangar. Once they were assured there was no one in the hangar they both stowed their automatics in shoulder holsters. There was a small cubicle in a back corner and a restroom with a shower. There was no sign anyone had been inside. The men checked the inside of the airplane; it was empty. "OK, Dick Tracy," said Lenny, "where to now?"

"Drive to his office. We can look around inside. We might find something to tell us where he is." Juan was looking at the list again. "Wait a minute. Do you remember Galen always ate at that little restaurant on a side street near his office? I think it's only a block or so from his office. He went there every day for lunch. Go there and I'll check to see if he has been in lately."

Lenny stopped in front of a small neighborhood café. The sign above the door read GASLIGHT CAFÉ. There were shrubs and a small patch of grass in front making it look more like a home than a place of business. Lenny waited in the car while Juan went inside where he was met by a perky waitress.

"Table for one?" she asked.

"No, thank you. I'm just trying to locate a friend of mine. He comes here all the time. His name is Galen Mason. Do you know him?"

"Oh, yes, we all know Mr. Mason. Strange you should ask about him, though," said the waitress.

"Why is that?" asked Juan.

"We, the other girls and I, were just wondering this morning why Mr. Mason hadn't been in for more than a week. He sometimes misses a day or two, but he has never gone this long without coming in for lunch. Has something happened to him?"

"He does work for our company and we haven't seen him either. Did he say anything to you about leaving or going on vacation?"

"Not that I recall, but I'll ask the other shift when they come in this afternoon. Do you have a number where I can reach you?" asked the girl.

Juan took a card from his vest pocket and a ten dollar bill from his pants pocket and handed them to the waitress. "Call me at this number if you hear anything or if he comes in again."

"Sure; OK," she said pocketing the money and card as Juan walked out the door.

"They ain't seen him either," said Juan as he climbed into the sedan. "Let's go to his office."

The men spent more than an hour in the office searching files and papers and looking in every conceivable hiding place in the office. The file cabinets had all been locked, but the keys were on the ring given to Juan. All the files seemed to be complete, however neither Lenny nor Juan could confirm that fact. Chico would have to get someone with accounting experience down here to verify the accounts. Mason had been a strange duck. There was nothing personal in the office, not a certificate or picture hung anywhere in the office. The only item there was a city business license. There were two comfortable chairs in front of a nice metal desk, a computer and a coffee pot. There was nothing written on his desk blotter, nothing but pencils in the desk drawers and only a pencil sharpener a tape dispenser and a stapler on the desk. It was as if Mason had no personality at all. No sign of relatives or a girlfriend. Nothing.

There was one item left on the list Chico had given him. Seaboard Gym. Mason was a member there. Lenny found it not far from the office and parked in front while Juan went inside. An attendant in sweat pants and tee shirt bearing the Seaboard Gym logo met him as he entered.

"May I help you, sir?" he asked.

"I hope so. I'm looking for my friend, Galen Mason. Has he been in today?"

"Normally I wouldn't tell you, but in this case the answer is no. I've wondered where he is. He has a locker here and comes every day during the week. Six o'clock every day. But he hasn't been here in the last ten days or so. Fred, the owner, and I have wondered where he is. You don't suppose he was hurt or in the hospital, do you?"

Juan took another card from his vest pocket and handed it to the attendant. "Give me a call if he comes in, will you?"

"Sure thing," said the attendant, reading the card and finding only a name, Juan Casillo, and phone number.

Back in the car he made a check mark by the name of the gym. "He ain't been here neither. Let's go to the hospital and see if he was admitted."

There is only one hospital in the area and it was six miles from the gym. On the drive across town Juan tried to imagine where Mason could have gone. After they checked the hospital they would go to his home and try to find some clue as to what could have caused his disappearance. There was no record of him at the hospital. The two men drove to Mason's home and found it as non-personal as his office. It was as if this man had no life outside of work. There were no nail holes in the walls where pictures had been removed. Nothing to indicate he had ever lived in the place. The two men were in the home for more than an hour without finding anything

Back in the car Lenny shook his head and commented, "It's like this Mason guy never existed. He didn't just clean up after himself. He didn't ever have anything of himself at his office or his home. Even the garage floor looked as if it had been mopped and waxed. I've never seen a place like this."

"Me neither, Lenny, I'm beginning to think he lived this way so's he could make a run for it if he had to. In this business we all try to figure out an escape route. I got one and I'm sure you have too, but I ain't never seen a person who could live as clean as this guy. It ain't natural." Juan was shaking his head and looked back at Lenny, "I guess we had better try to explain this to Chico. I think I'll leave that up to you."

Lenny chuckled. "Thanks, Pal."

After listening to the narrative from Lenny, Chico rubbed his chin, thinking. "Did you check around in his neighborhood and his office building and ask if he had any friends or girlfriends or people he associated? He was a pleasant sort of guy and I can't imagine him not having any friends. Keep looking. Check the court house and city hall. There has to be something where he applied for a business license or when he got his accounting degree. He has to have a past and we have to find it."

"OK, Chief, we'll keep looking."

Chapter 6

Dan Hanson was in his office early on Monday morning. He made the coffee in the small kitchen area, poured a cup and sat at his desk. He reflected on the fishing trip with Captain David and how much at ease he had felt while out on the fishing boat. He was about to get up and refill his coffee cup when the front door opened. It was Alma. She was wearing a stylish outfit, all earth colors, and high heel shoes. She took off her sweater and hung it in the small closet in the hallway.

"Good morning, Mr. Hanson," she greeted when he emerged from his office.

"Good morning, Alma. Do you want some coffee? I'm getting some for myself."

"I shouldn't, but I will drink one this morning, thank you." She went to her desk and sat down. There were only a couple of items for her to finish this morning and she pulled the files from the cabinet while she waited for her coffee. Moments later Dan arrived at her desk with two steaming cups of brew.

"I forgot to ask, do you use cream or sugar?" he asked. He had brought a small napkin and placed it under the cup.

"No thank you." She moved the files to one side and picked up the cup. "How was the fishing trip?" she asked.

"I was about to thank you for arranging it for me. I have been under a great deal of stress in recent weeks. I had a great time and caught some fish, but most importantly, I was able to relax for an afternoon. Captain David is a terrific young man."

"Yes he is. I've known him and his folks since I came to town. They are really nice people. I'll introduce you to them when they get to town." She carefully sipped her cup again. "Do you have anything for me to do this morning?"

"Yes, I have the business license on my desk. You can get a frame and hang it on the wall behind your desk. I would like for you to do some research for me. I plan to fly to Anchorage and Fairbanks later this week. I would like you to get me the business names and management names of potential clients. You don't have to solicit anything, just get me the names in order for me to introduce myself when I meet with them."

"There are several industrial publications where I can get that information for you," she commented. "I might suggest you drive to Anchorage, unless you're going to rent a car there, which could be tough this time of year. The reason I say this is that the city is a huge sprawling area and some of the businesses you will want to contact will be in Palmer and Wasilla, roughly 40 or 50 miles from downtown Anchorage."

"I think I am going to need a tour guide, Alma. I hope you don't take this the wrong way, but would you be interested in making the trip with me?"

"When do you plan to go?" she asked.

"I think Wednesday through Friday. If you decide to go we'll need two rooms at a decent hotel for those nights. And, will you get Owen Sutton on the line for me?" With that he took his empty coffee cup to the small kitchen sink in the little break room. He rinsed his cup and returned to his office.

"I have Captain Sutton on the line, sir," said the voice on the intercom.

"Good morning, Owen," greeted Hanson.

"Dan, good timing, I was just dialing your number. I have an emergency transport and the medevac plane from Anchorage can't arrive in less than two hours. The doctor said that may be too late. Can I impose on you to make the flight?"

"Of course, meet me at the hangar. I'll go pre-flight right now." He hung up the phone and walked to the front office.

"I have to make a flight to Anchorage. I'll be back in time for lunch, I hope. I have my cell phone if you need me." Without stopping he walked out the front door to his Jeep.

He had done his walk-around by the time the ambulance arrived. He had the plane on the apron and was disconnecting the electric tow bar when it arrived. Hanson climbed into the pilot's seat and waited for the medics to secure the patient. A medic and a doctor were to attend the patient during the flight. When the ambulance was clear of the aircraft Dan started the engine and asked for clearance to taxi for takeoff.

"Are you buckled in?" he called to the back.

"We are," was the reply.

Dan added power and the big single engine plane began to move. He climbed straight out and when above the hills turned to the north and west. He stayed offshore and above the Inlet waters for a smoother flight. He was cleared to land at Anchorage International Airport and was directed to a waiting ambulance at a hangar to the east of the main terminal. Two Anchorage medics loaded the patient into the ambulance and the Homer doctor went with the patient.

"Do you want me to wait for you, Doc?" asked Dan.

"No, I don't know how long I will need to be with him."

Dan turned to the medic saying "Strap in and I'll close the door. You can ride up front in the right seat if you care to."

On the return flight he quizzed the medic about the frequency of these medical flights. The medic explained they were frequent in the summer when tourists flooded the town, but it slowed in the winter. Dan used an inland route for the return to Homer, sightseeing and familiarizing himself with the landmarks. It was an interesting trip in which he saw several moose and two brown bears during the flight. He was more captivated with the far north with every passing day.

The medic helped him put the Caravan back inside the hangar. Dan closed the door and offered the medic a ride back to the fire station. After dropping the medic off Dan went to the office. The door was closed and locked when he arrived. He thought it strange, but assumed Alma had gone on some errand. He used his key to open the door. He was startled to see an overturned desk chair and the telephone lying on the floor.

Cautiously he made his way down the hallway, checking each door and room. He peered into his own office to see a horrific sight. Alma was tied, naked and bleeding, to the top of his office desk. She was restrained with duct tape, her legs to one end of the desk and her arms to the other. Her face was bloody and swollen. He reached for his cell phone and punched the 911 numbers.

"911, what is the nature of your emergency?"

"This is Dan Hanson. I just returned to my office and found my receptionist tied and badly beaten. I need an ambulance immediately." He gave the address. "I'll need the police, also. Hurry."

"They are on their way, sir."

Dan found a pair of scissors in a desk drawer and cut the tape from her arms and legs. There was a jacket hanging on a coat rack behind the door, which he used to cover her nude body. She was unconscious and still bleeding. Her swollen face was grotesquely misshapened.

The police officer, Gary Fritz, was the first to arrive with the ambulance and medical personnel immediately behind. Fritz went, at once, to the injured victim. "She's in bad shape, Mr. Hanson. Please go out to the front office and I'll be right with you." The medics were now entering with medical supplies and electronic monitoring devices. They went to work quickly inserting an IV port and injecting fluids. One of them got on the radio, reporting vital sign numbers to the doctor at the hospital. Another medic came out to the front office to get the name of the victim and a short explanation of what had happened.

Fritz waited until the medic returned to the rear office to begin his questions. "I know this is a stressful time for you, Mr. Hanson, but I need as much information as possible in order to find the persons responsible for this. Do you have any idea who may have done this?" he asked.

"No, I don't. I returned from a flight to Anchorage and found the office door locked. When I came inside I found the signs of a fight or something. I started checking the office and found Alma, my receptionist, tied up with duct tape on my desk. You saw her; she's severely injured. I called 911, cut the tapes off of her and covered her with the jacket." Dan was becoming emotional. "As soon as they take her out of the office I'll let you do your investigating and evidence gathering."

"How long has Alma Petersen worked for you?" he asked, writing the answers on his pad.

"Only about a week. I only just opened my office here."

"Do you know if she had any enemies?" asked Fritz.

"Like I said, I didn't know her well, but she was doing a wonderful job for me. She did tell me she had some kind of disagreement with her former employer, but I don't really know anything about that. I'm new in Homer and don't know many people here."

Two medics went to the ambulance to bring in a gurney. The officer and Dan stepped out of the way to allow them to pass. Officer Fritz followed the medics down the hall to assist with loading the victim, Alma, onto the gurney. The medical kits and IV bags were placed on the gurney and wheeled to the ambulance, which was backed up to the front door of the office. The four men loaded the stretcher into the ambulance and began closing it up.

Officer Fritz came back into the office to speak with Dan Hanson. "May I have the key to the office? I am going to have to follow the ambulance to the hospital and return later with another officer to check for fingerprints and gather any evidence we might find."

Dan went to the front desk and found Alma's keys in the top drawer. "Here, take this set. It's her keys to the office. I need them back when you are finished, because they also have the keys to the file cabinets on them. We don't have any files in them yet, but I will need them later. Tell the doctors I'll be responsible for the medical bill. I want her to have the best treatment they can get for her."

"I understand, Mr. Hanson. I'll tell them. Now I have to ask you to leave the office in order for me to secure the scene. Thank you." Fritz was firm in asking Dan to leave. Once the office was secured the officer followed the medics to the hospital.

Not really knowing what to do Dan drove to the fire station to find Owen Sutton. Owen was in his office, his desk cluttered with reports to be written. His out basket was filled with reports already written. A coffee cup sat, one third full of cold coffee, on the edge of his messy desk.

"Have you got a minute to talk, Owen?" asked Dan.

"Sure, Dan, come on in and have a seat."

"I can't stay. I'm on my way to the hospital to check on Alma. You must have heard what happened. She looks to be in bad shape. I'm really worried about her."

Owen stared at his desk a moment, "Don't take it personally, Dan. The police will find the guy who did this and arrest him. We have a good police force here in Homer. They'll get him."

"I suppose, but I can't help feeling responsible, somehow. I like Alma. She's doing a great job for me. I want her to have the best medical treatment possible. If she needs to be flown to Anchorage, I'll do it."

"I'll let them know. In the meantime, you need to take it easy. Let the doctors do their job. Go to the hospital, and the nurses will let you know of her progress. Just stay out of the way and let them do their job. OK, Pal?" Owen wanted to reassure Dan, but didn't think he was getting through to him. "My medics will be coming back to the station shortly and I'll try to find out how she's doing."

Two hours later a nurse came to the waiting room to take Dan for consultation with the doctor on duty.

"Someone beat her severely, breaking her jaw and cheekbone. Her eye socket is damaged and she has two broken ribs as well as an unknown internal injury. The severity of the head injuries and the number of other injuries make it difficult to treat her in this facility. We think she should go to the hospital in Anchorage where a number of specialists can work on her at the same time. She will need reconstructive surgery on her face and jaw. We can't do that here. She is stable right now and we have her sedated. I understand you've been doing mercy flights for the hospital. If you want to fly her to Anchorage I'll call the hospital and arrange for an ambulance to meet you there. I'll fax the medical records to the hospital for the doctors there to examine and determine her treatment. The advance notice will speed the treatment and I believe the damage to her face needs instant care. What would you like us to do?"

"Make the call. I'll go to the airport and get the plane ready. Get her to the plane and have two medics tend her during the flight. They will have to return to Homer on a commercial flight because I'll be staying in Anchorage until they tell me she's going to be all right."

"Good enough, Mr. Hanson. I'll start the ball rolling right now. We will have her at the airport in less than an hour." The doctor stood and began barking orders at the nurses.

Dan had finished his pre-flight when the ambulance drove onto the apron at the hangar.

Chapter 7

Dan Hanson had been able to get a room at the Hickel House, an area of the hospital for housing family of patients. Except for a few hours' sleep and showers, he had spent the entire time on the floor where Alma Petersen was being treated. She had endured several surgeries on her face, ribs and abdomen repairing the damage done in the attack. It was now the third morning following the attack and her doctors had said they would allow her to awaken this morning. Dan paced the hall while doctors examined her and administered medications to aid her awakening. It was shortly after noon when she began to stir.

Dan was sitting in the room reading a newspaper when she finally came completely awake. She moaned and shrieked with pain as she came back to consciousness.

"Take it easy, Alma, you're in the hospital. You're going to be all right. Your jaw is broken and it's wired closed. Be careful when you talk. You will have a lot of healing to do, but you're going to be as good as new. Just lie quietly and rest. "I'll be here with you." There was compassion and caring in his voice.

"What happened to me?" she uttered through swollen lips and wired jaws.

"Don't try to talk now, Alma. You were attacked in the office. We need to find out who did this to you, but that can wait until you are stronger." He was standing beside the bed now, "Stay quiet now. I'm going out to get the nurse. I'll be right back."

He stepped into the hall and motioned for a nurse to come to the room. "She's awake," he explained.

The nurse hurried into the room and began examining the patient. She pressed the button on the small radio pinned to her collar to call the nursing station. "Call Doctor Burton and let him know his patient in 533 is awake."

Dan stood on the off side of the bed from the nurse and held Alma's hand gently. Within minutes the room filled with medical personnel followed by the doctor who had operated on her facial injuries. There was a flurry of medical activity in the room with little attention paid to Dan. A nurse stood by with a computer on a roll-around stand making notations of every comment made by the doctor and his nurse. Different medications were prescribed, mostly to combat infections and pain. The doctor was in the room for more than a half hour with the nurses remaining much longer. Alma was more awake and aware now. Finally everyone was gone except Dan.

"What did they do to me?" asked Alma.

"Someone came into the office and attacked you. They broke a lot of bones and did a lot of damage to your head and face as well as your rib cage. I brought you here to the hospital in Anchorage where specialists could repair your injuries. I thought we were going to lose you, but you're a fighter and made it through. You said 'they.' Did you see the men who did this?" Dan was anxious to get any information he could to give to the investigators.

"Yes, but I didn't know them. There were two men. One was thin and had on a suit. The other was shorter, but big and mean. They asked me some questions about a man named Mason. I didn't know anyone by that name, but they didn't believe me and started hitting me. I remember they drug me to your office and tore off my clothes. The big man hit me some more and that's all I remember." She was weakening now, "Do you know who these men are, Dan?"

"No," he lied, "but when I find them they will pay dearly for doing this to you. I am so sorry you were hurt. I don't know how I can ever make it up to you."

"Thank you for being here, Dan. It means a lot." She closed her eyes and tried to smile, but the pain was too great.

"Go back to sleep now, Alma. I'll be here when you wake up again."

She smiled a little and turned her head to the side to ease the pain. The pain medications were making her sleepy now.

When she dozed off he stepped into the hall and dug out his cell phone. He dialed the number on the card Gary Fritz had given him.

"This is Gary," he answered.

"Gary, Dan Hanson. She's awake, or at least she was for a few minutes," reported Dan.

"Oh, that's good news. Was she able to say anything about the attack?"

"A little, but not much detail. She said there were two men, one taller and thin, the other shorter, but large and mean. She said they kept asking about someone by the name of Mason. She told them she didn't know anyone by that name but they didn't believe her and kept beating her until she lost consciousness." Dan paused to compose his building anger. When he was able to continue he gave a report on her health. "The doctors did a wonderful job of rebuilding her face. It's still swollen, but it looks like her only scars will be behind her hair line. I don't know what internal injuries they treated, but they said she had two broken ribs. I'm staying here until she's feeling better."

"Thanks for the up-date, Dan. I'll have everyone keep an eye peeled for these two, but it's not much to go on. Is there anything you need to have me do for you before you return?"

"No, I'll just leave the office closed for the time being. Alma and I were making plans to go out and solicit business for the office when this happened. All that is on hold now. I would appreciate it if you would keep an eye on the office in case they decide to break in again."

"Will do," said Fritz. "Keep me posted on her progress. I'll see you when you get back."

"I'll stay in touch. Thanks Gary."

Dan had not told all he suspected about the men who attacked Alma. He didn't know how they managed to find him, but he was going to have to find them before they found him. These were men prone to violent endings. Dan knew he would have to get them before they could get him.

By the fifth morning Alma's condition had improved to the point the doctor was recommending she begin physical therapy. The swelling in her face had begun to subside and she was regaining some of her beauty as well as her vanity. She was asking for a comb and brush as well as lipstick and make-up. The nurse said she would be back later with a comb and brush, but would not allow her to use make-up of any kind fearing it would affect the healing of her surgical scars.

"The doctor worked very hard to prevent any scarring on your face and we don't want to spoil his labors, now do we?" said the nurse as she left the room. "We'll get you up and walking this afternoon. I'll bring a wheelchair to take you down to physical therapy. We want you to start slow and work up to exercise. Those ribs are going to slow you down for a few days, but we'll keep you busy."

When the nurse left the room again Dan stood beside her bed and held her hand. "I have a few things to do while I'm in Anchorage and I'm going to leave you with the nurse for a while. Is there anything I can bring you when I come back?"

"Yes, could you find me something more stylish than this hospital gown to wear if they're going to parade me up and down the halls?" she asked.

"Sure, and is there anything else, magazines or books, anything?" Dan asked.

"No thank you, Dan. You have been a honey, taking care of me and sitting with me. You go and do your errands and I'll see what kind of torture they have in mind for me."

The nurse came into the room pushing a wheelchair. "OK, Miss Petersen, let's go for a ride," she said as she tossed back the sheets and helped her sit up.

"OK, Alma, I'm leaving, but I'll be back this afternoon. You have my cell phone number if you need me." Dan left the room as the nurse maneuvered the wheelchair close to the bed.

In the lobby of the hospital he found a phone and the number for National Car Rentals. He gave the voice on the other end the information she needed to fill out the rental agreement. She said they could deliver the car to the hospital and he could have the driver bring him to the office to sign the papers and pay the deposit.

As he waited, Dan bought a local paper and turned to the want-ad section. There were several garage sales listed and he circled the ones advertising guns. The rental car would have a GPS to direct him to the proper addresses.

By late afternoon Dan had purchased two semi-automatic weapons and found shoulder holsters for each. He found ammunition at the garage sales, also. He paid cash for the weapons. In the car he examined each gun with care. The larger one was a Colt Commander .45 caliber in almost new condition. The other one was smaller and easier to conceal on his person. It also had four extra magazines loaded with 9mm hollow-point cartridges. The carbon fiber frame made it light weight. Satisfied with the condition of his new guns he drove to a gun shop and purchased ammo for the .45 and plastic gun cases for each.

His next stop was the Sears store. He didn't have any idea what size clothes Alma wore, but the clerk helped him pick out what he thought was right size. He bought her stylish blue pajamas and matching robe, a pair of slippers and a sweat suit. The clerk called it a warm-up suit. Finally he walked down the hall in the large mall and found a book store where he purchased a hard cover copy of the new Danielle Steel romance novel.

It was getting late now. Dan drove to the airport and placed the two plastic gun cases, with weapons inside, in the Caravan and locked the door. He drove back to the hospital and parked near the Hickel House.

Alma was sleeping when he returned to the room carrying two large shopping bags containing her new wardrobe. He had been in the room for nearly two hours when a nurse came in to awaken her and give her some medications.

"Hi, Dan. How long have you been back?" she asked, still groggy.

"Not long. How are you feeling?"

"They wore me out down at physical therapy. It hurt a lot, but by the time I came back to the room the pain was easing off. The therapist said it would get better each day." She smiled at him. "Thanks for being here, Dan."

"You're welcome. I bought you some things, and I hope they fit." Dan stood and retrieved the two large shopping bags. He placed them on the bed for her to look through the goods inside.

"Everything is perfect. Thank you. You can take the cost out of my next paycheck, if you still want me to work for you." She held up the pajamas, admiring them. "I'm going to put these on in the morning after I get cleaned up."

"I'm glad you like them. Don't worry about the cost. I owe you that much. One other thing, Alma, I'm picking up the cost of the medical expenses. I can't help you with the pain, but I can pay for your treatment. I feel so terrible about your getting hurt while working for me. If there is anything you want or need I'll be happy to take care of it." He reached under his chair and pulled out a smaller plastic bag, which he handed her. "Here, this should keep you entertained for a few days."

She took the book from the bag and studied the cover. "Thank you, Dan. I haven't seen this one. I love her writing." She placed the thick book on the bed beside her. "I may never get well. I'm beginning to like all this attention."

"I'm afraid I will have to go back to Homer for a couple of days to check on the business and to talk with the police. The nurses and doctors will see to it that you behave yourself." Dan patted her arm while holding her hand with his other one.

"When are you leaving?" she asked.

"I'll come see you in the morning before I go. Feel free to call me anytime. I'll be back in a few days after I clean up a few loose ends."

Chapter 8

When he returned to Homer, Dan pulled his Jeep out of the hangar and, after refueling, moved the Caravan inside. Once the door was closed he took the new handguns from the plane and disassembled, cleaned and oiled them, carefully inspected the internal workings and reassembled both weapons. He adjusted the harness of each shoulder holster to fit him before strapping on the 9mm Springfield Armory semi-automatic.

The men Alma had described were employees of his former boss, Orlando Perez. How they were able to trace him to Homer, Alaska was a mystery, but their purpose here was not. Although Dan had never been a part of the illegal portion of his business he knew Perez would not let him live knowing the ins and outs of the Bluefin Seafood workings. He had made up his mind that since he was not able to outrun Perez's men he would have to fight them. For that he would need help. He called Gary Fritz.

"Gary, Dan Hanson. Can you come to my hangar right away? I have something important to discuss with you."

"Sure, Dan, I'll be there in ten minutes."

Hanson was nervous about what he was going to tell the policeman, but he had not committed any crimes in Alaska or, for that matter, in Florida either. The money he embezzled never existed on any tax rolls. He knew it wasn't right, but his rational was that it was stolen from a criminal. He decided the best thing to do was eliminate the embezzlement issue from his story.

Dan had left the main door ajar and sat where he could watch the entry. Gary poked his head in the opening and called out, "Dan, are you in here?"

"Come on in, Gary. Close the door." It was cool in the hangar as well as quiet and private. "Can I get you a Coke or something?"

"No, I'm fine," said the policeman as he approached the small table in the corner of the hangar. "What's on your mind, Dan? You sounded urgent on the phone."

"This is going to take a few minutes, Gary. I had hoped I would never have to tell this story, but my old employer has found me and his men are the ones who beat Alma so badly. I can't let that go unchallenged. These men are dangerous, killers actually." Dan didn't know where to start his story.

Gary took a notebook from his pocket and placed it on the table. "I think you had better start at the beginning."

"To begin with, my name was Galen Mason. I am an accountant by profession and education. Twelve years ago I was hired by a Florida seafood company to keep books for them. That was Bluefin Seafoods. For a long time I didn't know anything about the sideline the fishing fleet was carrying on. I began to suspect when the total cash flow far exceeded what should have been realized from the fish business. I tried to ignore it all and just do my accounting job. The owner of the business, Orlando Perez, approached me and asked if I would like a huge pay raise. Of course I was interested. He learned I was a pilot and he offered to buy a small twin engine plane for me to fly when doing business for Bluefin Seafoods. It was a great offer. In return he wanted me to fly shipments of cash from Florida to banks on the off-shore islands. At first I didn't think it was a good idea, but I was blinded by the offer of having my own airplane to use for travel. I'm not proud of my decision, but I took the offer. I thought if I just minded my own business and kept my mouth shut I could pretend not to know about the other business."

"Wait a minute, Dan," said Gary. "Where was all this extra money coming from?"

"I'm coming to that," replied Dan. "Perez had a huge fleet of commercial fishing boats. These boats would meet boats from several South American countries out on the open sea and take on illegal cargo. Occasionally it would be a person entering the U.S. illegally, but usually it was drugs, cocaine, marijuana, meth and heroine. I never saw any of that side of the business myself. The cargo was transferred to smaller, faster boats before they came back to port. These boats would take the cargo up various back-channels and put on trucks for delivery to processing plants around the east coast. It was a huge operation. Like I said, I never actually saw any of that part of the business, but I did help Perez filter a lot of the cash he made through the Bluefin Seafood business. It's called money laundering. Perez liked me and paid me well. I liked being paid and kept my mouth shut." Dan hung his head in shame.

"Do you have any proof of all this?" asked Gary Fritz.

"No, only what I learned by listening. My only direct contact was to make a flight once a week to one of the off-shore islands where Perez had bank accounts and make deposits for him, very large deposits. I told myself it was OK and I wasn't breaking any laws, but after years of this, I couldn't lie to myself any longer and devised a plan to get out. I wanted to disappear without a trace and thought I had done it until those two goons showed up and nearly beat Alma to death. I know these men. They are enforcers for Chico Miranda, Perez's right hand man. The tall thin one is Lennie Pierce. He does the thinking. He usually dresses in a suit. The other one is Juan Casillo. He's a mean one. I've heard he likes beating people to death. These men are killers, and we need to deal with them carefully."

"Hold on, Dan. This is a police matter. There is no WE involved here." Gary didn't know just how to deal with the man he knew as Dan, but he did know catching criminals was a job for the police. "I can't allow you to run around like some kind of vigilante. We have laws. That's why we have police. You have to let me handle this."

"That all sounds nice Gary, but these two won't let it happen that way. These men would kill you without even blinking. I won't interfere with any investigation you have going on, but sooner or later they will find me and come after me. When they do I'll defend myself." Hanson tried to make his position clear to the policeman.

"Are there any warrants issued for your arrest in Florida or anywhere else?" he asked.

"None I know about," replied Dan, shaking his head. "I never intended to bring any of this with me. I don't know how they found me. I spent years devising an escape. I changed my identity. I tried not to leave any trace of myself, and I left an obscure trail that should have been difficult to follow. Do you remember the plane in the Inlet incident a few weeks ago?"

Gary nodded.

"When I left for Kodiak I put phony numbers on my plane. I landed in Kodiak and took them off before I came to Homer. That was my final charade to change my identity. I wanted to start a new life and a new business here in Homer where no one knew me. It was working pretty well until these two found me."

"If there are no warrants on you I have no reason to arrest you. I hope it never comes to that. You've been a great asset to Homer and I would like to see you stay, but the law is the law. I can't ignore it. I am going back to the office and check out the names you gave me. I'm certain they have rap sheets in Florida if they are the kind of men you say they are. I'm asking you to keep a low profile and let me do the hunting." Gary wanted it to be friendly, but he was serious about his warning.

"There is something else, Gary," said Dan.

"What's that?" asked Gary.

"These men are killers. They probably think Alma has died from her beating. If they learn she's alive they will not stop until they finish the job. I'm telling you now; I brought this danger to Alma and I'll protect her from further harm with any means possible. And, you need to be cautious when you start looking for Pierce and Casillo. They'll kill you as quickly as they would anyone else."

"Thanks for the advice, Dan, but remember what I said about being a vigilante. I'll get back to you if we have any news on the whereabouts of the two "Goons" as you called them." Gary left the hangar with mixed feelings about Dan Hanson.

Dan sat in the cool hangar for a long time trying to determine how Chico's men had found him. He had gone to great lengths to sanitize his office and home before leaving. He had gone to his office as Galen Mason and left it as Dan Hanson. He had hitched a ride with a trucker at the local truck stop and rode north seventy miles where he bought a Greyhound Bus ticket to Wichita, Kansas where his new Cessna 208 was waiting. He spent two days with a flight instructor learning to fly the turboprop and mastering the electronics of the new plane. He thought about every step he had taken and was unable to determine where he had slipped up.

Finally he gave up. "It doesn't matter how they found me out, only that they did," he thought. "The important thing is to protect Alma. The only way to do that is to find Pierce and Casillo and eliminate them." In exasperation he left the hangar and drove to his office. He spent two hours cleaning the blood from the floor and his office desk. He swept up broken glass and spilled paper clips, righted the overturned furniture and thought about the horrors Alma had suffered from this senseless attack. He thought it best to let Gary Fritz find the two men who had tracked him down.

He was sitting at Alma's desk, thinking, when he decided to call the hospital and check on her. A nurse answered the telephone in her room. He explained who he was and asked for Alma.

"I'm sorry, sir, they took her back to surgery earlier and operated again."

Dan was shocked, "Is she out of surgery now? Is she going to be OK?"

"I can't tell you more than I have already told you, but I can tell you she is downstairs in recovery right now and will be taken to ICU when she's awake."

"I'm in Homer right now and it will take me nearly four hours to drive to Anchorage. When she wakes up tell her I'm on my way." Without waiting for an answer he ran from the office, locking the door and hopping into his Jeep. Black tire marks were left on the new paving in front of the office when he sped from the parking lot. He passed nearly every car on the highway along the route to Anchorage. Finding a parking space close to the entrance he walked quickly to the lobby of the hospital. With a map of the building that he found, Dan made his way to the ICU wing.

The nurse at the station in ICU wanted to know his relationship to the patient. Once satisfied with his identification she told him the doctor was in the room with the patient. He could go in once the doctor was finished.

She said the doctor would explain her condition when he came from the room. Dan paced the hallway for fifteen minutes, unable to sit quietly and wait. Finally the doctor emerged from the room. He was standing at the nurse's station making notes on a chart when Dan approached him.

"Are you Mr. Hanson?" asked the physician.

"Yes, I called earlier from Homer and drove up as soon as I heard. How is she, Doc?"

"She had a ruptured spleen and she was bleeding internally. We removed her spleen, but she isn't out of the woods yet. We will keep a close eye on her for a few days. You can go in and see her, but don't stay long. She needs to rest. Let the nurse know where you're staying in case we need you during the night." The doctor went back to writing his notes.

"Come with me, Mr. Hanson," said the nurse, leading him to the room.

The swelling in her face had diminished somewhat and the bruising had lost its deep blue color and was now a light green. Her jaws were still wired together, but she managed to say hello.

"Don't try to talk, Alma. I'm going to stay in town as long as you're in the hospital. I want you to get some rest and start healing up so I can take you home."

She nodded, smiled and closed her eyes.

At the nurse's station he asked if they could check to see if there was a room available at the Hickel House. There was. He moved his SUV to the parking area on the other side of the hospital grounds. It was late and he was tired. He called the ICU desk and gave them his room number before collapsing into bed.

Chapter 9

Alma had slept most of the next day. Dan sat on an uncomfortable chair in a corner of the room while the doctors and nurses came and went. By late afternoon she awoke again. He stood near her bed and held her hand. She seemed weaker than she had the night before.

"Hi, Dan," she managed to say.

"Hi, Alma, are you feeling any better?" he asked in a quiet tone.

"I hurt everywhere. What did they do to me this time?"

"You had a ruptured spleen. You were bleeding internally and the doctors took it out to stop the bleeding." Dan squeezed her hand, "I'm sorry I brought this trouble to you. I don't know how I will ever be able to make it up to you. I'll explain it all later, but for now you only need to rest and heal."

"You mean you know who did this to me?" she asked with surprise.

"Yeah, I know." He hung his head in sorrow. "I'll explain when you feel better. Is there anyone I can call to let them know how you are doing?"

"No, I don't have anyone. I've been on my own for a long time now. I thank you for caring, Dan. You're being here makes it easier." She closed her eyes and fell asleep.

Dan was asleep in a chair next to the bed when the alarms began to ring and beep. He awoke suddenly to the sounds. Nurses began to run into the room, crowding around the bed and frantically administering medications. One nurse touched his shoulder. "You had better wait outside, sir."

In the hall he watched an army of medical personnel enter and leave the room. He paced the hall for nearly an hour when a nurse came out to talk with him.

"I'm sorry, Mr. Hanson, we lost her. Her body just couldn't take all the trauma of her injuries. She passed quietly." She spoke in a quiet tone attempting to console him. "You may go in and see her if you wish. You are the only one on the list of individuals to be notified in this event. I would like you to stop at the nurse's desk before you leave. We will need to know which funeral home you would like for us to send the body. Please accept my deepest sympathy, sir."

The sadness he felt would soon fade to a deep anger. Dan went to his room in the adjoining building and tried to sleep. It was no use. He gathered his personal belongings and notified the desk he was checking out. In his Jeep he reached under the seat for the 9mm hidden there next to the .45 Colt. He strapped on the shoulder holster before leaving the parking lot. A stop at one of the coffee stands to purchase a twenty ounce double shot espresso to drink gave him some fortitude as he made the long drive back to Homer. It was very early in the morning, but the sun was shining brightly.

Dan needed a plan to confront Pierce and Casillo. He knew it was foolish to approach the two men together and tried to think of a way to split the two in order to attack them one at a time. He also realized he was going to face resistance from the Homer Police Department in the form of Officer Gary Fritz. He must either keep his plan secret from Fritz or include him. It seemed better to include the officer than attempt to avoid him.

It was noon when Dan unlocked the office door. He reasoned that the two hit men would be watching the office or hire someone do it for them. The Colt Commander was hidden in a computer bag he carried into the office and stashed it in a desk drawer. He was making coffee when there was a knock on the front door. Risking a peek around the doorway he saw Gary Fritz, in uniform, standing at the door. Dan walked to the door to let the officer inside.

"Good morning, Gary," Dan offered as he opened the door.

"Good morning, Dan," he replied. "I saw your car here and came in to apologize for my rudeness when we met at the hangar. Sometimes I let my badge get in the way of my manners. I'm sorry; I didn't mean to offend you."

"Forget it, Gary, I understand. I know you are required to play by different rules than me. That is going to be especially true now."

Gary was puzzled by the comment. "Why do you say that, Dan? I thought we were on the same side here."

"We were until this morning."

"Why, what happened this morning?" asked Gary.

"Alma died of her injuries around three this morning." Dan's eyes filled with emotion as he spoke. "I only knew her a short time, but she had become my friend, my right hand and the one I depended on to find information for me. She was wonderful as well as being a beautiful young lady. We didn't have a relationship outside the office, but given enough time we may have had one in the future."

"Ah, Dan, I didn't know. I'm sorry. I wish there was something I could say to make it better for you, but I know there isn't. I will say that I will do everything in my power to arrest these two men." Gary felt Dan's pain and was sincere in his condolences. "I got copies of the rap sheets on these two men. They are bad men. They are suspected in the deaths of at least a dozen men. They are wanted in Florida and Georgia for assault and suspicion of murder and wanted in Texas for the murder of a Mexican drug lord; I'm still waiting for the report on that one."

"These guys are relentless, Gary. They will be somewhere around Homer until they find me and eliminate me. I don't plan to be a sitting target for them. I know I can't take them together. Somehow, I'm going to have to split them up. I was hoping to get you to help me do just that."

"It looks like we're back on the same side, but, again, I have to tell you I won't be a party to your vendetta. I am going to arrest them and take them to trial." Gary echoed his previous message.

"I know, Gary, but I know how I am going to deal with them. My warning to you is that they are extremely dangerous men. Don't underestimate them. We have to devise a plan to separate them and take them one at a time. I don't know how to do that, but I think it's the only way we're going to take them."

"I'm willing to work with you, but you know where I stand." Gary was firm on his course of actions. "Now, it's time for you to level with me about your past. Did you know Pierce and Casillo in your previous life?"

"Not directly. I had met them at parties and meetings, but never did any business with them. They work directly for the manager of Bluefin Seafoods, Chico Miranda. Chico handles all the fish business and is the blind operator between Bluefin Fisheries and the drug trade being done on the open ocean. He is responsible for keeping the lines clear and distinct. When an event happens to blur the lines Chico sends Pierce and Casillo to eliminate the problem. Over the years I had kept clear of the drug business and only dealt with the commercial fishing industry, which Orlando Perez used to launder great sums of cash. I did the best I could to not know where this cash was coming from. I had myself convinced that ignorance was innocence. Pierce and Casillo were part of the reason I could no longer participate in the charade. That's when I devised an escape plan and ended up in Homer. I knew it was a dangerous scheme and I could be found out, but I never counted on someone like Alma being a victim."

"As I see it," began Gary Fritz, "our first order of business is to locate the two men. I would bet they're keeping an eye on the office and waiting for you to return. They may already know you're back in town. I don't know how we can separate the two men, but if we can locate them I might be able to have some officers take one of them for questioning."

"It might work," said Dan, "but it also might get you officers hurt. You are right about part of it, though. First we have to find them."

"I can start by taking my patrol away from your front door. I'll be in the neighborhood, though."

Gary drove away from the office building and Dan went to the little kitchen to pour a cup of fresh coffee. His plan to expand the business was put on hold and he now concentrated on getting the two killers out of the equation, either by killing them or arresting them. He preferred the former. Once that was done he planned to return to Florida to deal with the two men who ordered the hit: Orlando Perez and Chico Miranda.

Sitting at his desk he realized he could not see the front door of the office. He found a phone directory and called a local security firm to come and install a large, round, convex mirror in the hall opposite his office door near the end of the hallway. He was told they could come down and install it right away.

He was on his second cup of coffee when the phone rang. It was Captain Owen Sutton.

"I just had a call from Gary. He told me about Alma. He also said you wanted to handle the killers on your own. He warned me about getting involved. Alma was a good friend of mine and my family. It appears you need some help and, if you'll have me, I'd like to be in on it."

"You have a family, Owen. Are you sure this is a wise choice?"

"I was an Army Ranger before I was a firefighter. I know about danger and being hunted down. If you want me I'll come down to the office and we can talk about it privately."

"The coffee is on, Owen. Come on down." Dan felt an immediate sense of relief. He was no longer going to be alone in the fight.

The security company was in the office installing the magnifying mirror when Owen arrived. They waited until he finished the installation before sitting down to formulate a plan of attack.

"Do you have any kind of defensive arms in the office?" asked the fireman.

Dan opened his windbreaker to reveal the 9mm in the shoulder holster. "I also have a .45 in the desk drawer."

"Extra magazines?" inquired Owen.

"Four for the nine and two for the forty five," Dan answered.

"Good, can you hit anything with them?"

"I'm not Annie Oakley, but I do OK."

"Just checking. I have a couple of security cameras that work in low light. I can put one in the office and the other in the hangar. They will send images to your cell phone if they record an intruder. That way you get a warning when someone comes inside while you're gone. It won't stop anyone from entering, but you'll know if someone is inside. I'll have the same message sent to my phone and I'll respond with you when there is an intrusion. Don't try to go it alone either here or the hangar."

"Thanks Owen, I never would have thought of that. We might just make a good team. We'll need to be if we encounter Pierce and Casillo. These guys make their living beating people up and killing people. They are professional enforcers and good at what they do. I only say this again because I don't want you to become one of their victims. We will need to attack them together or not at all." Dan had seen the hit men in action in the past and knew how dangerous they could be. The recent attack on Alma was evidence of their viciousness.

"I just thought of something, Dan. The one guy has a Mexican name. Does he look Mexican?" asked Owen.

"As a matter of fact he does. He looks like he eats too many re-fried beans and tacos. He's the mean one of the two."

"Do you think it would work, if we find them, to have the police department pick up Casillo and take him to the station to identify him, you know, to be sure he isn't a terrorist or illegal alien?

"Do you think Gary would go along with the idea?" asked Dan.

"I'll bet I can talk him into it." He picked up the desk phone and called Gary Fritz at the station. They talked for only a minute and Gary said he would take part in the ruse.

"OK, Partner, we're set. Now all we have to do is find them. They're probably staying in a hotel using false names. I think we're going to have to canvass the hotels and find someone who has seen them. I also think we need to do this together. There's a chance that while we're out looking for them they may spot us. I would like to get a jump on them if we can."

Dan was pleased with the reasoning and military training Owen displayed. He was going to be a good partner in this adventure.

"How about if I take you and your wife to dinner tonight?" he asked his new partner.

"That would be great. Where would you like to go? I'll call my wife and let her know."

"Meet me at the hangar at six and I can fly us to Anchorage. I've heard the Club Paris has great food."

"I'll let her know and see you at six."

Chapter 10

In the back of the parking area of the Kachemak Islands Park headquarters, two men sat in the cab of an old, rusted, 1989 Ford pickup truck. They took turns looking through binoculars at the little office building up the street. Cars and people had been going in and out of the office since before noon. Now there was only one car in front of the office. It was the Jeep Cherokee Dan Hanson was said to drive. The men watched for another few minutes before deciding to approach the office to make sure this really was Galen Mason, now using the name of Dan Hanson. Lenny Pierce was driving as they moved to the other side of the main road to the Homer Spit. Lenny drove through the parking area, turned around and returned to the front of the office, parking next to the Jeep. They sat in the Ford trying to see who was inside the office, but the tinted windows of the building would not let them have a clear view.

They were about to exit the truck when a Homer City Police car stopped behind the old pickup. Two officers stepped out of the car and walked to the side window on the driver's side of the truck. Lenny rolled down the window for the officer.

"What's the problem officer?" asked Lenny.

"Oh, no problem, sir, we're just checking identifications on strangers. We do this in the summer when the fishing fleet comes in. I don't think you have anything to worry about. May I see your driver's license and vehicle registration, please?" The officer was very polite.

"Certainly, officer," commented Lenny, digging for his wallet. "We just bought the truck and haven't changed the registration yet. I do have the signed title, though. Will that do?"

"I think so, sir. Let me see it."

While the first officer inspected the documents the second officer spoke to Juan Casillo through the open window. "May I see your identification, sir?"

Juan fumbled for his Florida driver's license and handed it to the officer. The officer read the document, but did not return it to him. "I'm sorry sir, but I am going to have to take this one to the station for verification. I don't have the means to check it from the patrol car. Would you mind riding to the station with us. It won't take long?"

Casillo looked at Pierce with questioning eyes.

"Go with them, Juan. I'll come pick you up in a few minutes."

Pierce sat in the old Ford truck for a full five minutes. Sitting in front of the office he could see down the hallway to a wall in the rear of the building. There was no movement inside and no lights were turned on. No one entered or left the office while he was there. He was troubled by the interference of the Homer Police Department. The cop's story didn't seem right somehow. In the end he decided this was not the time to confront Galen Mason. He started the truck and drove to the other side of town where the police station was located and waited outside for Juan to emerge. In less than five minutes Juan was outside looking for his partner. He scanned the parking area of the police station before walking to the truck.

"What was the deal, Juan?" asked a puzzled Lenny Pierce.

"I don't know. They took me inside and asked me to sit down while they checked me out. I waited in a chair at the front desk until they came back out and handed me my license and said I could go. This whole deal seems phony to me, Lenny. I think they're just checking us out because of the girl. She was a looker and must have had some friends in the department." Juan scratched his shaved head. "They don't have anything on us or they would have arrested us. I think this was a warning to tell us they're watching us."

"I think you're right. I sat in front of the office for a while and couldn't see anyone inside. I was hoping to get a look at this Hanson guy to make sure he really is Galen Mason." Lenny blew out a long exasperated sigh. "Let's get some beer and go out to the cabin and lay low a couple of days."

When the two men returned to their rented cabin three miles out East End Road they carried an armload of supplies inside. Lenny put some of the things in the refrigerator and the rest in the cupboard. He went back to the refrigerator and brought two beers to the table where Juan sat.

"What now, Lenny?" asked the big man.

"I'm not sure. Obviously we can't just walk in and do the job like we planned. They're watching us. I'm going to have to think about it for a while. You got any ideas?"

"No, I don't, Lenny. I'm like you; I think the cops are looking at us for beatin' that girl. It was kinda fun though, wasn't it?" Juan snickered.

"Well, my friend, don't get too comfortable. We still have a job to do." Lenny was the thinker of the pair and realized their task had just become more difficult.

Juan finished his beer and tossed the empty can in the trash container beside the kitchen range. "I'm gonna go lay down a while. Let me know if you come up with a plan."

Lenny finished his beer and tossed his empty into the same trash can. He went to the refrigerator for a second beer to drink while he tried to figure out what to do next.

When the Homer police took Juan to the station and he sat in the hall they called Owen Sutton to advise him of the stop. Sutton was at home and told the officer to release him in ten minutes. Sutton had been at home and needed the time to come into town and tail the two men to where they were staying. He had followed them to the grocery store not far from Dan's office. They were inside the store for nearly a half hour and came out with each man carrying a large grocery bag. Owen followed the old Ford pickup three miles up East End Road to an old log cabin where the men pulled in and unloaded the groceries. The cabin was clearly visible from the road. He found a place to park where he could see the front of the cabin and the pickup. When he was sure the men weren't going to leave soon he returned to town and Dan Hanson's office where Dan unlocked the door and let him inside.

"Well, "Plan A" didn't work out so well, did it?" Sutton joked.

"What do you mean, Owen?"

"Homer PD spotted the two goons when they parked in front of your office and were sitting in their vehicle, an old Ford pickup. They picked up Juan and took him to the police station, telling him they wanted to check his ID. It was a good plan and the two were separated, but it was too soon and I wasn't prepared. The cops called me to let me know and I came down and was able to follow them to the cabin they're living in. Now we know what they drive and where they're staying. It's a start." Owen had a huge smile on his face.

"Don't underestimate these two, Owen. Right now they are probably sitting in the cabin wondering why they got stopped. It won't take long for them to figure out it wasn't just happenstance. These two are smart and you can bet they are sitting out there trying to come up with a new plan."

Sutton nodded in agreement. "We lost the only witness when Alma died or we could have just arrested them when we found them. I think you are totally correct in thinking they will find another way to attack you."

"I don't think they'll come back here. They know the police are watching my office. My only other regular stop is the hangar. I think they'll try there next. It will be more difficult because there is some security at the airport. Not much, but a little. I think I need to put some kind of alarm on the hangar door and perhaps security cameras like you have here in the office." Dan wrote a note on his desk pad. "I also think I need more firepower at the hangar. I don't want to get into a gunfight in the hangar and shoot up my airplane. I would rather stop them at the door, if I can."

Again, Owen was nodding agreement. "I think you're on to something. We need to get a couple of twelve gauge shotguns for inside the hangar. I think 00 Buckshot is the best ammo for there, nine large pellets in each shot. I'll arrange for those this afternoon."

Dan pictured the inside of the hangar before commenting. "The hangar is usually dark, no windows. I could make a shooting platform above the little living area in the back of the hangar. It would have a good view of both the large hangar door and the smaller man-door. There's a portable work light in a locker in the back. If I set the work light near the door and didn't turn on the overhead lights it would give me an advantage from the overhead loft."

"You're beginning to think like a Ranger, Dan," Owen joked. "It wouldn't take much to set up a motion detector outside the door to give you a little warning when someone is coming inside."

"All right, then. Let's go to town and get some supplies and set out the welcome mat." Hanson was beginning to feel more secure about his own defense and the man who was helping set it all up and who he hoped would help man the new fortress.

By early evening everything was in place; motion detectors were at the man-door, the work light was set up facing the doorway, a cot was lifted to the storage area above the kitchen/office area below, sandbags were stacked to make a bullet proof barrier above the office area and two shotguns loaded with buckshot rounds rested against the sandbags. There were two powerful spotlights lying next to the shotguns. Under the bed was a case of bottled water and a first aid kit.

"I think we're ready, Dan. You can sleep a couple of hours and I'll take the first watch. They won't wait for darkness this time of year, but I think they will want to wait until most of the daily traffic has quit. I would expect them sometime after ten tonight. Do you want to go to town and get something to eat before we settle in?"

"I think we had better eat something. It could be a long night. I can make coffee here at the hangar. Let's go eat and leave your car at the station tonight. You can ride back here with me. That way they won't see the extra vehicle out front. I would rather they didn't get too suspicious before entering." Dan knew Lenny Pierce was a cautious, but bold killer who always planned his hits carefully. "I do expect them to try soon. They know the police are watching them and will want to get this done and get out of town as soon as possible."

"How do you think they will make the raid?" asked Owen.

"I'm only guessing, mind you, but I think Lenny will pick the lock on the door. Juan will be the first one through. He will probably have a flashlight of some kind to spot his target and to find the light switch. Both men will get away from the doorway as quickly as possible. They will split up and work their way toward the kitchen below us. They will do this quickly, they've done it before. They won't speak to each other, just efficiently search for the target, me. If they see either one of us or any movement they will shoot. This is a dangerous plan, Owen. If you want to back out now is the time." Dan knew he wouldn't leave, but felt he should give him the choice.

"Let's go get something to eat and move my car before the fun starts." Owen knew the risks, but chose to ignore them. "I'm going to call my wife and let her know I'm working tonight."

Chapter 11

An hour later Sutton and Hanson were back in the hangar getting into position. "Get some rest, Dan," advised Owen Sutton. "I'll take the first watch. Just hand me one of those bottles of water and I'll take up my position by the barricade. You will probably hear them if they come in, but if not, I'll poke you with the shotgun barrel."

"Thanks, Owen, I need some rest. I didn't get much sleep while I sat at the hospital with Alma."

"She was a good gal, Dan. My wife and kids loved her. We'll miss her a lot."

"I've been thinking, when this is over I'm going to have to go back to Florida and finish some business there. If I don't come back again I'll have a lawyer contact you. I would like you to close the office for me. The title for the new Jeep is in the glove compartment. I've signed it off and if I don't return it's yours. It won't repay you for all you have done for me, but it's a start. Just my way of saying thanks." Dan pulled a cotton blanket over his shoulders. "I'll try not to snore too loudly."

It was 2 a.m. when the motion detector beeped. Owen turned it off and tapped Dan on the shoulder with his gun barrel. "Someone is outside," he whispered.

It was very dark in the hangar and Dan fumbled for the shotgun and light lying beside his cot. He found them and quietly moved behind the sandbag barrier they had built.

"You take the one on the left and I'll take the one on the right when they get inside. Do you have the light switch?" Dan whispered.

They saw the door being pushed open and the silhouette of a large man entering and stepping to the right as he entered. He was followed by another man who stepped to the left and closed the door behind him. The man on the left shone a flashlight on the walls attempting to find the light switch.

Owen flipped the switch turning on the work light that faced the doorway. Both the intruders tried to dodge the light without success. "Drop your weapons," shouted Owen.

They could now see the first man at the door who crouched to the right as he came inside; it was Juan Casillo. Casillo fired a handgun in their direction, missing them in the darkness in which they hid. Owen fired a shotgun blast in the direction of Juan, but was shooting too high, missing by inches.

Lenny saw the flame from the muzzle of the shotgun when Owen fired and fired his handgun in the direction of the shooter. His slug hit the sandbags in front of Owen but not injuring him.

Dan saw Lenny fire and took quick aim at his position. He pulled the trigger. Lenny screamed in pain.

"You all right?" called Juan.

"Yeah, but I got it in the leg. Move right, I'll go the other way," Lenny replied.

Juan was hidden, but not safe. He had dropped behind an open-top drum used as a trash barrel. Twice he poked his head out to find a target and shoot, and twice the barrel took a load of buckshot. There was also a bright light shining in his eyes each time he peered over the top of the barrel.

Lenny had worked his way to the far left side of the hangar. The Caravan made a good shield for him. Trailing blood from his left leg he worked his way past the landing gear of the large plane. The belly pod under the fuselage prevented a view of his movements by the men behind the sandbags. Lenny crawled along on his belly until he was under the plane and able to see where the shots were coming from.

Lenny called to Juan, "Keep them busy, I'm making a move."

Juan didn't answer, but fired two shots over the top of the barrel and ducked down once again. Placing a new clip in his automatic while he was out of sight, he reached up again to shoot over the top of the barrel, but when he did Owen saw his arm movement and sprayed the top of the barrel with a load of buckshot. Several of the pellets struck Juan's gun hand. He screamed in pain, but retrieved the fallen weapon with his left hand. It wasn't damaged. He decided to make a break for the door. Quickly he jumped from his hiding place and reached for the door handle. It was a fatal mistake. The next load of buckshot struck him in the center of the back, killing him instantly. His body lay bleeding in front of the door.

"Juan, you OK?" called Lenny from under the airplane. There was no answer. Lenny slid back out of sight on the far side of the big red and white plane, working his way toward the rear of the craft where there was little light. He moved slowly and carefully hoping to get a glimpse of the shooter above him. The spotlight used to target Juan was still burning, illuminating the two hooters. Lenny stepped out quickly and fired at the closest of the two men and returned to his hiding place behind the airplane. Lenny worked his way back to the front of the Caravan where he could see Juan lying face down in a pool of blood.

Lenny felt his anger mounting. He fed a new clip into his handgun and stepped into the open behind Juan's body. He began spraying lead toward the barrier above the kitchen and moving toward the area, hoping he could reach a spot under where the shooters were barricaded. The instant he paused his shooting there was return fire. Owen stood up and directed two blasts from his 12 gauge toward the advancing gunman. Lenny raised his arm to fire again when Dan stood and fired. Lenny was knocked backward violently, collapsing on the floor.

"Cover me. I'm going down and check on them," said Owen as he turned to climb down the little ladder on the side of the kitchen wall.

"Got it," replied Dan, standing with his weapon aimed at the two men now lying on the floor at the front door.

As he moved into the open Owen kept his shotgun aimed at the men. There was no movement by either of them. Owen kicked a gun from near the first man and walked to the wall where the light switch was located. He flipped the switch allowing both men to see the damage done by the buckshot to each of the attackers.

He lowered his weapon and reached for his cell phone to report the incident to the police.

Once done with the phone he turned to Dan, "Come on down. We got 'em."

Dan was shaking violently from the adrenalin rush as he climbed down the ladder to the hangar floor.

"I know these two men, Owen. I would never have given us a chance at besting them in a gunfight. I owe you my life." Dan was weak from the realization they had beaten the two killers. "I'm going to the table and sit down."

Now they could hear the sirens approaching. Within a minute the hangar was filling with Homer policemen and Alaska state troopers. Owen handed his shotgun to one of the city policemen before joining Dan at the small table in the back of the hangar. Police Chief Ed Garrison was now coming through the door.

He surveyed the situation quickly as he entered. "OK everyone, listen up. I want two Homer PD officers and two troopers in here to investigate. Everyone else get outside. We have a crime scene here and we have too many people in here." He pointed a finger at two Homer officers and motioned for them to leave the hangar. He turned to a trooper sergeant who was doing the same thing with his men. He spoke to the chief and advised him of his leaving and said he would be available if more help was needed.

One of the trooper investigators began to take pictures of the scene; the bodies, weapons, spent shell casings, the sandbag barrier and blood trails around the hangar floor. The other trooper confirmed the two men on the floor were dead.

Gary Fritz had been at home, sleeping, when the call came in. He jumped from bed and dressed in uniform. Now he was entering the hangar to take charge of the investigation. The chief left the scene in his hands and went back to the office. Fritz made an assessment of the scene, making notes in his little book. As he approached the table in the back of the hangar he said hello to the two gunfighters seated there. "I thought I told you two to let me handle these two."

Owen Sutton spoke up first. "We were willing to let you handle it, but they came looking for Dan in the middle of the night, and we defended ourselves. We didn't go out looking for them."

"I can see that," said Fritz. "I want you two to come with me to the station and we'll get your statements. These officers will stay here and do the investigation. Come with me, but be careful where you step. I don't want the scene contaminated."

For the next two days Dan was not allowed inside the hangar. He spent those two days at his office in town when he wasn't at police headquarters making or clarifying his statements. Owen was back to work at the fire department. Dan had used the time alone to assess his own situation. He knew his old employer, Orlando Perez, would be sending someone else to finish the job Lenny and Juan had started.

Owen had taught him a valuable lesson. You must either attack or be attacked. He decided to attack. A plan to stop Perez was not an easy task. Perez was a cagey target. He knew he could get in to see Perez and be able to kill the man, but getting away would be impossible. Chico Miranda would have someone follow him wherever he went and extract revenge, even though killing Perez would give Chico an instant promotion to boss.

No, this could not be a full frontal attack. It must be clandestine and well planned. But, before he could leave here he must take care of a few loose ends. He had reviewed Alma Petersen's employment application. She had not listed any next of kin or contact numbers. He called Owen Sutton. "Hi there, Owen, have you calmed down yet?"

Sutton laughed, "A little, but I'm still jumpy, how about you?"

"Had it not been for you I would have been the body lying on the hangar floor. I can never repay you for your help and advice." Dan was still weak from the experience and sincere with his thanks. "Have you got a minute to come by and talk? I have a couple of questions for you."

"Sure, when?"

"The sooner the better, Owen. It has to do with Alma. You know, making arrangements and such."

"I'll buy lunch at the Duncan House if you're hungry."

"That sounds good to me. I'll meet you there."

Duncan House is a small family style restaurant on the main street of the uptown district. The building is old and decorated in antiques and local art. The food is very tasty and the prices are very good. The two men met in the parking lot and went inside together. A young waitress led them to a booth toward the rear of the restaurant. After she brought them the iced tea they ordered. Dan began to explain the meeting.

"I had a call from a mortuary asking when I wanted to schedule a service for Alma. I don't know what church she attended. I don't know who her friends or relatives are. She didn't list anyone on her work application. I was hoping you could help me out with some of that."

"I asked my wife about her family and she said Alma never mentioned them. We don't know where she came from. She was always a loner. She was quiet and pleasant and everyone liked her. I know my wife and my kids adored her. I can have the police run a background check on her, but unless she has a criminal record I doubt it will tell us much."

"I think we had better do it anyway. Otherwise I am going to have to order a cremation and have her interred in the local cemetery. She struck me as a nice person and she deserves kind treatment. I'll pay the expenses, but she should have someone besides you and me to say goodbye." It was sad, Dan thought, to be alone when you leave this earth.

"I'll see what I can find out for you." Owen saw the hurt on his friend's face, but knew no words could comfort him. "Alma chose her lonely life, Dan. She never let anyone inside her small world. I think she must have been hurt awfully bad at some time during her life and this was her defense against it happening again. She liked you and I think she was closer to you than she ever got to anyone."

Dan was shaking his head, "I only knew her a few days, but I liked her, too."

"Have you set a timetable for leaving?"

"Not yet, but it will have to be soon. My old boss will get word about Lenny and Juan and find someone else to do the job. I don't want to bring that kind of situation here again. I have to go out there and confront him before he does." Again Dan was shaking his head with remorse for the trouble he had brought to this small community. As soon as the service for Alma can be arranged I'll plan to leave."

"Will you be coming back?" asked Owen.

"Yes, I'm leaving my airplane here and if I survive this trip I'll be back to continue putting this office to work. You have my cell phone number, but please don't call me. I'll call you to let you know what's happening. If you don't hear from me within a week of my leaving it means you never will.

The Jeep will be yours and I will leave a letter in my desk telling you what to do with the office and the airplane."

"You had better call, old buddy, I'm beginning to like you."

"You have been a good friend, Owen. Let's get the memorial for Alma out of the way and go on from there."

Chapter 12

A somber service was held at the gravesite with only Dan, Owen and his family there to hear the pastor give a short prayer. It is said the funeral is for the living; a final goodbye and closure to a lost life. There was little comfort here for Dan or the Sutton family. After the service the only words spoken were from Owen as the group walked back to where the cars were parked.

"See you later, Dan," said Owen.

Dan Hanson only nodded his affirmation. He went to the hangar and packed what little personal gear he was taking with him. He had stopped at the Kachemak Gear shed to buy a large plastic shipping box in which to pack both his handguns and magazines. He didn't know if it was legal to pack ammo with the guns, so he unloaded all the magazines, cleaned his weapons and packed them in the new gun case. He placed a new lock inside the box to be attached after it was inspected by TSA at the airport. He caught the late flight from Homer to Anchorage and checked in at the airline desk, declaring his weapons and signing the receipt for the officers.

At a newsstand he purchased an *Alaska Magazine* and a *Fish Alaska Magazine* to read later. The wait was long and boring. He avoided speaking to anyone while waiting for boarding time. Once on the plane and his carry-on bag stowed in the overhead bin he sat quietly looking out the window at the crews scurrying around on the ramp. He sat through the flight attendant's briefing and checked his seatbelt. After takeoff and before the airliner had reached cruising altitude the flight attendant came around to ask if he would like something to eat or drink. He said no, leaned his seat back a little and closed his eyes. It was a long flight to Denver where he would change planes and continue on to Miami.

In Denver there was a delay for boarding his Miami flight. The late night flight had become an early morning flight. Dan's main worry wasn't the late arrival in Miami, but if his checked bag would arrive on the same flight.

It was nearly noon when he picked up the plastic pistol box and walked to the National Car Rental counter. He was able to rent a Jeep Cherokee like the one he owned and felt comfortable driving it. His first stop was a sporting goods store on the east side of town where he purchased two boxes of ammunition, one for the .45 and one for the 9 mm. He found a motel, out of the main business district, went to his room and began reloading all the magazines with new cartridges. He wore the shoulder harness for the .45 Colt and tucked the smaller, lighter 9 mm into a pancake holster on his belt. He concealed the hardware with a nylon windbreaker. On his way out he stopped at a vending machine to purchase a bottle of water. It was warm in Miami.

His plan was to confront Perez without warning. Dan drove to the cannery where Perez had his office. The young receptionist tried to ask him his business, but he only said, "I have an appointment" and continued to the office door. He entered without knocking, closing it behind him.

A shocked Orlando Perez looked up in shock. "Where have you been, Galen? I have had people looking all over for you."

"Yeah, I know. Lenny and Juan won't be reporting in soon." Galen Mason pulled the Springfield from the holster on his belt pointing it at Perez. "Call Chico and get him here, alone. Don't be cute on the phone."

"OK, OK, Galen, whatever you want." He picked up his desk phone and dialed. "Chico, get to my office as quick as you can."

It took several minutes for Chico to drive from his office in another part of the docks to the more public office of Orlando Perez. In the outer office he stopped at the desk of the receptionist. "What's going on, Lucy?"

"I don't know Mr. Miranda. Some man came in and said he had an appointment and went into Mr. Perez's office without even knocking."

"Who was he?" asked Chico.

"I don't know, sir. I never saw him before."

The already suspicious Chico was now becoming cautious. "What did he look like?" he inquired.

"He was tall, slim, nice looking. He had a nice square chin, you know, strong looking."

"Galen Mason," muttered Chico as he turned toward the door. He drew a handgun from his shoulder holster and reached for the office door knob. He pushed the door open quickly and stepped inside, but Mason had anticipated his entry. Chico scanned the room quickly. Seeing Mason he swung to his right pointing his gun at Galen. Mason fired, striking Chico in the chest.

He fell to the floor, dropping his gun as he went down. Mason took two steps to pick up the fallen gun.

Perez used the distraction to reach into his right hand desk drawer for a .357 Smith and Wesson he kept there. Mason picked up the weapon from the floor while Perez pointed his revolver at him.

"You know, Orlando, this was a terrible incident," commented Mason.

"What makes you say that, Galen?" was the reply.

"The way Chico came running in here and shooting you like that."

"He didn't do any such thing, but I'm going to kill you for killing him."

"Oh no, Perez, you shot Chico before you died." Mason still had Chico's weapon pointed at Perez.

"That's enough of this crap, Galen. Drop the weapon. Lucy has called the cops by now, anyway."

"You're right Perez. It's time for me to go." He squeezed the trigger of Chico's gun twice hitting Perez once in the chest and once in the neck. Perez dropped his weapon on the floor, still in his chair.

Galen Mason took a handkerchief from his pocket and wiped his fingerprints off the gun then pressed it into the hand of Chico Miranda who lay dead on the floor. He then walked behind the desk, picking up the .357 to put it back in the drawer where it had been before. After wiping the fingerprints off his own 9mm, he pressed it into the hand of Perez, then dropped it on the floor where the .357 had landed. Once done he walked to the office door to survey his work. He nodded to himself, "Yup, they shot each other," he thought.

Satisfied he opened the door to speak to the receptionist, "You had better call 911. Your boss and his right hand man just shot each other." With that he walked toward the entry door.

"Wait a minute, who are you?" she called out behind him.

He didn't answer, but kept on walking. His Jeep was parked a half block away and by the time he made it to his car the police were arriving and entering the offices of Bluefin Seafoods, Inc.

Dan drove back to his motel and went inside, shaking nearly as badly as he was after the shooting in his hangar. It had cost him his 9mm Springfield, but it was worth it. He couldn't think of any other members of the company who could identify him by sight. He lay on the bed, but couldn't sleep. After a few minutes he gave up and sat on the edge of the bed to call the airline to arrange a trip home. Yes, he thought, Homer was now his home. He had friends there.

He packed his .45 Colt and shoulder holster inside the plastic gun case for the return trip to Alaska after taking the ammunition out of all the clips once again. Looking at his wristwatch he noted he had three hours until boarding time. He stopped at a nice restaurant for an early dinner and ordered sword-fish and wild rice with a dinner salad and white wine. He suddenly realized he was relaxed and felt good for the first time in many months.

After eating he sat in his rental car and called Owen. "I'll be back tomorrow afternoon," he reported.

"Good, do you want me to pick you up at the Homer Airport?" asked Owen.

"That would be great. I'll call you from Anchorage to let you know what time I'll be getting into Homer."

"Did everything go as planned?" asked a curious Sutton.

"Yes, thanks. I've liquidated my holdings down here. I'll tell you about it when I get home."

While watching the local news on television in the airport and waiting to board his flight he saw an item about a gunfight in Miami resulting in the death of two local businessmen. The report said there had been a witness to the shooting, but he could not be found. A receptionist at the business verified the findings of the police department. No motive for the shooting was given.

"It worked," thought Dan, "and now, at last I can get on with my new life."

The return flight to Alaska was a different route than the one he had taken to Miami. He was now returning by way of San Francisco to Seattle and Anchorage. There were no long layovers on the return flight and with better connections the trip took two hours less than the trip south. When the flight attendant came around he ordered a glass of scotch whiskey. He thumbed through an airline magazine while sipping his drink, which made him sleepy and he soon dozed off. He was awakened in time to change flights in San Francisco.

It was early morning when Dan arrived in Anchorage. The commuter air-line counter wasn't open so he went to the coffee shop for breakfast. After an hour he had a ticket on an early flight to Homer. He called Owen to give him an arrival time. It felt good to be back without having to look over his shoulder to see who was chasing him. He decided his first order of business would be to call Captain David and book a halibut fishing charter. In fact he would book two seats and treat Owen to a fishing trip in gratitude for helping him get free of his past.

The next two weeks were like being in heaven. He had plenty of money, but if he didn't have a source of income he thought people would be curious about how he was supporting his lifestyle. He had begun to organize his office and had interviewed several applicants for a replacement for Alma. None of those interviewed measured up to the proficiency Alma had delivered. He was becoming frustrated with the interview process when, one early morning, a new applicant came to his office.

Her name was Leah Cooper, a tall brunette who walked with purpose in her stride. She was in her mid-forties, neatly dressed and well prepared for the interview.

"Have you lived in Homer very long?" asked Dan.

"Only three years, this time; I was raised here, but left when I went to college. I was married right after school, but it didn't work out. I lived in California and Colorado for a while and later moved to Oregon and worked for a big fruit company. I liked it there, but things slowed down and I was laid off, so I came back home. I've been working on the Homer Spit for a cannery, but it's cold in the building and I don't like it. I want to find a warmer office."

"This office will be a consulting firm. I am just opening and I'll need some help with screening clients. I hope to entice clients from all over the state. I am confident the business will be successful, and I am looking for someone willing to grow with my company. If I hire you, you will be in charge of the office. I don't know, at this point, what the duties will be in the future, but as for now they will be to help build a clientele. There may be a little traveling involved at some point, but those expenses will be paid by the office."

"I'm sorry, but if this is a telephone solicitation position, I'm not interested." She was emphatic in her comment.

Dan liked her decisiveness, "I want someone to be in full charge of the office. I want the new girl to research companies around the state as clientele, but I will do any soliciting myself."

"Oh, that sounds exciting. I think I would like doing it." So far she had not asked about the wages.

"I'll tell you what I'll do, Miss Cooper, I'll hire you on an interim basis, say, three months. If at the end of that time either of us is dissatisfied we can part company with no hard feelings. Are you interested?" he asked the new prospect.

"That sounds very fair to me, Mr. Hanson. Please call me Leah." She held out her hand to shake on the deal.

"I hope it works out for both of us, Leah. Welcome aboard. When can you start?" asked the new boss.

"Right now, if you need me. I'm not doing anything else."

"You know, that would be great. Come back here to the kitchen and get a soda or some coffee and we'll talk about some of the things that need to be done."

Once she had gone out of the office to sign on to the bank account, he called Captain David.

Chapter 13

In Miami there was confusion at Bluefin Seafood, Inc. The foreign cartel, fearing an interruption of their pipeline to suppliers in the U.S., sent a man to take control of the fish processing plant and its fishing fleet. This new man, Diego Garcia, had been in the higher echelon of the cartel for many years. He was the one responsible for all distribution of drugs for the cartel in the western hemisphere. A stubby little man with a bad temper and a short cigar clenched in his teeth, one he never smoked, only chewed.

With both Orlando Perez and Chico Miranda dead there was no one to investigate what had taken place in the offices, but it seems it was not the first strange occurrence at the fish plant in recent times. Not long ago the head accountant for the company had disappeared without a trace. Perez had not been able to locate him or learn what had happened to the man. He had simply vanished. Chico vowed to find him and put two men on the problem. Now the two men he sent had disappeared. Diego spent many hours thinking of possibilities, but could only surmise these men had been eliminated by some local rival.

Lucy, the receptionist, was the only witness to the events in the office that day. She had worked in the office for only a matter of weeks and had no knowledge of the clandestine workings of the business. When Diego questioned her about that day she became extremely nervous and threatened to quit the job. Diego offered her a large raise and a bonus to stay on. It was enough and she stayed, still frightened.

Diego Garcia had brought another man with him when he came to Florida. His name was Thomas Finn. Finn was a Columbian, but carried the name of one of his ancestors who was Irish. Finn took over that portion of the business once controlled by Chico Miranda. It was Finn's job to keep the drugs moving from the transfer of the product on the open ocean to delivery to the transporters operating in the backwaters of the coastal region. Diego had brought two other strong arm specialists with him from Columbia. They were his foremen and ran the drug transfer operation. It was their responsibility to see that all cargo transferred on the high seas made it safely to its destination. They were very good at their jobs.

These two 'foremen' were brothers from Mexico who spoke perfect English. Raised in Cabo San Lucas, the brothers learned the language of tourists. As young men they began robbing and strong-arming drunken American tourists. They had caught the eye of several local drug dealers who hired them. Their proficiency propelled them to the employ of Thomas Finn. Fernando and Phillipe Lopez were as ruthless as they were loyal. If a dirty task needed doing Finn sent the Lopez brothers.

The police in Miami had been satisfied with the result of the investigation, announcing to the public Perez had called Miranda to his office for some unknown reason. When Miranda arrived the two men argued. The argument erupted into a gun battle and the two men shot each other; case closed. Incidents like this took place on the docks frequently, bad guys killing bad guys, no big deal. No one seemed to know who the visitor had been, but the evidence clearly showed the two men, Perez and Miranda, had killed each other.

Diego Garcia called Thomas Finn to his office for a conference. He was not satisfied with the lack of answers being presented to him.

"I think we have a big problem here, Thomas," noted Garcia. "You and I are strangers here, and we have no answers as to what took place in Perez's office. For all we know this could have been done by one of the other cartels. I don't like being without answers."

"Do you have a plan of some kind to get to the bottom of this problem?" replied Finn.

"No, I don't, but I am uneasy to drop this. For all I know we may have an enemy here we don't know about. I don't want to seem paranoid, but there are too many things I don't have answers for. We can fight what we can see, but we can be killed by what we cannot."

"Here's what I'll do, Diego." Finn had only one open lead and was about to present the idea to his angry boss. "Lucy says there was another guy here when Orlando and Chico, according to police, shot each other. She described him pretty accurately, but had never seen him before. I think we need to concentrate on this man. He may not be involved, but he will be able to tell us exactly what took place. I'll have the Lopez brothers look into it and find him. Another strange thing about this whole business is the disappearance of the accountant. Nobody is even asking questions about him, nobody. I would have thought the police would have been interested, especially after the shooting here."

"Good point, Thomas. The operation is working well and I see no reason to change anything, but if the killings are done by some other cartel, then you and I will be the next victims on the list. I would rather that didn't happen." Garcia took the chewed stub of cigar from his mouth and pointed the end at Finn. "Put your bird dogs to work and don't let them stop until we find the guy who was in the office and the accountant."

"I'll have them start right away, Diego." With that he stood and left the office not knowing for sure where to start.

In his own office at the docks he summoned the Lopez brothers, explaining the suspicions of Diego Garcia. "I want you two to find out what really happened in that office. There was a witness, but no one knows who he is and he's disappeared. I want you to learn what happened to the accountant, Galen Mason, who also disappeared some weeks ago. There are two other men missing also, the men you replaced, Lenny Pierce and Juan Casillo. People don't disappear without a trace. We have four men who, they say, did just that. Find out what happened to them and where they are now."

"We'll need the addresses of the four men as a place to start. The accountant must have had an office or home where he worked. The two men Chico sent looking for him must have had a home or office where they worked. I'm sure someone has looked there before, but we need some place to start." Orlando Lopez was a thinker and had begun to formulate a search plan. "What do you want us to do with them when we find them, assuming they are still alive?"

"Find out what they know before you eliminate them," said Finn.

First stop for the Lopez brothers was the offices of Galen Mason, CPA. The office was as it had been when Mason left it. Even the trash basket next to his desk had his last trash in it. It took the rest of the day to search the office, and it appeared he had only one client, Bluefin Seafood, Inc. The man had been a meticulous record keeper. It was obvious the records and files had been searched before. There were file folders with labels denoting the contents, but nothing remained in the files. Phillipe Lopez was the computer whiz of the two and went to work on his computer files. There was no reference either in the file cabinet or the computer, to the illegal activities being carried on by the Bluefin Group. It was strange that there were no personal files regarding Galen Mason. All such files had been deleted and erased. Fernando Lopez was searching the desk when he found a business card tucked under the desk pad. On it was the name and phone number of a salesman for Cessna Aircraft Corp., Wichita, Kansas. As he searched the office he noted a calendar on the wall with an airplane picture on it. Fernando called Garcia on his cell phone.

"Diego, didn't Perez own an airplane?" he asked.

"Yeah, it's owned by Bluefin. They keep it at a small county airport just out of town in their own hangar there. Why?"

"Maybe nothing, but I found a card from a Cessna salesman and there's a calendar on the wall with airplane pictures on it. It made me wonder. We're nearly done here and I think we should go out to the airport and check to see if the company plane is there." Fernando wanted to follow up every lead.

"OK, let me know what you find." Garcia hung up, but was pleased to learn they had unearthed something new.

Finding nothing else the Lopez brothers locked the office and left the building. Phillipe said he was hungry and they stopped at a small diner while on the way to the county airport. An hour later they entered the electronic gate to drive onto the airport property. The Bluefin hangar was the big blue one on the end to the left of the gate. They found the airport security officer and explained they worked for Bluefin and needed to enter the hangar, but had no keys.

"Let me check with the office at Bluefin Seafood and if they say it's OK I'll take you down there and let you in. I'll have to stand by while you're in there, you understand, for security reasons." He was pleasant and accommodating.

Five minutes later the guard opened the main door to the hangar to allow the two men to enter. Inside was the small, twin engine plane Galen Mason had flown so many times to the island banking destinations. Fernando looked inside the airplane as well as in the baggage compartment. Phillipe searched the small office area at the rear of the hangar and looked through the laptop on the desk. The only information in the laptop was maintenance records for the aircraft in the hangar; likewise, for the small two-drawer file cabinet. There were only aircraft log books and records. There were two lockers without locks. One contained a pair of coveralls and the other was filled with odd parts for the airplane. After an hour of looking they had found nothing and left the hangar for the security guard to lock up.

"It's getting late, Fernando," said Phillipe, yawning and stretching. "Let's call it a day and start again tomorrow."

"Good idea, Phillipe. It's too late to call the number on this card today anyway. I'll do it in the morning."

After breakfast at a local IHOP the two brothers once again took up the search. Their first order of business was to talk to Lucy and get a first-hand description of the witness to the shooting. Fernando took careful notes and thanked her for being so observant.

The second order of business was to call the number for the Cessna salesman in Wichita. "We are trying to determine the whereabouts of one of our company employees. His name is Galen Mason and was a licensed pilot who flew the company single engine on business. We found your card on his desk and wondered if you know him?" Fernando was polite in his questioning.

"I'm sorry sir, I don't recognize the name. I talk with a lot of potential buyers and I don't remember them all, but I don't think I have talked with anyone by that name." David Wheaton was a smooth talking salesman used to conversing with high rollers willing to spend millions on a new airplane. "Oh, wait a minute! I had another call regarding that name a short while back. I told them the same thing. I've never heard of Galen Mason. Those other men described the man they were looking for and I did sell a Cessna to someone who looked like that. Only his name wasn't Mason. It was Hanson, I think. I can look it up, but I'm sure his name was Dan Hanson. He was a really nice guy and a good pilot. He finished his Cessna training course and took possession of the new airplane. That was several months ago, though."

"You say those other men described him. Do you remember what he looked like?" asked Fernando.

Wheaton described the buyer. The description also matched the one Lucy had given them of the witness to the shooting in the Bluefin Seafood offices.

"Do you have any idea where the plane or the owner might be today?" Fernando inquired.

"Sorry, I sure don't. The plane could be anywhere in the world. It was the new model with the stronger engine and belly pod. I remember the owner asked to have a large fuel cell installed in the belly pod. That request is not unusual for owners wanting to make long flights to Alaska or Northern Canada or even South America. We do it all the time."

"How would I go about finding the airplane?" Fernando was excited about the new lead. "I'll look up the aircraft registration number, but I have no idea where to look. You might call the FAA and give them the number to see if he filed a flight plan to a specific destination. Hold on just a minute and I'll look it up." Moments later he was back on the line to give Fernando the registration number for the Cessna Caravan.

"Thank you, you have been very helpful. If for some reason the owner should call you for something, would you please call me on this cell phone number? I would appreciate you not mentioning my inquiry to him if he calls. Thank you."

"You're welcome, sir. Have a good day." A salesman to the end.

Chapter 14

The death of Alma Pedersen weighed heavily on his mind. He had hoped he would feel some relief when he extracted revenge upon the two men responsible. Dan had taken a terrible risk by returning to Florida where someone could have recognized him, but it appeared as if he had pulled it off. Since returning to Homer he had thrown himself into his work at the office. Leah Cooper, his new receptionist, was working out well. She had compiled a large list of potential clients and was notifying each one on the list she would contact them with the date Mr. Hanson would be in their city. He planned to visit each area by flying his own Cessna and renting a car in order to contact the names on the client list she had composed.

Dan walked the few steps down the hall to ask Leah to come to his office. He filled his coffee cup and returned to his desk. She was only steps behind him.

"Yes, Mr. Hanson, what is it you want?" she asked.

"I have been reading this material you put together, Leah, and I've decided I would like you to accompany me on this recruiting tour. I will be speaking with business heads each day and will need someone to attend to the details as they arise. I can't think of a more qualified person to do the job. Would you be interested in going along? After all, it will be an 'all expenses paid tour' of Alaska."

She studied her shoes a moment, considering the offer. "When would you like to leave?" asked the receptionist.

"Let's see, today is Thursday, how about Monday? Can you be ready by then?"

She was nodding her head, "Yes, I'll be ready. There are some things I'll need to finalize on the list of clients before we go and some shopping I need to do in Soldotna before I can leave, but I'll be ready by Monday."

"I want you to know how impressed I am with the work you've done in putting this trip together. I believe this will be a successful trip and we'll be picking up several new clients. I also think we will need to hire another receptionist to allow you the time to work with the new clients. I'm hiring an administrative assistant for those responsibilities and would like you to accept the position. It would come with a nice pay raise as well. Are you interested?"

She studied her footwear again, "I'll take the position under the condition that I am only an administrative assistant. I'm not interested in any after-hours work, if you know what I mean. I'm sorry, but I don't do that kind of work."

"Leah, you have just confirmed that I've made the right choice. Welcome aboard. You will no longer be on an hourly wage, but have a guaranteed monthly salary. The hours will sometimes be long, but you are free to come and go as you wish and work the hours needed to get this new venture under way. If and when the business warrants it we will hire someone to help you with the paperwork we will generate in this effort. We'll hire you an assistant, so to speak."

"That sounds nice, Mr. Hanson. I hope all of this plan works out. I like working for you and I like the job. It's been fun so far." Leah was telling the truth, she was having a good time doing the groundwork for Dan Hanson.

"I have drawn up an employment contract of sorts," he said as he slid a copy of the contract across the desk. "This outlines your new salary and benefits. It also has a formula for estimating a year-end bonus plan based on how much new business we generate. Take your time studying it, and if you agree, sign it and bring it back to me." Dan was happy to have the new assistant and excited to launch his new consulting business. "If you like the terms and sign the contract you will have to hire your replacement at the front office receptionist desk."

The remainder of the week was busy. Leah had advertised for a receptionist to replace her in the front office. She had read and signed her new contract and placed it on Dan's desk. Applicants began to come to the office almost immediately. There had been eleven applicants interviewed by Friday. Only one had real qualifications, looks, appearance, manners and a desire to make the office look successful. She had recently moved to Homer from Anchorage where she had worked as a receptionist and secretary for one of the administrators at Providence Hospital. She was married, but the couple had no children. Her name was Donna Stanton and her husband was Doug. He had been promoted to manager of the local bank a block from Dan Hanson's consulting office. Leah interviewed her twice and decided she was the one to replace her at the front desk. She said she could start right away.

Leah spent the weekend tutoring her in the affairs of the office. She provided all the cell phone numbers for contacting both her and her boss. The two walked to the bank and filled out signature cards in order for her to buy office supplies. It would be a short break-in period, but if she had questions, the new girl could reach Leah on the cell phone.

Dan had worked on plans for the trip until Friday when he went to the hangar to get the airplane ready for the trip. The weather looked to be good for the next two weeks, at least in the areas he intended to visit. He stocked the plane with bottled water, snacks and Cokes. He opened the cowling and inspected the engine. Using a ladder he climbed up to inspect the pins on the controls. He checked to be sure all the lights were working and did a thorough inspection of the entire Cessna. It was full of fuel and ready to go on Monday.

While in the hangar he put together a travel bag with clean clothing and shaving gear. They would be staying in hotels where Leah had secured reservations on each leg of the trip. This was beginning to look like a very expensive journey and Dan hoped the new business he generated would warrant the time and effort as well as the expense. He felt excited and relieved about the trip, feeling certain he had solved the problems of his past and was free to pursue his future. He didn't need the money, but he wanted to feel useful and had a desire for success.

Monday morning Dan opened the hangar door and moved the Cessna outside. He put his Jeep inside the hangar and closed the door. Everything was ready to go when Leah came to the hangar. She had a large suitcase on rollers, which Dan stowed inside the cabin of the craft. The airplane was configured to take ten passengers, but with just Leah and him there was plenty of space. He planned to stop in Anchorage allowing Leah time to do some shopping before heading out to more remote parts of the state where the shopping opportunities were limited.

After her three hour shopping trip she returned to the airport to load her treasures. "Necessities for the trip," she explained.

It was now noon and time to fire up the plane and head directly to Valdez where they had an evening meeting scheduled with several potential clients. Leah had rented a banquet room in the hotel for the conference. The flight plan to Valdez was by way of Whittier down Prince William Sound and up Valdez Arm to the city of Valdez and the Valdez Airport. The trip, including some sightseeing, took just over two hours with spectacular view of the scenery and glacier lined mountains. The air was smooth and the sun was bright. Dan had never been over this part of Alaska and enjoyed the trip as much as Leah. They landed at Valdez and were assigned a transient parking spot. Dan tended to the tie-down of the airplane while Leah went to the terminal to pick up the rental car. She was allowed to drive the rental through the gate to where the plane was parked in order to load their bags.

As Leah had just exited the airport gate in the rental car, her cell phone chirped. It was Donna Stanton, the new receptionist.

"Is everything OK?" asked Leah.

"Oh, yes, just fine, but there were two men here a little while ago asking for someone by the name of Galen Mason. I told them there was no such person in this office. They didn't believe me and described this Galen man. The description they gave matched Mr. Hanson perfectly. I didn't admit that to the men, but they seemed upset when they left the office. I told them Mr. Hanson would be out of the office for several days. After they left they sat in their car for a long time before driving away. I don't know if this is important, but I thought I should let you know."

The telephone was routed to Bluetooth and the speaker in the radio. "I heard your report to Leah, Donna. I would appreciate it if you didn't give them any information without telling me first. Leah made you aware of the receptionist I had who was attacked and died from her injuries. I don't want to take a chance on you being hurt. I want you to call the Homer Police and get hold of Gary Fritz. He investigated Alma's death. He'll be aware of the possibilities and offer some protection for you. I also want you to call Owen Sutton. He is a fireman with the Homer Fire Department. He's a friend and will sort of keep an eye on you. I'll call him to let him know also. I don't think there is any danger for you, but I don't want to take any chances."

Donna now sounding frightened, said, "Mr. Hanson, I don't want to be involved at all if there is going to be danger in the office."

"I understand, Donna, but there shouldn't be any danger for you. I'll call Gary Fritz and Owen myself and let them know you're frightened and want protection. In the event the two men come back, call Homer Police immediately and close the office. I don't want you to be hurt or threatened." Dan was worried about who these men could be. He and Owen had taken care of the two men who killed Alma. There must be a new boss in charge at Bluefin Seafood.

Dan took his own cell phone from his pocket and found the number listed for Gary Fritz.

"Sergeant Fritz," the officer answered.

"Gary, its Dan Hanson. I'm in Valdez and just had a call from my new office girl. She had a visit from two men a few minutes ago and she was frightened enough to call me. Would you go down to the office and talk with her?"

"I'll go there right now. I'll call you later and let you know what's happening." Fritz spoke with urgency knowing the recent events in the office.

"What's going on?" asked Leah.

"I'm not sure, but Gary is going to the office to talk with Donna. As long as we're here in Valdez we'll go ahead with the meeting tonight as scheduled. If there is some threat going on in Homer we can go back in the morning. If not we'll finish up here and move on to Glennallen tomorrow afternoon."

Dan had thought his problem past had been resolved, but now here it was facing him again.

Leah and Dan checked into their rooms at the hotel and found the room where the evening meeting was to be held. It was adequate. Dan ordered refreshments delivered to the meeting room to pacify the potential clients. With a written outline and visual aids to punctuate this presentation, he was confident this would get some of those who were present interested enough to want follow-up meetings with specific information for each of their businesses. The response to the presentation was remarkable. Eight had signed up to hear the presentation and fourteen attended. It was a good sign, especially from this small community.

The meeting had just concluded and Dan was busy shaking hands when the call from Gary Fritz came. Dan stepped into the hallway to answer his phone.

"We located the two men, Dan. I talked with them, but I don't know what they want. They are definitely up to no good, and they're looking for you. They called you Galen Mason, but they described you right down to the little scar on your left thumb. I don't think they'll try anything like happened to Alma, but I also don't expect them to leave Homer until you return. Donna seemed satisfied we would be looking after her and said she'd keep the office open. In my opinion it should be safe for you to go ahead with the schedule you have now. These guys know we're keeping an eye on them and they know you're out of town, but also know you'll be back. I would hate to see another conclusion like the other one at your hangar."

"Thanks for being so thorough, Gary. I'll ask Owen to sort of look out for Donna, too. We just finished the meeting here in Valdez and had a great response. I think this is going to work out well." Dan was trying to decide if it was safe to continue on with the meetings tour. His call from Gary indicated it was probably safe to continue with the scheduled meetings around the state. It would take a week to make the entire circuit. It was possible the two men would leave Homer by the time he returned, not likely, but possible.

Chapter 15

The rest of the tour was also successful with a good turnout at each meeting and attendance better than expected. From Valdez they flew to Glennallen, Tok, Delta Junction, Fairbanks for two days and finally back to Anchorage for two days. In each location Dan had passed out printed material and asked those interested to fill out registration cards with their name, the name of their company and what goals they intended to meet. At each meeting he collected the cards as a reference for future calls and to be included in mailers, which would go out to all who filled out the cards. His business and investment plans were simple and straightforward, a tactic which interested most of the small business owners attending the meetings. At the end of each meeting Dan conversed with anyone interested and wanting more information. The meetings usually ran late with interest running high.

The final night in Anchorage both Dan and Leah were exhausted. Dan asked Leah where she would like to eat dinner this final night on the road. She said she had never been to the Club Paris on Fifth Avenue. At dinner Dan thanked her for all the work she had done to make this a successful business trip. "I want you to take a couple of days off when we get back to Homer. You've worked hard putting this together and while we were on the road. Remember, you're on salary now and get paid even when you don't come in to the office."

She laughed as she sipped her wine. "That's right, I forgot about that," she said. "I want you to know that when we started this trip I didn't know what to expect, but I have been pleasantly surprised and impressed with each of your presentations. I now see that you really do know what you're doing and that this isn't just a scam. Until a few days ago I didn't know if I was going to stay with you or not. Well, I'm convinced and you can count on me for as long as you want me in the office."

"I must say you've proven your worth to me, too. This trip should make your annual bonus look pretty good. Of course it depends on how many of these cards turn out to be paying clients. This investment business is the culmination of a lifetime of accounting experience. It's something I've always wanted to do. I have to thank you for your part in making it possible." Dan sipped his black coffee feeling relaxed for the first time in many years. "We can start a little later tomorrow morning. If there is any shopping you want to do before we go to the airport we'll have time. Come on, let's get out of here."

It was nine a.m. when Dan's phone rang. It was Gary Fritz, "Good morning, Dan, did you have a good night?"

"Yes I did, Gary, thank you for asking. Are you planning to wreck my morning?"

"I hope not, but I wanted to tell you those two bozos asking questions in your office last week are back in town. One of our patrol officers found them snooping around your hangar and stopped them. He asked for ID and they came up with Mexican passports. They say they're commercial fishermen looking to buy a boat to fish the Bering Sea. My officer spends a lot of time at sea, fishing, and he said these guys don't know a crab pot from an anchor. They didn't give a local address." Gary had finished his short report. "I just wanted to pass this information on to you in case they are someone you may know. You know, kinda like those two who visited you and Owen at the hangar last time."

"I don't think I know them, but thanks for the warning, Gary. I'll be careful. Leah and I will be back in Homer this afternoon. I'll come in and talk with you when I get back."

"I'll be looking forward to it, Dan."

"If you see Owen would you tell him I could use a hand putting the plane in the hangar if he has the time? I'll call him when I get fueled up." Dan Hanson wanted to talk with Owen about a plan in case these men had the same mission as those they encountered in the hangar a few weeks ago.

"When will it end?" he asked himself. "When will it all end?"

An hour later he and Leah loaded their luggage into the rental car and headed to the airport. Leah said she had done all her shopping on the first leg of the trip and didn't have anything else to purchase. They turned in the rental car and were given a ride to the Executive Aircraft hangar where his Cessna was waiting. He did a preflight check and walk-around of the plane all the while worrying about the two men who could be waiting in Homer when they arrived. He tried to shake off the uneasy feeling, but it stayed with him.

Once in the air Dan climbed to 4,500 feet as he crossed Turnagain Arm. His plan was to skirt the mountains high enough to view the glaciers, but stay on the west side of the peaks. This would make it a beautiful sightseeing trip and allow him the opportunity to familiarize himself with the terrain on the eastern edge of the Kenai Peninsula. The sky was blue and the air calm and cool near the mountains. At this altitude they could see the vast expanse of the Harding Ice Field. It was spectacular. Dan noted the entire peninsula west of the mountains was only a few hundred feet in elevation, but the mountains formed a formidable barrier rising more than 7,000 feet in some places. This barrier blocked the harsh Pacific storms from reaching the Kenai River and Kasilof River valleys giving the peninsula mostly pleasant weather patterns.

Dan flew along the mountains crossing Fox Ridge at the head of Kachemak Bay where he began his descent to Homer. He reported his intent to land at the Homer Airport and began his landing checklist. After landing he taxied directly to his hangar on the south side of the airstrip. Owen was standing next to his pickup at the hangar, awaiting their arrival. He had opened the big door and moved the two vehicles out of the hangar. Dan waved from the cockpit as he cooled the engine and prepared to shut down. He was glad to be back in Homer in spite of uncertainty awaiting him.

Owen was waiting near the aircraft door when Dan unlocked and opened it. "Welcome home," he called out as the two emerged from the big single engine plane.

"I didn't expect a welcoming committee," said Dan as he placed wheel chocks under the tires.

"Gary let me know you were coming in, and I asked the FAA folks to let me know when you reported in. I thought you might use an extra hand putting the bird back to bed. Did you have a good trip?" Owen was full of questions, avoiding conversation about the two strangers with Mexican passports.

"We had a great trip," interjected Leah.

Dan pulled the baggage from the plane and helped Leah carry hers to her car. He tossed his own bag into his Jeep and would later put it in the hangar. He returned to the plane where Owen was waiting. Leah thanked him for letting her take the rest of the day off, and he mentioned that he would check in with Donna at the office before ending his day. Leah started her little Toyota and drove on home. Dan and Owen watched her as she drove away, waving as she went.

"OK, Dan," Owen began when the Toyota was going out the gate, "what's the story with the two new goons in town?"

"I honestly don't know. I've never seen them as far as I know. If they were sent by the people I used to work for they have more diplomacy than the last two. At least they didn't go to the office and beat up the receptionist."

"Do we need to get ready for another assault like the last one?" asked Owen.

"I don't know what to expect, to tell you the truth. I wish I did. I guess I had better put the shoulder holster back to work, but until I can talk with these two, I really don't know who they are or who they work for. It could be dangerous, but I think we have to wait until they tip their hand and we know what they want. We can't just go around blasting strangers because they look suspicious. I think they'll show their hand as soon as they hear I'm back in town, if the same old employer sent these two."

Owen placed his hand on Dan's shoulder. "We got lucky last time, old friend, but we may not be so lucky this time. Call the fuel truck and let's put the bird in the hangar. I'll even buy you a beer and you can tell me how much money you made on this trip."

Once he had taken care of the Cessna and closed the hangar Dan drove to the office to confer with Donna, his new receptionist. She was at her front desk with several folders open, working diligently. She looked up when Dan opened the front door.

"Oh, hello, Mr. Hanson, welcome home."

"Thank you, Donna. I just came by the office to check with you to see if there was anything urgent I need to take care of before calling it a day. Is there any coffee in the kitchen?"

"No, sir, but you go sit down and I'll make some for you." She stood and moved toward the hallway leading to the small kitchen. "How was the trip, sir?"

Dan followed her down the hall as far as his office. "It was great. I think it will generate a lot of business for the office. I give the credit for the success to Leah. She researched and created a client list and arranged all the meetings before we began the tour. The whole thing went like clockwork and we were able to get a sizeable number of business owners wanting follow-up information." He was seated at his desk when she entered with a steaming cup of fresh coffee. "Have a seat, Donna. We must have things to talk about."

She placed the cup on a glass coaster on his desk before sitting in the upholstered chair in front of the desk. She took a steno pad from under her arm and placed it on her lap. "Yes, sir, I have quite a list here. Do you want to do this now?"

"First of all I need to know about the two men who came in asking for me. Did they say who they represented?" he asked.

"No, sir, they didn't say who they were or what they wanted. Actually they weren't looking for you. They said they were looking for someone by the name of Galen Mason. I told them there was no one by that name in this office. The taller of the two started to describe this Mason person. The description matched you perfectly, but, again, I told them there was no one by that name in this office. I'm sorry, sir, but for some reason I didn't like their looks. And, given the Alma Petersen incident, I didn't think it wise to volunteer any information. Officer Fritz said I did the right thing. I've been frightened ever since they came into the office. The Homer Police Department has been patrolling the area regularly and I heard they picked them up just to identify them, but I'm still a little scared. Am I in any danger, Mr. Hanson?"

Dan picked up his coffee cup and took a drink before attempting an answer. "I don't think you're in any danger, Donna. I don't know who these men could be. I promise that if there is any hint of danger I'll do my best to keep it out of the office. I don't know what I can do to ease your mind, but I will have Officer Fritz keep an eye on you to insure your safety. This situation will be the first item on my agenda. The success of this office depends on our ability to be strong and reliable. Customers will pay us a large sum of money to protect their investments and it is up to us, in this office, to deserve that trust. You did the right thing by not giving those men any information. I will remember your loyalty and I thank you for what you did. I will have a meeting with Gary this evening to discuss the matter." In truth, Dan didn't know what to do about those two men.

"I feel better already, just talking with you." Donna was still uneasy but no longer felt alone. "There are a few other things to deal with, two new clients want your services, locally, and there have been several calls from businesses in Soldotna asking for you. It seems you already have a trustworthy reputation. None of this list has to be dealt with today. I just wanted to discuss those two men because they frightened me."

"You did the right thing, Donna. I'll do my best to resolve any problem with the two men. Please be patient. I need you in the office. You would be nearly impossible to replace. I don't want to lose you." Dan knew the men were here for him and there was little chance of danger to her, although that didn't work out for Alma Petersen.

Chapter 16

Dan met with Gary Fritz at the Homer Police Station. Owen Sutton joined the meeting shortly after Dan arrived. The trio sat at Gary's desk in the station for a briefing from a report sent by DEA, the federal Drug Enforcement Agency.

"This is a confidential report and I don't want this information leaked to the public," Gary began. "When our officer stopped these two men the other day they had Mexican passports. The officer ran the information through the National Crime Information Center to see if they were wanted anywhere in the country. There were no warrants issued for either of the brothers, but we received this report from DEA who has dealt with them in the past and sent us the information they have."

"They aren't wanted in the lower forty-eight?" asked Owen.

"No, but that doesn't mean they haven't committed any crimes. It only means they haven't been caught. The report states they are suspected in a number of killings in Mexico, Columbia and Florida, but there is no evidence to prove it. The man the brothers now work for owns a commercial fishing business in Florida called Bluefin Seafood, Incorporated. DEA suspects the company is importing drugs into the United States from Columbia and other South American countries. Again, there is no evidence to prove it's happening. Their names are Fernando and Phillipe Lopez. Born in Mexico, they moved up in the cartel by beating and killing dealers and others for the cartel bosses. They were very good at what they did and were hired by Thomas Finn, one of the bosses for the Colombian Cartel."

Dan held up his hand to stop Gary's report. "I have to tell you something, Gary, but this information can never get out of this room. I warn you that if you ever tell anyone and I'm asked about it I'll deny everything. Am I clear about that?"

Owen had heard some of this revelation from Dan in the past, but Gary was shocked by it. "What are you saying, Dan? Do you know these men?"

"No, Gary, but I am the man these guys came here looking for. My name, before I had it changed, was Galen Mason. I was the accountant for Bluefin Seafood, Inc. I never knew about the drug business the company was involved in and only dealt with the fish business. I began to suspect when my boss, Orlando Perez, had me transport large sums of money out of the U.S. to several off-shore banks for deposit. I did this for a long time as part of my accounting duties. I learned about the illegal part of the company by bits and pieces. After several years I was able to figure out what was happening. Bluefin Seafood had a fleet of fishing vessels operating on the Atlantic Ocean. The fishing fleet did well and furnished the fish for the seafood company. What I learned later was that while on the open ocean the fleet would also meet and receive illicit cargo transferred from other vessels. The fishing vessels would drop that cargo off in a backwater rendezvous on the way to the cannery to unload the fish.

Gary Fritz, amazed by the story, said, "Do you mean to tell me you worked for the drug cartel in Florida before coming here?"

"No, I'm not saying that at all. I worked for Bluefin Seafood. It was a legitimate corporation making a great deal of profit. The drug end of the business was handled by another man, Chico Miranda, totally separate from the fish business. I worked for the fish company for several years before I even suspected there was another side of the corporation. After I confirmed my suspicions to my own satisfaction, I began to make a plan to disappear without a trace. It took a long time to arrange, but I thought I had gotten away with it until Pierce and Casillo came looking for me. I don't know how they found me, but they did. I thought it was over when Owen helped me get rid of them. I guess I was too optimistic, because we now have the Lopez brothers here looking for me. I'm sorry. I never intended to bring this kind of wrath to this community."

"Did you know all this, Owen?" Gary asked the fire captain.

"Not all of it, but he had told me about the two goons who came to the hangar and tried to kill us. I thought then, and I think now, that what he had done was justified and done for honorable reasons. You know this man, Gary. You know how much he has done for the community of Homer in the short time he's been here. I'd hate to see you try to make him out to be the bad guy." Owen had suddenly become defensive on Dan's behalf.

"Hold on, Owen," said Dan. "I have to take the blame for bringing this mess with me. I never intended to get anyone hurt, but Alma is dead and Pierce and Casillo are dead, all because of me. And now there are two new killers in town looking for me. Yes, I'm responsible for all this."

Owen was about to speak, but Gary held up his hand, "Hold on a minute, both of you. Let's not worry about who is to blame. Let's try to figure out what to do about it." He turned to Dan, "OK, Dan, how much of this can I take to the DEA agents?"

"I would just as soon you wouldn't connect me, Dan Hanson, with my old persona, Galen Mason. The rest you can give to the DEA, but there's no proof for any part of this story. You're not dealing with some street punk here. These are ultra-successful cartel members. They don't deal in small numbers. They deal in the millions of dollars. They have no conscience. They will kill anyone they think will threaten their organization. There is no evidence against them because they kill all the witnesses." Dan was speaking softly, knowing his entire new world was collapsing around him. "One innocent person has already been killed and it's likely others will be hurt before it's over. I don't know how I can do it, but I have to put an end to this business. The only way I can see to do this is to go back to Florida and stop them myself. The problem is that the cartel is like a snake that can grow a new head. If I cut off one head another will replace it and do it quickly. The organization itself must be stopped in order to kill the snake."

Gary was quick to respond, "You can't go back to Florida and take on the cartel alone. You need the DEA and the federal government on your side. You're talking foolishly, Dan."

"I've thought about it a lot, Gary, and there's no other way. The DEA and ICE, the FBI and all the other agencies have failed to come up with any proof of wrong-doing by Bluefin Seafood or any of its personnel. The transfers are made out at sea and the product is unloaded before the boats reach the cannery. I worked in the company for many years before I realized what was happening. I don't know how, but I have to do something to stop this violence. I thought I could get away from it, but I only endangered more innocent people, including you and Owen. No, this is my fight. I have to do it."

Owen was next to ask, "Do you have a plan?"

"Not a plan, but I have enough inside information to get me close to the company operators. With a little luck I can eliminate them before they get me."

Owen was shaking his head. "That isn't a plan, it's suicide. You can't take on the cartel alone and expect to succeed. You need help, a friend, an ally, a backup."

"I know all that, Owen," said Dan, "but there is no way to lure the head men here to Homer. I have to go to Florida. Remember Florida isn't Homer. It's big with lots of people. A single person can get lost in the crowds. I think I can do that. You and Gary don't need to know my plan and in spite of what the two of you say the feds won't be any help. I'm the one to do the job.

This isn't revenge, its self-preservation. If I survive I'll be back to continue building my consulting business."

"If I can't talk you out of it I'll have to go with you. You can't possibly do it alone." Owen was emphatic in his statement.

"Don't even think about it, Owen. You have a family to take care of. You have a job and responsibilities to the community. You can't just walk away from all that."

"I've thought about all that, Dan. When do we leave?"

"I'm taking the Cessna in case I have to make a run for it. I'll get ready today and leave early tomorrow morning. If I can't talk you out of it, be ready to leave by five a.m.," instructed Dan.

"You're both crazy," said Gary. "The two of you have no chance. No a chance at all. You are both going out to be killed. I can't let you do this."

Dan looked at Gary with cold eyes. "I would rather not tell you any more of the plan, Gary. I don't want you to stop us. Please stay out of the way. I respect you and I don't want you to compromise your official position or interfere with my plan. Please, Gary, let Owen and me do what we have to do."

"You're both crazy. Get out of my office and good luck to both of you."

"I'll meet you at the hangar, Dan." Owen had to go home and explain to his wife his decision to go with Dan.

Dan could have taken a more direct route south, but had decided to take the Colt .45 and shoulder holster with them on the plane. Originally, he had intended to leave the gun in Alaska, but thought with so many people looking for them it would be wise to carry protection. Not wanting to land in Canada to refuel and be forced to a customs inspection he opted to take the coastal course to Seattle. It would be necessary to stop in Ketchikan for fuel, but that would give the men a chance to stretch their legs and to eat a good dinner before resuming the long flight.

During the flight he had decided to change his original flight plan and continued down the west coast to San Francisco and Las Vegas where Dan decided to spend a couple of days searching garage sales and a scheduled gun show to purchase more weapons. The time in the air allowed him to formulate a plan of attack.

Back in the air and navigating toward Florida, Dan spoke over the intercom system to Owen. "OK, Owen, it's time to share my plan with you. I want you to tell me what you think, and feel free to point out any mistakes you see."

"I wondered if you were going to share the plan with me or if I would need to act surprised." Both men chuckled.

"Here's the plan. I'm not stopping in Florida. I'm going directly to the Bahamas. I think I'm still on the Bluefin Seafood account at the bank there. I know the bank manager, after so many years of depositing large sums of cash with him. I plan to move all the cash from his bank. Bluefin and the drug cartel will be at a loss for working capital. It should make them a little angry." Dan chuckled again. "I'm hoping this will cause them to come after us and make some mistakes that we, you and I, as well as the Feds, can work to our advantage. If we can make them come into the open and attack us, then there will be probable cause for the feds to begin making arrests. According to Gary, DEA, FBI and Customs are all waiting for evidence they don't have in order to act. Maybe we can help generate that evidence. The new boss at Bluefin Seafood won't be happy when his checks begin to bounce. Especially if they are written to the Columbian cartel. Those folks have no sense of humor."

"How do you intend to get the money from the bank?" asked a curious Owen Sutton.

"That's why I brought a new suit. Bankers like men in suits. I'm betting the new managers of Bluefin Seafood have never changed the bank account for the off-shore money. I have the account numbers, and since the new company management assumes I'm dead I doubt they changed the account numbers or authorized signers. I'm betting I can get the bank manager to agree to a transfer by my authorization."

"That's a lot of 'what ifs,'" commented Owen.

"I didn't say the plan was perfect," quipped Dan.

"I admit I'm not much on accounting. My wife balances our checkbook because I can't. I'll have to trust you know what you're doing. So let's do it." Owen felt confident in Dan's assessment without a good reason to justify the feeling. The plane passed over Miami enroute to Nassau.

Chapter 17

I t was a beautiful, sunny, afternoon when the red and white Cessna Caravan landed and taxied to the transient parking area. A uniformed customs agent met them as they stepped out of the airplane. Dan had been through this ritual many times in the past.

"Good day, sir," greeted the friendly agent. He was quite pudgy, his good paying job a boon for his pocketbook and a curse for his waistline. "Do you have anything to declare?"

"No," stated Dan, "our luggage is in the belly pod. I'll get it out and you can inspect it if you wish."

"I should look in the baggage compartment, if you don't mind."

"Of course." Dan allowed it as he opened the baggage door on the pod and removed the two suitcases stowed inside while Owen stood aside, waiting.

The agent put his head inside the large compartment to look. "Very good, sir," said the customs agent as he stepped into the shade of the wing. "Now if I may see your passports."

Dan and Owen each took out a passport and handed it to the agent who scanned the first page of each one carefully.

"How long do you plan to stay in Nassau, sir?" he asked.

"We will probably leave tomorrow," answered Dan. "We have a meeting here in town this afternoon."

The agent nodded and initialed the documents. "Have a nice day and enjoy your stay in Nassau." He gave a sharp salute, turned and walked back to the main building.

"That was easy enough," said Owen, relieved there were no further questions.

"The customs agents see folks like us all the time. It's only a short flight from Miami and many small plane owners come here to fish and party. Come on, let's catch a cab and find the hotel. I have to change clothes before we go to the bank."

Owen seemed out of his element, "Are you sure this is going to work?"

Dan snickered, "We'll find out, won't we?"

The two men walked to a small gate in the fence near the main building and stepped outside onto a very nice palm-lined street. Dan stepped into the street and waved to a cab a half block away. The cabbie got out of the car to place the luggage in the trunk while Dan and Owen climbed into the backseat.

The cab driver was friendly and cheerful when he climbed back behind the wheel. "Where to?" he asked.

Dan gave him the name of a hotel not far from the airport. Upon arrival at the hotel Owen paid the driver with U.S. dollars. The two men registered at the office, each in a separate, but adjoining room. Half an hour later Dan tapped on the door next to his. When it opened the man inside, Owen, was wearing tan slacks and a tropical shirt. "I called a cab," said Dan. "It should be here any minute. It's not far from here to the bank. We should know within a few minutes if this plan is going to work or not."

"How much money do you plan to take out of the account?" asked Owen.

"I'm not sure how much is in there right now, but I don't plan to close the account, just move most of the cash to another bank."

The cab arrived and the man in the suit ordered the driver to take them to a Bahamian bank just over a mile from the hotel. Again Owen paid the cab with U.S. dollars. Owen found a bench in the shade of some bougainvillea as Dan entered the bank. He knew this could be a long wait.

A teller at the third window asked, "May I help you, sir?"

"Yes," replied Dan, "I would like to see Mr. McGruder, if he's in."

"May I give him your name, sir?"

"Yes, Mason, Galen Mason; Mr. McGruder will know me."

Moments later the teller came from an office at the rear of the bank lobby. He approached Dan, "Come with me, sir. Mr. McGruder will see you." The teller led Dan back to the office he had just come from. He stopped at the door and allowed Dan to enter. The teller went back to his window as Dan entered.

Angus McGruder had been with the bank for more than forty years. Now approaching 70 he had begun making plans to retire. "Mr. Mason, good to see you again. Come in and have a seat. Would you like some refreshment?"

"Oh, no, but thank you. I've come to make a change in our account with your bank, only temporary, mind you. I need to know the exact amount in this account right now." Dan slid a business card across the desk with the account number written on the back.

Angus McGruder picked up the card and read the number. "Miss Osecci, will you come in here a moment?" he spoke into the intercom. Momentarily a pretty black lady appeared.

Angus held out the card, "Bring me a statement for this account number, please."

She took the card and left the way she had come. Angus asked what plans he had for the account.

"There have been some awful happenings at the company offices in Florida. I have been tasked with safeguarding these assets until the situation has been stabilized. I'm sorry I can't give you more details, but I'm sure you understand."

"Unfortunately, I do understand. These things seem to be happening more frequently today. I am beginning to think I have picked the right time to retire. I don't envy your position in today's world. If there is any way I can assist you with the problem, please let me know."

"Thank you very much, Angus. You have been a great friend for many years. We'll miss you around here."

Miss Osecci tapped on the door and entered with a handful of account sheets. "This is current as of this time today," said the assistant.

"Thank you, Miss Osecci, that will be all for now."

McGruder thumbed through the sheets and found the line he was looking for, highlighted it in yellow and handed it to Dan. "As you can see, the amount is quite large at this moment."

"Yes, I see, more than one hundred ten million dollars. We will need to use this capital before we can re-deposit it back onto this account, but we will be renewing this account as soon as possible." Dan handed McGruder another card with another bank number written on the back. "I want to transfer one hundred ten million dollars to this account. We will leave the odd change in this account to keep it active until we are certain our other problems have been resolved. Is it possible to make this transfer immediately?"

"Yes, we can begin the transfer right away. It should be completed by this time tomorrow. You will have to sign some papers, of course, but I will have the transfer started now." He rang Miss Osecci again, "Have David Blake come in here, please," he ordered.

The two men sat in silence while waiting for Blake. When he arrived Dan chuckled inwardly. Blake was young, mid-twenties, black rimmed nerdy glasses and walking stiffly.

"Bring me the paperwork for a large transfer. Get the numbers from Miss Osecci. She will know the name of the authorized agent and both account numbers. Bring them back to my office as soon as you have them ready."

"Yes sir," said the little nerd as he left the office.

"I don't mean to pry, but I am curious, is everything all right with your company in Florida?" asked McGruder.

"Oh, yes, it has to do with a hostile takeover and my boss is just being cautious. I'm grateful for the nice day I get to spend here in Nassau, though."

"I envy you the trip. I plan to travel as soon as I retire. I have three more months and I will get a gold watch and lose my fancy office." Angus McGruder laughed. "It's time for me to leave. I'm becoming too cynical. If all my customers were as charming as you I could stay another five years."

"I know how it is when the joy goes out of the job. I wish you well. Do you plan to stay in Nassau?"

"My wife wants to stay, but we have a country home near Beisenstoke, England. Our son lives there with his family and Grandma wants to be with the grandchildren, but he won't come here. He is with Bank of England. Rather successful, as a matter of fact."

"You must be very proud, Angus. I wish I had a family, but I never took the time for it. Now that I'm getting older I regret the decision. I am going to grow old alone."

David Blake tapped on the open door and entered with a handful of papers. He spread them out on the desk in front of McGruder. "The signature page is the top sheet. The legal data is on the next two pages and the releases are the last two. Is there anything else I can do for you, sir?"

"No, David, this will do nicely, thank you."

Without any further comment David Blake exited the office using the same stiff stride he had used when entering.

"You can look through these forms, Galen, and if you're satisfied I'll have you sign this sheet." He held up the top sheet, which was the signature sheet that needed to be notarized and witnessed.

It took nearly ten minutes for Dan to read the entire document. As he neared the end he began to nod his head in agreement with all he had read. "This looks just fine. Angus, where do you want me to sign?"

"I'll witness the signature, Galen, but let me get Miss Osecci in here to notarize the document. Once that's done we will begin the transfer. I will be sorry to see you move this account, for obvious reasons, but mostly because I have enjoyed doing business with you for so many years. I will likely be retired when you re-activate the account. So, I will shake your hand and say goodbye now, while we are in private. It has been a pleasure, sir." McGruder stood to shake hands with Dan.

"I'll miss you, Angus. I hope you enjoy retirement. Good luck to you with your future." Both men were sincere with their handshake and wishes for the future.

The papers were all properly taken care of and Dan was assured the transfer was underway by the time he left the bank. Outside Owen was seated in the shade, now drinking a tall mango drink of some kind.

"How did it go?" asked an anxious Owen.

"We're done here. We can have some dinner and a couple of drinks and relax tonight. The transfer will be done by morning and we can fuel up the plane and fly off to another tropical paradise. I'll bet by the time the transfer is completed someone from the bank will have called the boys at Bluefin Seafood to report the transfer. That's when things will begin to get exciting."

"Did you find out how much was in the account?" asked Owen Sutton out of curiosity.

"I just transferred one hundred ten million dollars to my account in the Virgin Islands." Dan related the total amount in a passive voice.

Owen nearly shouted the figure, "ONE HUN—" realizing what he was doing he looked around to see who was listening. Now he spoke barely above a whisper, "One hundred ten million dollars! I didn't know there was that much money in the entire world. From now on you pay the cab fares."

"Let's go to the airport and fuel up. I'll check the plane out and we will be ready to leave in the morning. After that we can find a nice restaurant and have dinner. How does that sound to you?"

"A hundred and ten million dollars?" this was incredulous to Owen.

"Remember, this is drug money. Money gained from criminal activity. We can't allow them to get it back. That means the new managers at Bluefin Seafood and subsidiaries are probably going to be a little upset." Dan was being facetious, but he knew, firsthand, just how ruthless these men were. The task they had undertaken had just become extremely hazardous. Everyone connected with Bluefin Seafood would be on the lookout for the person who stole their money. This in turn would put both the Mexican and Columbian cartels on their trail.

Dan realized from the start he would probably never survive this plan, but he didn't want the same fate to befall his friend, Owen. He would have to send Owen back to Alaska at some point: hopefully alive.

Dan paid cash for the Cessna's fuel as well as the rooms, the dinner and drinks the two had consumed as well as the cab fares. It was late when the two returned to the hotel for the night. He had checked the weather and learned the flight tomorrow should be sunny and warm and barring an encounter with any strange affects crossing the Bermuda Triangle, it should be a relaxing flight.

Chapter 18

The following morning Dan and Owen boarded the Cessna for the five hour flight between Nassau and St. Thomas. Dan was confident in his navigational skills, but the GPS navigational system in the Caravan took all the work out of the over-water flight. A five hour flight is long in any airplane as is a single leg of 920 miles especially over the open ocean. The two men were prepared with bottled water, Cokes and sandwiches in a cooler, strapped into a passenger seat behind the cockpit. Dan had tuned in a satellite radio station in case they ran out of conversation on the long trip.

After flying two hours over the Atlantic Ocean Owen was bored and sleepy, moved his seat aft to keep his feet away from the rudder pedals, and went to sleep. Dan smiled at his ease and peace. It had never been that easy for him to fall asleep. Owen slept for nearly two hours. Islands were appearing on the horizon in several directions when he awoke.

"Where are we?" he asked, stretching his arms and back.

"Less than an hour out. I'll be entering controlled airspace soon and will have to report in. We'll be in U.S. territory in a few minutes."

Minutes later Dan contacted Cyril E. King International Airport to report his arrival. The last thirty minutes of the flight was busy for the pilot. He was given clearance to one of the runways and a radio frequency to switch to after landing. The runway was very long prompting Dan to ask permission to land long, reducing his taxi time by several minutes. Permission was given and upon touchdown he was instructed to change to ground frequency. Ground control gave him instructions to transient parking and informed him U.S. Customs officials would meet them at the parking area. He was to have his passport ready when they arrived. The official welcome back to the U.S. was short and painless. The customs official walked the men to the entry gate and wished them a nice day.

Dan waved down a taxi and asked him to take the main highway to a nice hotel near the airport. It was only a few short blocks from the hotel to the Banco Popular De Puerto Rico on Charlotte Amalie Road. Dan had been here many times before to deposit cash into his personal numbered account at the bank. The manager in the bank knew him by sight, but he had never developed a friendship with the man. That may all change today when his deposit of one hundred ten million dollars was added to his account. That should be enough to impress even this snobbish man.

Dan lay on the bed and napped for an hour. When he arose he showered and put on his suit once again. It was now late afternoon. He called a taxi to take him the short distance to the bank and asked Owen to wait in the roomuntil he returned.

The deposit could not readily be traced because of the number status of the account and Dan felt safe entering the public building. He walked to a small cubical and asked to be taken to the office of Darwin Costner. The young executive asked for his card and marched to another cubical, larger and with doors, where the manager was busy checking on a very large deposit made this morning. The young clerk gave the manager Dan's card and said something to him. The manager was nodding. The young man returned and led Dan to the office where Bank Manager Costner was waiting.

"A pleasure to meet you Mr. Hanson," greeted the manager. "We were surprised by the size of the deposit arriving this morning. Your account already had a sizable balance, but you are now our largest depositor. Thank you for your confidence in our bank. Come in and have a seat."

Costner led the way to the back office from where he directed his kingdom.

"I am in the consulting business, as you can see from my card. I am about to make a very large real estate purchase on behalf of my clients. The purchase price will come out of today's deposit, but the remainder will be my profit and I will leave that amount in this bank. You have been very accommodating to me over time and I appreciate it." Dan was lying, of course, but Costner was stumbling over himself to be helpful; making him look very proficient with the bank executive committee.

"Is there anything I can do to help you with this transaction, Mr. Hanson?"

"As a matter of fact there is. It's late today, but tomorrow morning I will be bringing my associate in to be added to the signatures authorized to use this account."

"Come directly to my office when you come in. I'll be happy to assist you with the signatory change. Just tell my receptionist, Claudia, and she will show you into my office. Do you know what time you might be here?"

"Whatever is convenient for you; however there will be one other item we must consider. The federal government will be looking to get a cut of this transaction. If possible, I would like your auditors to contact them and negotiate a fixed amount to be paid in taxes. Remember, after I make this land transaction I will be keeping the profits here in your bank. The less we pay in tax the more profit we will realize. I'm sure you understand. Your auditors deal with the IRS on a regular basis and would have a far greater influence there than a single individual such as me. It would do me a great service if your bank would represent me with the IRS." Dan had no interest in personally speaking with any of the federal representatives. He had enough of a problem with Florida drug lords.

"It is highly unusual, but I think I can instruct our accounting department to get you an amicable settlement. We have a direct line to those who levy the tax and I think we can have this settled by the time you come in tomorrow. Because of the tax item I would like to meet you here in my office at eleven tomorrow morning. Is that satisfactory?" Darwin Costner had dealt with the IRS on many occasions, but seldom did he have a request for him to pay the tax. This, he thought, would give him a great deal of leverage with the feds.

"I thank you, Darwin. You have been very helpful." Dan had another thought as he was about to get out of his chair and relaxed once again. "I do have one request. After the tax question is settled I want to reward my assistant for his loyalty and hard work. He's the one I am bringing in to add to my account as an authorized user. His name is Owen Sutton and I want him to have an opening balance of five million dollars in his own account. This will be a numbered account over which he has full authority. Again, I want there to be no tax liability toward this account. Will you be able to have that taken care of by the time we arrive at eleven in the morning?"

Darwin was making a note on his desk pad. "Oh, yes, everything will be ready for his signature when you arrive. It is a distinct pleasure doing business with you, Mr. Hanson. Usually clients want us to avoid the tax issues, but you are meeting them head on. It is a refreshing change. If there is anything further I can do to be of assistance, please let me know."

"I think we have covered all we can do today. I thank you for being so accommodating." Dan rose from his chair and held out his hand to shake the hand of the bank manager. "Do you suppose I could impose on you to have your receptionist call me a taxi?"

"Of course, Mr. Hanson, and the bank will cover the fare."

Back at the hotel Dan knocked on Owen Sutton's room door.

"We need to talk, Owen," said Dan.

"Sure, Dan, come on in. How did things go with the bank?"

"The manager was so impressed by the numbers he nearly wet his pants. However, I was able to accomplish a couple of things. The money arrived and tomorrow morning I'm taking you to the bank to have your name added to the account. I've also ordered them to open a private numbered account in your name. I'm depositing enough cash in that account to assure your kids a first-rate college education. There will be enough left over for you and your family to take a nice vacation. This will be after-tax money. Free and clear. It's the only way I have to repay you for helping me. All you have to do is live long enough to spend it."

"I can't take money from you, Dan." Owen was surprised by the gesture.

"That's up to you, Owen, but the money will be there for you, like it or not." Dan wanted to continue with the agenda he had planned without opening an argument with his friend. "We're going to be busy tomorrow. We have an appointment with the bank in the morning at eleven. You will be signing onto my account allowing you to use the account without my signature. This is a safety measure for me in case I get taken out. You will also sign for your own numbered account. I have the bank negotiating the tax settlement we must pay for bringing this money back into the U.S. I expect it to cost around thirty-five percent of the one hundred ten million. It's a lot of money, but we can't be dodging the feds as well as the cartel goons. As far as the bank knows this cash came from investors in my consulting business. We have just laundered a mountain of cash. It will be ours, legally if not morally. But, if you steal from a crook, is it a crime?"

"I don't know what to say, Dan," Owen was humbled by all this information. "I know nothing comes without a cost, so when do we get the bill?"

"I stopped at a lawyer's office, and I'm having a new will prepared and registered with the court. If this turns out badly I want you to take a large portion for yourself and donate the remaining amount to the City of Homer. There will be enough to build a new boat harbor, buy new fire trucks or a library or whatever they want to do. The city has been good to me in the short time I have been there and, if I don't survive, I want to repay some of that kindness." Dan was speaking from his heart. "I haven't been able to find any relatives or family of Alma Petersen, but, if I'm not around and some are found, I want them compensated for her death. I feel responsible. She was a terrific lady."

"You talk like you are planning to die. Get that notion out of your head. You can't quit fighting, EVER. You have to assume you'll survive. It's the only way you can win. Now, where do we go from here?" Owen was passing on lessons he had learned in the military, valuable lessons, to be sure.

"I'm not planning to die, Owen, just accounting for possibilities. We have a lot of things to take care of tomorrow. I think we should rent a car. The concierge in the hotel can help with that. We will need to go to the lawyer's office and sign the new will before they can record it. At eleven we are to meet with the bank manager to sign those documents and open your new account. He will have a figure from the feds about the tax assessment. I'll pay it, whatever the amount. Once done at the bank we can come back to the hotel and change clothes for the trip back to Florida. The plane should have been fueled this morning, but I'll check it before we take off. I'll file a flight plan for Miami, but I don't intend to land there. We need to find a small airport out of town with easy access in case we need to leave in a hurry." Dan scratched his head, thinking, "The first thing we need to do when we get back to Florida is hit some garage sales and buy more weapons and ammo. I'll need your help with that."

Owen was chuckling, "You know, I became a firefighter for the excitement. Had I known being an accountant was this exciting I would have pursued a different career."

The following morning, driving the rental car, and after stopping for a hardy breakfast, the men stopped at the law offices to sign Dan's new will. That done, they drove to the bank to meet with Darwin Costner. Both Dan and Owen were in suits to impress the banker.

"Our auditing department was able to get a reduced tax rate on the total assessment. The government agreed to reduce the tax rate by ten percent because you were willing to settle in advance of any litigation. I hope this will be satisfactory, Mr. Hanson."

"Yes, a commendable settlement. Thank you for your assistance in this matter, Mr. Costner."

"I have the forms here for you to sign giving us the authority to pay the taxes due. Just sign the top copy, please." Costner handed the paper to Dan who signed it.

"Good, now the matter of the additional signer of the account. Mr. Sutton, if you would please sign the card and the form opening your account as well as the card to be used as verification as a signor on Mr. Hanson's account. We will need a mailing address and a telephone number where we can reach you."

Owen wrote the information on a separate sheet of paper after signing all the mandatory forms making him a millionaire. It took several minutes to process the forms and make copies for Dan and Owen. Once done, Darwin Costner bid them a pleasant trip home.

The two travelers returned to the hotel to change their clothing and prepare for the flight to the mainland. They returned the car to the airport rental office. Dan checked the fuel levels and found the tanks to be full. It was two in the afternoon when the red over white Cessna Caravan departed Cyril E. King International Airport. While it was still daylight they landed at a small county airport several miles north of Miami. Dan used the airport loaner car to get to the local motel and rent rooms.

"This may be our last peaceful night," Dan told Owen. "We had better enjoy it while we can. In the morning we can look in the paper and find an old SUV to buy and return the loaner to the airport. Once we have transportation we can begin to look for weapons, but tonight, let's have a drink and celebrate being rich."

Chapter 19

Dan purchased a local newspaper outside the IHOP where they were going to eat breakfast. He found the want ads and after ordering coffee he opened the pages to the vehicles for sale. There were two that caught his eye, an old Ford Bronco and an also old, but with low mileage, Chevy Blazer. He circled items on the page and went to the garage sale pages of the paper. The list was long. He began by circling the ones advertising guns and ammunition. Breakfast came and he put the paper aside. The two had little conversation during the morning meal.

Later, outside the restaurant, Owen asked, "OK, Partner, where do we start?"

"I found two possible SUVs for sale. The first one isn't far from here. I want to take the loaner back to the airport as soon as possible. It's too easy to trace back to us. If we buy a used vehicle we can run it around on the old license plates for as long as we'll need it. Let's get started."

The first SUV, the Ford, looked terrible and filled the air with blue smoke when it started. Dan had used the key to start the old Bronco, but once it started Owen got his attention and motioned for him to go on to the next one on the list.

It was several miles to the next location, but Dan was familiar with the area and found the address easily. He spoke with the owner of the Blazer, a widow, who informed them the car belonged to her husband who recently passed away. She just wanted to get rid of it. It was clean and well kept. The sticker on the windshield noted that the oil had recently been changed. Dan drove the car around the block to check out its running condition. Upon his return he asked the widow the price. He paid cash and tossed the keys to Owen, instructing him to follow him back to the airport where he would return the loaner car.

Dan took the wheel when they resumed their quest. Owen read the want ads. "Is there any particular order you want to attack the garage sales?" he asked.

Dan pulled to the side of the road. "Give me the paper and I'll number the ads from the closest to the furthest. That will save us a little time. Just give me the address for each one as we go. I used to live near here and I know the area pretty well."

The men started down the list of sales buying several guns, both handguns and shotguns. At the first three sales they found four .45 semi-automatics. Two were Colt Commanders, one was a Smith and Wesson stainless steel while the fourth was a Kimber, almost new and still in the original box. There were holsters with the Colts and the Smith, but they would have to find one for the Kimber.

The next listing advertised assault rifles for sale. This one was a treasure chest of weapons. Dan found two AR-15's with nylon carry cases. The same young owner had cases of ammo and more than twenty clips for the rifles. He told Owen he was a survivalist, but his wife was about to have a baby and he needed money for the medical bills. He admitted he was reluctant to sell the guns. They also bought a Mossberg 12 gauge shotgun with a folding stock. It came with several boxes of 00 buckshot loads.

As they worked through the list of garage sales they were able to pick up nearly everything they needed including two ballistic vests. The body armor could be very important to them on this mission. By late afternoon they had filled the back compartment of the Blazer with guns and equipment. Dan suggested they find a secluded place and test fire them all.

"I don't like surprises," he said.

Several miles from town, on a side road, they found an abandoned gravel pit where it was safe to shoot. Owen proved to be an expert with the shooting and sight adjustments. He was also expert at taking the guns down for cleaning and inspection. By dusk they felt they were ready to begin.

Sixteen miles west of the abandoned gravel pit where they had been shooting was a huge sporting goods store. They were able to pick up most of everything else they thought they would need including good boots. The two men thought they were well outfitted with these final purchases. After dinner at a local restaurant the men returned to the hotel for the night. Dan had showered and was about to climb into his bed when there was a knock on the door. He slipped into his pants to answer the knock. It was Owen.

"I just got off the phone with my wife," Owen reported.

"How are things at home?"

"Things are fine. I talked with both the kids and both of them wanted me to bring them something. You know how kids are. The wife wants me home, of course, you know how wives are." Owen was now inside the room. "What I wanted to tell you was that Gary Fritz left a message with her for us to call him. It has something to do with what we're doing, but he didn't tell her what it was. I told her to call him and let him know we would call him tonight."

Dan looked at his wristwatch. "It's still early in Alaska. Let's give him a call now." The two men went to the phone resting on a small circular table at the back of the room. Owen knew the number without looking it up and dialed it. When Gary answered Owen punched the button for speaker in order for both men to listen to the conversation.

"Hi, Gary. Shirley said you left a message for us to call you. What's up, Buddy?"

"I'm glad you called, Owen. Is Dan with you?"

"Yes, I'm right here," said Dan into the speaker phone.

"You had better get some paper and a pencil. I have a lot to relay to you. Several phone numbers and instructions from the DEA and ICE. The two of you have caused a panic at DEA and Customs. They want you two to stop what you're doing and leave the situation up to them."

"Tell them we can't do that, Gary. They aren't doing anything and I don't like the idea of sitting on my hands and waiting for them to make a move." Dan sent the feds a clear message.

"I told them you would say that. They told me to ask you to wait until they could get some manpower in the area. They said they didn't want a bloodbath in the streets and innocent people getting hurt or killed. I have to say I agree with them, Dan. You and Owen can't take on the Mexican and Columbian cartels on your own. They have the manpower, the firepower and the skill to fight you. Don't do it. You'll both be killed without getting the job done. Don't do it, Dan." Gary was pleading with the two men knowing they would, in all likelihood, refuse.

"I know the feds. They'll stop at nothing in order to prevent us from doing what they couldn't. Tell them to forget it. I would be happy to work with them, but I am not quitting. When they ask why tell them they failed to keep Alma safe. They failed to keep Owen and me from being in a shootout at my hangar and they're admitting they have no evidence to confront them with. Their organizations are powerless to do anything. I don't have the same policy constrictions blocking my actions. I may get killed in the process, but the men responsible are going to be running for cover, and if I catch up with them, they'll be ducking bullets. I hoped they would do the job, but so far, they haven't and don't have any legal reason to act. I guess that's not quite accurate. They will come after me and Owen for doing what they have failed to do. By the time you deliver that message I'll have ditched my cell phone to keep them from tracing us with a GPS locator. If they want to find us, tell them to follow the blood trail. I won't be calling you again, Gary, for your own good and your safety. Thank you for trying to help. I hope to see you soon." With that short note Dan ended the call.

Owen was stunned by the conversation. "I think we just jumped out of the airplane without a parachute," he said curtly.

"We can't fight a war with an enemy in front and one in back. Once the violence starts they'll have to be on our side in order to protect the public. Our enigma is to figure out how to get the goons from Bluefin Seafood and the drug dealers operating up the bayou to start shooting first. When they do we'll have a right to defend ourselves. Great plan, don't you think?" Dan took the cell phone from his pocket, placed it on the floor and stomped it until the small parts and plastic housing were destroyed.

Owen found his phone and did the same. Once done dismantling his cell phone he looked up at his partner. "I have a lot of confidence in you, Dan, you earned my respect that night in the hangar, but I can't help but think we're getting in over our heads. How do you plan to get those hoodlums to come to us? You realize the two Lopez brothers we encountered in Homer will be here by now? Do you have a plan?"

"Yeah, I have a plan, but I don't think you're going to like it." While he talked he took off his windbreaker, adjusted one of the shoulder holsters and put it on. He put the windbreaker on over the nylon webbing and reached into the bag on the backseat of the Blazer for one of the Colt Commanders.

"Let me guess. You're going to their offices and spit in their eye," commented Owen.

"Pretty much; I'm going down to the Bluefin Seafood office to tell the new boss I shot his predecessor and stole one hundred ten million dollars from his bank account. I'm pretty sure that will get his attention. I also think it will make him mad enough to put the dogs on the street looking for us. I'm hoping he'll react brazenly enough to make a mistake and cause the DEA to take notice."

Owen was shocked at the plan, "Are you sure you want to play it this way, Dan? I don't see any way we can fight all that cartel firepower. Do you have an escape plan?"

"Nope, I'm counting on them coming after us in such force and we become a public nuisance and the feds will come to the rescue." Dan finished adjusting the shoulder holster and adding extra clips filled with ammo to his pockets. "How do you like the plan so far?"

"Your mother must have been frightened by a Kamikaze," stated Owen. "This is suicide."

Dan was grinning broadly, "I hope the boys at Bluefin Seafood see it that way. I'll drive down there. When I get out of the car to go inside, I want you to get behind the wheel and when I come out, with you driving, we go two blocks down the street and turn left. We will be out of sight and can slow down. It'll take them a few minutes to mobilize, giving us a head start."

"I don't like it, Dan, but you know these guys and I don't. I have to trust you. I'll be there to back you up." Owen still had mixed feelings about the plan.

"There is one other thing, Owen."

"What's that, Dan?"

"If the plan fails I want you to get out. I want you to leave all the guns and armament in the car. Go to the Cessna and get the black nylon Pilot's Bag from the cockpit. In it there's a copy of my will leaving everything I own to you. You will have control of nearly ten million dollars in my account and eighty two million five hundred thousand dollars-after tax money we took from the bank in the Bahamas. The only request I have is if any relative of Alma Petersen ever comes forth you must compensate them for the loss. The rest is yours to do with as you see fit."

"Don't ever talk like a loser Dan. You've already set me up with more than I could have ever done on my own. I told you before, you won't win if your surrender before the battle. We fight this battle together and we fight to the end." Owen didn't like the way this conversation was going.

"I know this isn't a perfect plan, but we have to get the bad guys into the open where the DEA can legally act. I don't know another way to do it. Do you?"

"I guess not, Dan, but I had to point out some of the risks. Now, let's change seats. I'll drive from here. I assume the first stop is the Bluefin Seafood office on the docks."

"One last thing, Owen, if things go bad and I don't make it, you get away. Don't try to be a hero or save me. You have a family who needs you. They're more important than this plan." Dan got out of the car to let Owen get into the driver seat. Once back inside the Blazer he said, "You've become the best and most trusted friend I've ever known, Owen. I hope we win this battle, but in the end I don't want you injured. Now, let's go stir the pot and make someone mad."

Owen nodded in agreement and put the car in gear, "You'll have to give me directions along the way, Partner."

Chapter 20

Owen drove the Chevy Blazer with Dan giving him directions to the offices of Bluefin Seafood, Inc. The offices were located on the north end of a long, tall, industrial building on the docks where fishing boats unloaded their catch. Inside the fish were processed, frozen and packaged for shipping and delivery to customers over the entire United States. On the opposite side of the huge building were loading docks where trucks were backed to load frozen fish products, mostly to retail stores and restaurants on the east coast. It was a busy place with heavy truck traffic.

The parking area for the customers and staff entering the Bluefin offices was fenced, but the gate remained open during business hours. Owen saw a handicap parking spot near the front door of the office where he backed in to facilitate a speedy exit.

"Wish me luck," said Dan as he stepped out of the car.

Inside the office complex he walked directly to the rear where the office, formerly occupied by Orlando Perez, was located. The receptionist looked up as he entered the outer office. Lucy, the receptionist, was shocked to see a person she recognized. She reached for the telephone to announce Dan's appearance, but was stopped when Dan took the handset from her and replaced it in its cradle. He never spoke to her, but wagged a finger indicating she was not to call her boss.

Frightened, she pushed her desk chair back from her desk and stared at Dan. Dan smiled back at her and again wagged his finger at her. She nodded slightly, but sat perfectly still.

Dan strode purposefully to the inner office door and flung it open. The man at the desk inside looked up, startled by the intrusion. Within that short instant of surprise he closed the door behind him.

"Who the hell are you?" demanded the man behind the desk.

"You would know me as Galen Mason." Dan stood quietly near the door.

Diego Garcia turned slightly in his chair.

"If you reach for that gun in the drawer I'll blow your head off like I did Perez and Chico Miranda," said Dan in a calm voice.

"What do you want?" demanded Garcia.

"Oh, I think you know what I want. You sent those goons to find me. Perez sent the ones before and they came up short, too. I came to tell you I'm the one who just cleaned out your bank account in the Bahamas. I'm the one who killed Perez and Miranda as well as the two men they sent to kill me. And, I'm the one who will kill you if you don't back off." Dan delivered the message in a calm and icy voice. "I know you'll call whoever you have running the processing plant and he'll send a couple of enforcers to find me, but they didn't get the job done when they came to my office and they won't get the job done here. BACK OFF OR DIE." warned Dan.

"You're an idiot," said a red-faced Perez. "You can't get away with this. I want that money back in the bank today. Do you understand me?" Perez' voice had raised a full octave.

"You're the one having trouble understanding. I already have your money. I have already killed the last two bosses and the two watchdogs they sent after me. I don't take well to threats and I should kill you right now, but I want you to deliver my message to the cartel. Shut down the drug operation and get out or I'll shut you down. You know what I'm capable of doing and know I don't make idle threats. Do it NOW or die." As Dan started to open the office door, he noticed a slight move by Perez. Holding his windbreaker open slightly, Dan said, "I told you, don't make a move for the gun in the desk drawer or you will die today. Deliver the message." Dan found the door handle and opened the office door.

He backed into the outer office where Lucy, the receptionist, was still seated in her chair backed away from her desk, clearly frightened. Dan heard the intercom on her desk ringing as he walked from the office. He didn't run, but walked with a fast pace down the hall and back to the entry door of the office complex. As he exited the offices he heard the Blazer engine idling. He stepped inside the car and said, "I think we had better leave now."

Owen pulled the shift into gear and raced from the parking area, turning right, driving two blocks and then left. Once out of sight of the Bluefin offices he slowed to legal speed. Dan gave him directions to a coffee shop a few miles away.

Owen kept a watch on the rear view mirror, but didn't see anyone following them. "Well, are you going to tell me how it went?"

Dan was grinning, "If the DEA has anyone watching the Bluefin Seafood plant they're now wondering what caused all the commotion at the office.

I'll bet there are people running everywhere there, looking for me. I feel sorry for the poor office girl, I think her name is Lucy, I'll bet she just got fired."

"Or killed," offered Owen. "They don't seem to be big on severance pay."

"You're right, I didn't think about that, but I can't change it now. That Perez, the guy in charge now, strikes me as a cold-blooded cartel killer. We'll have to lay low for a while until the wheels of justice get into motion. When we finish lunch let's go to the airport and fire up the Cessna. Where would you like to vacation for the next couple of days? St. Thomas?"

"Since we can't go home and see the family I guess St. Thomas would be really nice. Do you want to go back to the hotel before we leave?"

"No, I think we need to be gone as soon as possible. We can leave the Blazer at the airport, but we'll take the firepower with us, just in case." St. Thomas was a good choice, being a U.S. Territory there will be no customs inspection. "Owen, I want you to consider going home. There's going to be some killing and I don't want to get you involved. You have a family to think about."

"Come on, Dan, I'm already involved. If your plan works, and I hope it does, DEA and Customs should be mobilizing as we speak. If we lay low a couple of days we should have reinforcements when we get back. It may not be safe, but it will be Less perilous, I hope!

DEA supervisors had been at odds as to what to do with the information surfacing out of Homer, Alaska. The two men they had identified had fled the state. They had learned the Lopez brothers had fled back to Florida. In Miami the local supervisor was aware the brothers worked in the fishing industry, but their occupations were unclear. This morning something had happened to cause managers at Bluefin Seafood to panic. Bluefin Seafood managers associated with the maritime division of the company were called to the production offices for a meeting. The unusual thing about this was low-level enforcers were at the meeting. Word was sent out to field officers to learn what was happening within the Bluefin Seafood organization.

Mitch DeLong, a DEA field officer working the docks on the northeast side of Miami, was informed by one of his snitches of a threat made to the management of Bluefin Seafood. The seldom seen managers were huddled together at the corporate offices. Several enforcers in company cars left the packing plant in search of a man who had made threats to the company CEO, Diego Garcia. The informant said the man had come into the office and threatened to kill Mr. Garcia. Thomas Finn had mobilized his enforcers to find the man and bring him in. DeLong was certain the enforcers were paid hitmen, but had never found any proof he could take to court. *This may be what we need to make an arrest down here*, thought DeLong.

DeLong had several paid informants inside the company, but had never been able to gather any evidence from them. Drugs had long been suspected as the main product being sold by the fish company, but none had ever been discovered at the packing plant. Twice DeLong had developed informants through the local bar when the men drank too much on payday. Both times, after learning the drugs were being off-loaded away from the docks, the informants disappeared, never to be seen again. The agent had long suspected the enforcers were the ones responsible for the disappearances. These enforcers were supposedly security for the company, but they had never been seen at a checkpoint and often were absent when the fishing fleet arrived in port.

Mitch DeLong contacted the area supervisor to discuss the situation.

Ed Lewis was the local Miami area supervisor, "What do you think we should do, Mitch?" he asked.

"Without knowing the whole story, I don't know. One thing I do know, though. Something big is going on. I think we should set up a regional operations center and call in at least twenty men to coordinate the information. This may be the situation we've waited for to get evidence on Bluefin. They've never, in the past, panicked and sent their troops into the streets. They didn't even get this excited when the two top guys down there got iced. I never did like the idea they had shot each other."

"We need hard evidence. If you feel sure now is the time, we'll get it. I'll send Gene Blake over to you. He has a mobile command center at his disposal, but it would be better if it wasn't parked on the street. See if you can find a building from which we can operate. I can only give you ten men today, but if you get good information I'll pull a few off another job. Keep me posted and try not to waste this time. I don't want to have to report another dry hole to my bosses in Maryland." Ed Lewis was a good man and stood between the political bosses and the agents on the street. He had been threatened with loss of his job on several occasions, but in the end his efforts and those of his men had proven fruitful.

Within minutes Gene Blake contacted DeLong. "Have you found a place to park this van?" he asked without preamble.

"I'm headed there now. I'll have an answer for you within twenty minutes. It's a warehouse just four blocks from Bluefin's offices. I'll call you as soon as I find the owner. He owes me."

"It'll take me that long to drive there." Gene Blake was an old-timer in the DEA. Five years ago he had been shot and nearly killed in a raid up in Jacksonville. When he returned to work, he was unable to go back to full duty. Ed Lewis had just become the regional supervisor and once worked with Blake. He assigned him to surveillance duty and made him information coordinator for the district. Gene was now less than a year from retirement and would be sorely missed in his new capacity. As he neared the area where he was supposed to park at the warehouse, his cell phone rang.

"Where are you, Mitch?"

"Right in front of you, about half a block, the sidewalk on the right."

"Oh yeah, I see you."

"The warehouse is right beside me. I've opened the door. Go ahead and put the van inside."

When he spotted the open door he drove the truck inside and stopped the engine. DeLong closed the big garage door. "Tell the others to honk at the door and I'll open it for them. We can get all the cars inside out of sight here. There is a utilities room in the rafters with a skylight that opens and faces the Bluefin Seafood plant. We can put someone up there with binoculars to watch who comes and goes down at the plant."

"Will do, Mitch, good to see you again," shouted Blake as he climbed from the driver seat to walk to the back of the van. He opened the door, reached inside and toggled a master switch energizing all the equipment.

"Nice toy, Gene," DeLong commented just as a horn sounded outside the garage door.

"We'll be up and running in five minutes. There should be four agents in the car outside. I'll start assigning positions to them. You can go ahead with whatever you need to do. I can get you on the radio with this unit." Blake never looked up while talking, but was busy spinning dials and tuning radios.

"Get someone up in the loft as soon as you can. I want to know when Garcia or Finn leaves the office. I'm going to put a tail on them. I think we're ready for whatever happens next." DeLong knew Garcia and Finn were the key players in this plot, but he also knew the soldiers they had dispatched to the field were the dangerous ones. They would soon need more men.

Chapter 21

Mitch DeLong was inside the command vehicle with Gene Blake. It was getting late in the evening and none of the field agents had returned. The agent acting as lookout in the rafters of the warehouse was stiff and aching from the long hours and the confinement of his small, lofty perch.

"I'm going to have to come down to go to the bathroom pretty soon," the lookout said into his small hand held radio.

"I'll send you some relief as soon as someone comes back in. I'll also have someone bring you a sandwich and coffee. Hang in there." Blake cared for all the men he commanded.

"I'll go out and get him something to eat. I'll be back in ten or fifteen minutes. If no one has returned by then I'll go up and relieve him. He's had a long day." DeLong knew how it was to sit and stare out a small window at a doorway making notes of who came and went. Doing nothing is very stressful when you wished you were out on the street and getting involved, but it was all part of the job.

"Hold on," said the voice on the radio. "Someone just pulled up in front of the office in a Bluefin Seafood truck." There was a short pause. The door of the truck opened and a man stepped out. "It looks like that Thomas Finn character. Yeah that's him. He's going inside the office."

"Sit tight, Mitch, I'm going to call someone back here to relieve our lookout. He can stop for a sandwich for him. I need to get someone back here to tail Finn when he leaves the Bluefin office." Blake keyed another button on the console calling two of the team back.

"I'll go up and give our man a break. I want to see who else is showing up at the office." DeLong stepped out of the big van to begin climbing up the to the observation platform in the rafters. He had been watching for nearly a half hour when another SUV style vehicle stopped in front of the office. It, too, had the Bluefin Seafood logo painted on the door. DeLong recognized the two men when they exited the company truck. They were the Lopez brothers. Previous reports had indicated they were hit men for the Mexican cartel. The men were dressed casually and walked briskly to the office door and disappeared inside. Mitch surmised the men were all holding a high-level strategy meeting.

He heard the big garage door opening and a vehicle move inside. Two agents stepped out of the car. Before they could close the big door another car arrived and two more agents stepped out, one carrying a McDonald's bag. The men closed the big door. One opened the back door of the command vehicle to say something to Gene Blake. Another agent began to climb the ladder to the perch in the rafters where Mitch was sitting.

When he reached the top of the ladder he spoke to DeLong, "We've been following two guys from Bluefin Seafood all afternoon. They acted like they were lost. They zigged and zagged all over town. No pattern or method to the travel. I think they were just looking for someone and didn't know where to look or who it was they were looking for. Nothing happened. It was really frustrating. I brought you a burger; it's in the van. Take a break. I need to sit on a seat that isn't moving."

"Thanks Del. There's some kind of meeting happening there in the office. The boss is still inside and Finn showed up a while ago. Just now the Lopez brothers went inside. We haven't seen the secretary leave the office, so she must still be inside, working. I'm going to tell Blake to have the others come back here and have them follow everyone at the meeting to see where they go. Perhaps they're going to give up for the night." With that DeLong began his climb down to the warehouse floor.

In St. Thomas Dan and Owen had spent the day relaxing and sunning on the beach. They had strolled along the city streets looking at the shops and souvenirs. Owen bought tee shirts for his wife and kids. It was late afternoon when they returned to their hotel to take a little nap and shower before dinner. Dan Hanson had been unusually quiet all evening but broke the silence as they walked back to the hotel in the dark night.

"I think we had better plan to go back to the mainland tomorrow. The DEA must be on the job by now."

Owen just grunted. He was beginning to like life in this tropical paradise.

"I also think," Dan continued, "I will fly into an airport in Georgia where you can catch a flight home."

"Oh no!" said Owen quickly, "I came with you to back you up and I plan to do just that. You can't face this bunch alone. I'm staying."

"Listen to me, Owen. You have a family to think of. You can't stay down here indefinitely. Your family needs you. You did what you came to do; backed me when I was alone. The feds should be mobilized by now. We stirred the pot and made them come into public view. They will be looking for me and I intend to give them glimpses of the target, but I won't sit still and let them get the shot. When I had to do it alone I needed you to pick me up and take me to safety. You did it well and I thank you for everything you did here, but it's too dangerous for you now. You have to go."

"Dan," Owen said in a frustrated voice, "I can't let you be out there along with no help. I have to stay."

"That's the point, Owen. I am no longer alone. The feds now have something to investigate. I'll contact them and volunteer to be the bait they need to smoke out the cartel. I plan to try to be where they land the drugs back in the bayou. I know what to look for and it should be easy to find if they have a shipment moving into town. If I can find where they bring in the shipments the DEA troops can take over. The worst that can happen is the Bluefin outfit finds me first and kills me. But it has to be done. I can't live in Alaska or anywhere else as long as they keep tracking me."

"I see your point, but I don't like it."

"Trust me, it's the only way. You have to step out of it now, for the sake of your family. I have a new computer case in the Cessna with your name on it. In it is a new laptop computer with all the information I know about Bluefin Seafood. In there is also the numbers for your new St. Thomas bank account. You can use this money any way you wish. The taxes are paid and no one will question you about it. In the briefcase with it are files for you to use to access my bank accounts. This includes the big one we established. We talked about how I want you to use this money. You have been the best friend I have ever had. I can't let you be hurt."

"If you're that set on doing it your way, I guess I have to agree, but I still don't like it." Owen knew Dan had explained it clearly, but didn't like leaving him alone.

"I'm not suicidal, Owen. I plan to come back when it's over. I have a business to run in Homer," Dan joked. "In Georgia I'll go to a Walmart store and get us each a new prepaid cell phone. I want you to stay in touch, but it will have to be discreet."

"What time do we leave in the morning?" asked Owen.

Early the next morning the men ate breakfast at the hotel without much conversation. The hotel provided transportation to the airport where Dan did his preflight inspection before climbing into the pilot seat of the craft. He began his start-up checklist and put his headphones over his ears. Owen did the same.

Dan slapped him on the shoulder and said, "Let's go home, Partner."

Owen gave him a 'thumbs up' sign and they were on the way across the open ocean toward the mainland. Dan flew northward toward the Georgia coastline. The GPS presented him with a direct route to the Savannah/ Hilton Head Airport. Once on the ground he ordered fuel and a taxi. As he climbed out of his pilot seat he stepped into the rear cabin with Owen following. He stopped at the second seat on the right side to pick up a nice Samsonite computer bag.

"Here you go, Owen. There's some cash in there to hold you over for a while and get you home. You're a true friend. I've never known anyone like you. Thank you for what you did."

"I'm not yet convinced this is a wise move, but for what it's worth I count you as a friend also. Good luck, Dan."

"When the cab gets here we'll go to the Walmart for cell phones and then back to the airport to get you a ticket home. I won't stay to see you off, but I wish you and your family all the best luck in the world." Dan was aware this may be the last time he would be able to see his friend.

"Let's go get the phones and let you go back to Miami. I wish you luck, too, my friend."

Three hours later Dan was back in the Cessna winging his way back to the little airport outside Miami. It was dark when he landed and taxied to the hangar he had rented. As he taxied to the parking spot he saw no signs anyone had been there. That, at least, was comforting. It took a while to start the Blazer and put the Cessna inside the hangar. He stopped at a roadside restaurant on the way back to the place he had rented for some dinner. It was lonely without Owen. At his rented room he showered and lay down to rest. It had been a long day.

The following morning there was a light rain falling. Dan strapped on his shoulder holster and covered it with a light nylon jacket. It would protect him from the rain and hide the shoulder rig. He stopped at an IHOP for breakfast, sitting alone contemplating his next move. It was time to shake up the Bluefin Seafood bosses again.

In the warehouse down the street from the Bluefin offices the lookout in the rafters spoke into his small radio.

"Hey Gene, wasn't there something about an old Blazer in the first report we had?"

"Yes, there was. Whoever sped off in the Blazer is the guy who Set this com- motion into play. Why?"

"An old Blazer just pulled up in front of the offices down the street. The guy inside is alone and is now getting out of the car. He's about six feet wearing a blue windbreaker. Now he's standing in the street looking around like he's looking for someone."

"Keep an eye on him," said Gene Blake, "I'm going to have someone check him out." Blake keyed the radio and asked one of the officers in a car outside to move in and make contact with the newcomer.

Agent Art Spasky was the closest officer only a block away, parked on the street. Gene asked him to hurry and check out this suspect before he entered the Bluefin Seafood offices. Thirty seconds later Spasky skidded to a stop beside the Blazer. Dan had begun to walk around his Blazer when the agent arrived.

"Excuse me, sir, I would like to speak with you," called Spasky.

Dan turned to face the voice. "Who are you?" he asked.

"Come to the car and I'll show you my badge."

Dan hesitated only a second and walked to the white sedan. "What kind of badge do you own?" sarcasm dripping in his tone.

"I'll show you mine if you show me yours," said Spasky.

Dan reached into his hip pocket for his wallet with his driver's license inside. In return Spasky presented his DEA badge. Each inspected the other's identification.

"What's your business here?" asked Spasky.

"I'm applying for work," lied Dan.

Spasky opened his car door. "I think you need to get rid of the bulge under your left arm and get into my car. We need to talk and I need better answers."

"All right," said Dan, unzipping his windbreaker to make the Colt visible, "but I'm keeping my hardware for now."

"Get in," Spasky ordered. "I want you to meet some friends up the street."

"I'm not feeling friendly," spoke Dan.

"We won't be long. We just want you to answer a few questions."

Dan opened the passenger door and sat inside. Spasky spoke into the radio and drove off in the direction from which he had come.

Chapter 22

Art Spasky called the warehouse on the radio asking for Mitch DeLong to meet him outside the building. DeLong was waiting outside an office door when the agent pulled to a stop in front of the large building.

"Leave your cannon on the seat," ordered Spasky.

Dan complied and removed the Colt from the holster and laid it on the passenger seat. "Happy now?" he asked.

Spasky said nothing, but stepped out of the car and walk toward the man standing next to the building out of the misty rain.

"Dan Hanson, this is Mitch DeLong, special agent with the DEA. It would be in your best interest to cooperate with Agent DeLong." It was Spasky's way of introducing the two men.

"How do you do, Mr. Hanson?" Mitch held out his hand.

Dan looked into his eyes and decided to shake the outstretched hand. "Call me Dan."

"Fair enough, Dan. I think I know who you are, but I need to know what business you have at Bluefin Seafood? There's an investigation in progress here and I need to know how you're involved."

"What sort of investigation?" asked Dan.

"Sorry, I'm not permitted to discuss that with you," replied Mitch.

"Then, I guess, you don't need any answers from me. You just want me to go away and leave you alone." Dan didn't want to engage in a one way conversation.

"Mr. Hanson—Dan, you resemble a one-time employee of this company who disappeared some time ago. I was just wondering if you're that man."

"Do you have a warrant to arrest this missing man?" asked Dan.

"No, he's just a missing person we would like to talk with."

"I'm afraid I can't help you. I'm just here from out of town and looking for work."

"Are you looking for an accounting position?" asked DeLong.

Dan was startled by the question. DeLong obviously suspected or knew who he really was. "Let's cut to the chase, Mitch. I can help you, but you weren't interested when I tried to get this investigation going a long time ago. Because of you and your agency and the lack of interest I was involved in an attack on my person and nearly killed. My secretary was killed. If you aren't going to level with me now I'm not giving you a second chance to get me killed. I'm getting my Colt and leaving."

Dan was turning to leave when DeLong called him back. "OK, Hanson, come back. Let's go inside and talk. I think you have information I need and I don't want to see you injured in any way. I think we can help each other."

Dan opened the car door and retrieved his Colt, stuffing it back into the shoulder holster. But he stopped to stare at DeLong. "If you're serious I can help you, but if you try to play me again, I'm gone."

"Fair enough, let's get in out of the rain." The three men went into the warehouse, entering a small office in the front of the building. "Have a seat, Dan. Would you like some coffee?" DeLong took a seat behind the empty desk.

"No thanks," said Dan.

"So, you're one of the men who had the gunfight with Chico Miranda's men up in Alaska. You were very lucky to survive that one."

"I had some good help. Since you and your feds blew it all off and left me out there alone and got my secretary murdered, I thought it best to defend myself and was prepared. Now, you come along and want to kiss and make-up. Well, Mitch, it's going to have to be something more substantial from you to get me to cooperate with you. I don't like being a target."

"Ok, I understand, and you're right, but we had no evidence to allow us to intercede in the matter. I apologize, but neither the DEA nor the FBI was able to act until there was evidence of a crime and we had none. That has changed and we are now investigating real crimes. I'm asking for your help in the case, please." Mitch DeLong was sorry for what had happened to Hanson, but it was something he couldn't change. "Help us prevent another innocent victim from being injured."

Dan's plan was to get the DEA involved and to take down Bluefin Seafood and its illegal drug trade. He made the decision to get involved. "Ok, Mitch, but I want to be involved in the investigation. I want to see, first hand, that this takes place."

"Fair enough, how about we go back and start over as friends?" DeLong held out his hand to shake with Hanson.

Dan nodded and took the outstretched hand. "I have a file I can bring you. The same file I tried to give you before. It details the legal fishing industry and financial hijinks of Bluefin Seafood, Inc. The file outlines the financial dealings of the legal portion of the business. However, the totals reveal huge sums of cash entering the company and being transferred by Bluefin Seafood to an off-shore bank. I had learned that this cash was used to purchase giant shipments of various drugs from the South American cartels. The drugs were transferred to the Bluefin Seafood fishing fleet for transport into the U.S. and again reloaded on small boats for delivery to drug processing facilities in the backwaters of the Florida coast. It was an ingenious plan and has worked for many years. I was never able to learn where the drugs were taken once they were loaded into the high-speed small boats and delivered to the processing facilities, which was why I contacted you guys in the first place. I didn't want to be involved with the drug trade. I knew they would kill me if I tried to quit, so I faked my own disappearance and changed my name. I went to a lot of trouble to get this done and I don't want all my efforts wrecked." Dan stopped speaking.

"I'm truly sorry no one paid attention to you before. But, I'm paying attention to you now. I suspect the reason you weren't able to learn the location of the drug processing facilities was that they move them around to prevent detection. We, the DEA, have the same problem and, until this very moment, we didn't know this was a major entry point for drugs. I would like to have that file." Mitch DeLong had instantly realized his office and that of the FBI dropped the ball when the file was first presented. Had it been acted upon then it may have prevented a large number of deaths.

"I'll get the file and bring it to you. I have one immediate concern for you to handle, the new secretary across the street. Her name is Lucy. I've met the bozo now in charge there and I suspect recent revelations in the office are going to put her in danger. She's an innocent bystander, just like my secretary in Alaska. I think Lucy could wind up just as dead because of what she has seen in recent days. I want you to protect her. You can't let these new managers at Bluefin Seafood escape. I would prefer you just kill them, but I suppose you aren't going to do that. You know as well as I that these new managers are lieutenants in the cartel. They work for someone, too. If you don't stop the cartel you haven't solved the problem. It will only change its name and location, hire new faces and continue to do business. I want to stop the killing and money laundering. I want to stop the drugs. I want the public protected. I can't do this alone. I can eliminate the two men across the street, but that won't solve the other problems. So get Lucy out of there and go to work. I'll be back in a couple of hours with the file. You can even send "Ol' Starsky" there with me if you like, but I'll be back in a while with the file for you."

"Art," Mitch called, "Take Mr. Hanson back to his truck. I think we can trust him to bring us the file."

"Will do, sir," said Starsky, (Spasky).

Dan shook hands with Mitch again before turning toward the door. Spasky drove him back to his Blazer. He climbed inside and drove away without saying anything to Spasky.

Back in the warehouse Mitch DeLong was devising a strategy to remove the secretary, Lucy, from the Bluefin office. When Spasky returned he told him to take another officer and bring Lucy here for an interview. He would have two other officers outside the Bluefin Seafood offices in case there was any resistance by Diego Garcia or others to stop them.

As Art Spasky turned to walk out, DeLong pointed a finger at a young agent, George Wisnet. "Go with Art," he ordered. On his hand held radio he ordered Gene Blake to have Car 2, waiting outside the warehouse, to follow Spasky down the street to the Bluefin Seafood office.

Spasky and Wisnet drove slowly down the short distance to the Bluefin Seafood offices, parking in front of the entry. Wisnet walked back to Car 2 and asked the agents to wait until they came out with Lucy. "Stop anyone trying to follow us," said Wisnet.

The two men walked into the outer office where Lucy was seated. She sat behind her desk looking tired and worried.

"Can I help you gentlemen?" she asked quietly.

"Are you Lucy?" asked Spasky.

"Yes, I am. How can I help you?"

"I'm a federal enforcement officer and I would like you to come with us. We would like to talk to you." Spasky showed his badge to the lady.

"Oh my!" she said, startled. "What have I done?"

"This is an interview, Lucy, you aren't in any trouble. We just want to talk with you for a few minutes. Can you come with us?"

"I'll have to tell my employer, but yes, I'll speak with you. I must warn you I don't know much about what is going on around here. I'm new, you know."

Spasky nodded his understanding.

Lucy dialed the intercom on the desk phone. "Mr. Garcia, I have to go out for a few minutes." She paused a moment, "I have to go with some federal officers for some kind of interview."

An instant later the door to the inner office opened revealing a short, stocky man chewing a cigar. "Get the hell out of my office and leave my secretary alone," said the man.

"I assume you're Mr. Diego Garcia, the manager here. We have some questions to ask her and we'll bring her back shortly. We're sorry for the inconvenience, sir."

"You ain't taking her nowhere. Get out of my office."

"We are taking her, Mr. Garcia. I would suggest you not try to stop us." He spoke softly, but with purpose.

Garcia ducked back into his office to use the telephone. Spasky turned to Lucy. "Let's go, Ma'am."

She grabbed a sweater off the rack near her desk and moved quickly toward the door. Spasky held her arm as they walked. Wisnet walked backward until he reached the door, keeping an eye on Garcia. Once outside, Spasky led her to the car, opening the front door for her, then walking to the driver side and getting in behind the wheel. Wisnet motioned to the agents in the other car to keep an eye on the front door. Their training told them what to do.

As Spasky's car pulled from the curb a Bluefin Seafood pickup came into view. It stopped in the space just vacated by Spasky. Two men stepped out of the vehicle and marched toward the office door. Moments later they reappeared moving quickly to the truck. The two agents in Car 2 were standing by the front of their vehicle and had removed the key from the pickup. As they approached one of the agents held up his hand to stop them.

"Hi, fellas," he greeted them. "What's the hurry?"

"None of your business," said the taller of the two.

"I think it is my business, sir. I'm agent Diston with DEA." Diston showed his badge to the men. "We came to get a witness for an interview and it appears the two of you want to stop the process.

Why don't the two of you just sit tight a few minutes?"

"Go to hell!" said the tall guy. "We got things to do."

"Sorry you feel that way. I'll tell you what, I think you should show me some identification; to be sure we are properly introduced." Diston was using up time, giving Spasky time to get out of sight.

"Get out of my face," said the tall guy. "You don't have a right to come here and hassle me and my brother with no good reason. I'm leaving." With that the two men got into the Bluefin Seafood pickup, but the keys were gone. Fernando Lopez opened the driver door swearing and red faced. "Give me my damned keys," he demanded.

"You know, you'd get a better response if you were nicer to people." Diston was now having some fun with the men. "You should just calm down. You're too tense. And while you're relaxing you should take the bulge from under your jacket. I hope that bulge isn't a weapon, but if it is I want you to place it on the hood of your truck and step back. Perhaps your partner should do the same. His argument was punctuated by the second agent pointing his weapon toward them from the other side of the car.

Seeing the Glock pointed in their direction they began to comply, taking the weapons from under their jackets and placing them on the hood of the truck. "We got permits for these," Fernando said gruffly.

"Oh, I'm sure you do," said Diston as he stepped up to search the tall man while the other agent moved to do the same to Phillipe. "Please keep your hands on the top of your heads." Diston and his partner kept the men occupied and angry for several minutes. They had produced permits for the weapons they carried. Diston did a cursory search of the vehicle before saying, "Thank you for your cooperation, fellas. You can go now." He tossed the keys to Fernando before walking back to his car.

The Lopez brothers started the truck and sped off in the direction the other car had gone. Diston knew Spasky would have parked his car inside the warehouse by now. As they pulled away from the curb another Bluefin Seafood truck pulled in. They watched to see who had come to the office. It was Thomas Finn.

Chapter 23

With Lucy in the front seat beside him Spasky drove into the warehouse while another agent closed the big garage door. Spasky walked around the car to open the door for Lucy. He led her into the small office in the front of the garage, but through a door from the inside of the big building. Mitch DeLong was seated at the desk and stood when the lady appeared.

"How do you do? My name is DeLong, Mitch DeLong. I'm a special agent for the Drug Enforcement Agency. You are not under arrest and aren't in any trouble. We believed that you may be in some danger and thought we needed to get you out of the office. What is your name?"

"Lucy—Lucy Parsons." She spoke in a quiet and meek voice.

"Miss Parsons, we are here to help you, so please relax. Can I get you anything?"

"Oh, no, sir," said Lucy.

Mitch sat behind the desk once again. "Miss Parsons, we suspect there are illegal activities happening around Bluefin Seafood. We don't believe you are involved, but you may know something that will help us stop it. Have you seen anything suspicious since you worked there?"

Lucy hung her head, thinking. "I really don't know what is going on in that office. I've only worked there a short time, but strange things happen there all the time."

"What kind of strange things?" DeLong asked.

"I can't tell you that. My boss said I couldn't tell anyone."

"Your boss, you mean Diego Garcia?"

"Yes, sir, something happened the other day and he said I couldn't tell anyone. I'm afraid. I would have quit my job, but I was too frightened of what might happen if I did. I'm scared, Mr. DeLong, I'm scared to death."

"We can protect you, Lucy. We won't let anything happen to you." Mitch was trying to comfort her, but without much luck. "Do you have family here in Miami?"

"No, I'm from Minnesota and came to Miami with a boyfriend, but he left me. I had no money, so I took this job to get money enough to live on and buy a plane ticket home. I never should have come here." There were tears in her eyes now.

"It's important we stop these men, Lucy. If you help us I will see to it you get a ticket back to your home in Minnesota. We need to get you out of here. It's too dangerous." DeLong again tried to comfort her. "Have you seen anything you considered strange or illegal while you worked in the Bluefin Seafood office?"

"Yes," she said in a small voice, "the other day a man came into the office and went into Mr. Garcia's office without stopping at my desk. He was only in there a couple of minutes, but when he came out he left the office quickly and Mr. Garcia came out of his office mad as a hornet. He told me to call Mr. Finn and some others to ask them to come to the office right away. I don't know what the man said to Mr. Garcia, but he acted scared. There was a shooting in the office a short while ago and I kind of thought this may be connected to that shooting, but no one ever said anything about it to me. The men I called are all mean looking. I don't like them. We are the fish processing part of the business, but those men all work for the maritime division. They do the fishing and bring the fish to our processing plant. Mr. Finn is the boss at that part of the company. He frightens me. Him and his two thugs he always has around him." She had never looked up into the eyes of the DEA agent.

"Did you know this man who came to the office?" asked Mitch.

"I never saw him before, but he caused a terrible uproar in the office. Mr. Garcia was yelling at Mr. Finn and slamming things around in his office. It was awful. That's what scared me so badly. I'm afraid to quit my job because I don't know what they might do to me. I've already spent one whole night in the office. I don't know what to do." Again Lucy was crying.

"I'll furnish you protection. I don't want to see anything happen to you. We can get you a secure room as a hiding place until we can move you back to Minnesota. Would you like that?"

"Oh, Mr. DeLong, that would be wonderful. I have to get away from here."

"Good, Lucy, I'll begin making arrangements right now. I want you to sit here with Agent Spasky and give him all the information you know. He will be asking you names of people coming and going from the office and any small bits of information you may recall. It's those small items we piece together to make a picture. What you tell us will add to the picture and when we get enough we'll be able to stop whatever illegal activity is occurring there at Bluefin Seafoods. Thank you Lucy."

"Thank you, Agent DeLong. I've been very worried about how I was going to be able to get away from these men. I felt I was in danger of being killed. I never saw any real violence, but Mr. Garcia and Mr. Finn seem like ruthless men and they frighten me. Those other two, the brothers, carry guns all the time and I don't like the looks I get from the short one. He's creepy. I just want to go back home to my family."

DeLong walked around the desk to place his hand on her shoulder in reassurance. "I'm going to the back to begin making arrangements for you to do just that. I thank you for your cooperation, Lucy. Art, here, will take down all the information from you while I go start the ball rolling. If you need anything, just ask Art."

Lucy said nothing, but nodded in agreement. Mitch went out the back entry door and to the command vehicle while Spasky took his seat at the desk with a yellow legal pad in front of him. He introduced himself and the interview commenced. An hour later she was escorted to Car 2 and driven to a safe house to await her planned trip home to Minnesota. DeLong had called for a female officer to join the team and watch over Lucy until she could be sent home.

Dan recognized one of the agency cars as he approached the warehouse, returning with the thick file in hand. Mitch met him in the small office once again.

"I see you have the file with you," commented DeLong.

Dan placed the file on the desk saying, "Yes, and it's going to take you quite a while to go through it. There are copies of transactions by Bluefin Seafood, bank deposits, payrolls, expense sheets, and basically, all the financial dealings by the company for more than three years. You should pay special attention to the sales totals and the amount of bank deposits into the various banks, both local and off-shore. Like I told you before, the off-shore accounts were used to pay the cartels for the drugs being sent into the U.S. and loaded onto Bluefin Seafood fishing vessels out on the open Atlantic."

"This is exactly what we need to put these guys out of business and I thank you, Dan. I'm sorry the agency didn't listen to you when you first approached them. I can't change that, but I assure you we'll act on it now. Judging from the size of the file and the detail I see so far, you're right, it's going to take a while to sort it all out. Meanwhile I have a team working to put pressure on them. In the beginning we didn't have anything but suspicion to go on, but with the tidbits given to us by Lucy, the secretary, and this file I think we're finally going to bust this place wide open. There's another team working to find the landing point for the drugs. We have aircraft and agents in vehicles scouring the small inlets and bayous you indicated were probable entry points. This may turn out to be the largest bust we have ever made in Florida, thanks to you." Mitch was truly impressed with the detail he saw in the papers.

"What can I do to help?" asked Dan.

"Nothing, we'll take it from here. This situation is far too dangerous for you to be involved. I want you to go back to Alaska and let us do our job."

"No, I'm not doing that. I'm too involved to drop it now. Your outfit dropped the ball and it got my secretary killed. It got me and my friend involved in a gunfight, which, fortunately for me, we won. If you and your agency get weary of chasing Bluefin Seafood boats around the ocean and quit, leaving me and my friends in danger again, I may not be so lucky next time. No, I'm staying and I will be a part of it until the end." It was Dan's ultimatum.

"I'm sorry you feel that way, Dan, but I can't allow you to be involved. It would be too dangerous for you. Just go home and let me handle it," encouraged Mitch.

"I'm staying and I'm going after the cartel. I may get killed, but it's better than waiting for someone to sneak in at night and kill me when I'm not looking. I intend to hunt them down and keep them on edge. I intend to keep them looking over their shoulders all the time. I intend to be a thorn in their sides. And when they come after me I intend to defend myself."

"I can't make you leave, but I can arrest you for interfering with an investigation. You have a good reason, but I'll arrest you. The judge will probably release you with a warning, but you'll have a record and spend a lot of time in jail, waiting for court. I'm not joking here, Dan. You can't be involved."

"Ok, I'll tell what I'll do. You have the file with all the information I know. I'll give you two weeks to study the file and act. If Bluefin is still in business in two weeks I'm coming back to do the job myself. If, at that time, you attempt to keep me out of it I'll consider you the enemy and treat you the same as I'll treat anyone from Bluefin Seafood. Understand?"

"Oh, I understand, but you must understand, I don't take well to threats. I have the law on my side. Don't push or threaten me, Dan."

"It isn't a threat, it's a promise. The lady you allowed to be killed was a beautiful, efficient and wonderful person. Had she been one of your agents, what would you be doing about it? You would be pushing all the limits for revenge and calling it justice. Well, I'm calling it justice. You have two weeks." Dan stood and walked toward the door. "Two weeks," he said over his shoulder as he turned the knob.

Mitch sat behind the desk staring at the papers Dan left on his desk, knowing what Dan had just said was true, but he was bound by rules. There was no doubt Dan intended to make good on his promise to return in two weeks.

It would be up to Mitch and his team to finish this case in time or he would be forced to arrest a good citizen for something, as Dan pointed out, he would probably do himself.

Dan drove to his small room to pack his bag for the trip home. He opened his laptop computer to check the weather on the entire route back to Homer. This time he would take a more direct route across Canada. One other item he had to take care of was the several weapons he possessed. On his way to the small airport where the Cessna waited he had seen a small storage lot with locked storage units. He bought a packing box and placed all the firearms, holsters and equipment as well as the ammunition and clips inside. The box he bought was larger than needed in order to accept the shotguns. Nonetheless the box was extremely heavy. He taped it closed with duct tape and wrote his name on it. The box was deposited in the small storage unit and the rent paid. Now it was time to pre-flight the Caravan.

He stopped on his way past a Quick Stop store to purchase a small ice chest and some ice. He loaded it with bottled water and Cokes, chips and cookies. His plan was a two day trip and would spend one night in a hotel along the way. Dan's final act of readiness was to make an arrangement with the airport manager to leave his Blazer parked behind the hangar. He gave the keys and an envelope to the manager: "If I'm not back in two weeks the Blazer is yours. The title is in the envelope."

It felt good to climb into the Cockpit of the big single engine Cessna. He was looking forward to returning to Homer. Dan dialed Owen's number.

"I'm on my way home, Owen. See you in a couple of days."

Chapter 24

The weather was good and the air mostly smooth. He was flying west into the prevailing winds, but they were light and except for periods of mountain flying there was little turbulence. Once he crossed the border and entered Alaska he decided to alter his course toward the Gulf of Alaska and fly over Whittier and on to Homer. It was late in the evening when he arrived in front of his rented hangar. Upon landing he called Owen to ask him to meet at the hangar.

Dan had just closed the hangar door when Owen arrived with a cold beer in his hand for Dan.

"Here you go, Partner," said Owen, handing the beer to Dan. "Welcome home."

Dan accepted the cold brew and took a long drink before answering. "It's good to be home, Owen. How's the family?"

"They're fine and looking forward to seeing you. I called Leah Cooper to let her know you were returning. She was thrilled. She said she had a lot for you to do when you got back." Owen took a sip of his own beer, and asked, "How was the trip?"

"Long, but it gave me a chance to think. When I left here I had just finished a long business trip to start up my consulting business. I hope Leah has followed up on the requests that came into our office. It's time I started working for myself. I'll be in the office in the morning."

"How did it go after I left Florida?"

Dan chuckled, "I shook them up at the Bluefin Seafood office while you were there. When I came back I dropped in to say hello, but the DEA stopped me from going inside. I met with an agent named DeLong. He seems like a good guy, but he warned me about coming back. I gave him the files I had and he is working on them right now. I told him if he didn't have results in two weeks I was coming back and taking over again."

"What did he say to that?" asked Owen.

"He wasn't pleased." Dan tipped up the bottle and drained the last of his beer. "Can you give me a ride to the office? I need my Jeep."

"You bet, Dan. I'm glad you're home. With a little luck you won't have to go back to Florida."

"I meant what I told DeLong. If he hasn't solved the problem in two weeks I'm going back and do it myself. This time I'm not going to be able to act in a subtle manner. They will be ready for me and I'm going to need to shoot first. I probably won't survive this one. I hope the DEA gets the job done."

In Florida Mitch DeLong had been busy verifying the information in the files and ledgers Dan had given him. The information all checked out so far, but any crimes uncovered were committed by the previous management team at Bluefin Seafood. The corporation would still be liable, but not the present management. The best hope for a good conclusion and conviction was to find where the illegal drugs were being brought ashore for distribution. Mitch had a plan for that. He called one of his old friends, Glen Messer, at the National Oceanographic and Atmospheric Administration (NOAA).

Once the preliminary conversation was finished Glen asked, "What can I do for you, Mitch? You never call just to pass the time of day."

"You got me there, Glen. I'm working a case involving large amounts of drugs coming into the U.S. and I need some help. The information I have is that the drugs are brought out to sea and transferred to American fishing vessels while on the open Atlantic. The fishing vessels bring the drugs into the country with their blue water catch. Once in U.S. waters they are transferred again to fast, shallow water boats and taken into the backwaters of Florida to a distribution point where they're processed and packaged for distribution on the street. We haven't been able to learn the location of those landing points here in Florida. What I need is to have someone working the open ocean to watch for the exchange taking place off-shore. We want to follow the shipment into the backwaters and find the distribution point. We think they move the spot around making it almost impossible to locate. Is there a chance you can help me out with finding which fishing vessel to follow?"

"Drug interdiction seems to be one of our new priorities. I'll see what I can do for you. Fax me the identification numbers and names of any fishing vessels you suspect of being involved and we can look for them. If what you say is happening, our air surveillance should be able to pick up on them. We try to track any boats coming from South America toward the U.S. If the boats we are tracking head toward the boats on your list we might just catch the transfer in progress on the open ocean." Glen sounded positive about locating the delivery.

"I'll have the list for you by this afternoon. It will be quite long. They all fish for Bluefin Seafood, Inc. I just don't have the resources to pull this one off. Stay in touch and call me when you get to Miami." Mitch was elated by the news he was looking for and the help he was about to receive.

In the past NOAA was tasked with many scientific duties as well as identifying and investigating ocean-going vessels discharging pollutants into the ocean. Recent changes had placed NOAA under Homeland Security. When that change was made the duties of NOAA enforcement personnel were greatly expanded to include watching for illegal immigrants and drug transfers such as the one Mitch had just reported.

Thomas Finn was in Diego Garcia's office this morning conferring with the Bluefin Seafood boss.

"No one has seen the bookkeeper in the last few days," he reported. "My men say he was picked up by the feds, but they let him go. I think DEA is working on us pretty hard right now. Too many things are going wrong. Out in the back country there are strange trucks running around looking for something. My men have seen several of them. Your receptionist hasn't come in to work since they picked her up and took her away from here. The Lopez brothers had that run-in with the DEA in front of the office. Those boys don't like to be hassled. Taking all this stuff together indicates to me we're being watched closely. Luckily I haven't seen any sign of the DEA on my end of the pier, but they are looking in the canals. We need to either change strategy or shut down for a while. I know the boys in Bogota don't want us to close, but it's looking more like a good idea right now."

Garcia pulled the cigar stub from his lips. "I'll talk to the boss down south, but we need the new shipment coming in this week. I had calls from three area distributors over the past few days. Supply is running short in most places. We need this new shipment. Once we get the stock ashore and in place we can try building a new system for bringing the drugs into the States. Pass the word to your men to be extra careful. One other thing, Thomas: Find that girl, Lucy, and get rid of her. She's a flake and if she knows anything at all she'll spill it to the feds. Have the Lopez brothers find her and take care of her."

"I'll take care of it, Diego, but I don't understand how all this started in the first place. Perez and Miranda had a good thing here for a long time. There was money in the bank and the feds didn't even know we existed. Now we're dead broke and the feds are crawling all over the place. Where did it all go bad?" asked Finn.

"It was that damned bookkeeper. Diego should have killed him long ago. I want him dead, now! You tell Fernando and Phillipe to get it done. I don't care what it costs, I want him dead. My boss in Bogota is very upset with the situation here. It has cost him a lot of money. I've convinced him we can recover and pay in the future, but he wants this mess cleaned up. I want this mess cleaned up. Tell your boys 'don't come home 'till it's over.' Tell the boys in the swamp it's open season on feds. If they see a fed in the swamp, get rid of him. Make sure he's never found. We can't play around any longer. Get that new shipment moving. I don't want any of your men sitting on the dock or waiting around looking bored. We have to take care of this situation right now. This has turned into a war. A lot of people are going to have to die, but we will come out on top. Now, get moving, Thomas. There's a lot to do." Diego stuffed the cigar butt back into his fat lips.

"The Lopez brothers are like coon hounds. They will keep their noses to the ground until they tree the bookkeeper and bury the girl. It's going to cost a lot of expense money, though." Finn didn't like the idea of the expenses coming out of his budget.

"Give them each ten grand for expenses. When the new shipment comes in we'll have some free cash for such things. Now, get on it." Diego sat at his desk, angry and glaring at Thomas Finn as he walked from the office.

In his own office at the other end of the pier Finn summoned the Lopez brothers. They came to the office, but didn't sit. "I don't care how you do it, but we have to find the accountant. We have to eliminate him. He has information that can destroy this organization and he has stolen a great deal of cash from the company. We don't know where he is, but it will be your job to locate and eliminate him. You will also find and eliminate Lucy, the receptionist over at the big office. The feds took her away, as you know, and she hasn't been seen since. She is a loose end we can't afford." Finn tossed each of the men a fat envelope. "This is for expenses. I want the two of you to stay on the trail until the job is finished. Find and eliminate the accountant and the secretary. Do it quickly." Finn was explicit in his instructions and firm in his orders.

Fernando and Phillipe both stood and left the office without question or salutation.

Next on Finn's list of duties was to contact Bud Girard. Bud was in charge of the in-shore boat fleet and the distribution of packaged product from his mobile processing plant. He had a small army protecting his operation. Many of his guards rode motorcycles on the swampy trails he used to get the drugs distributed to wholesalers in populated areas.

"Hello, Bud, how's it going?"

"Oh, you know, win some and lose some. Mostly it's pretty quiet, but we need product. The buyers are getting antsy."

"Have you seen much enforcement activity in your area?" asked Finn.

"No, it's been quiet, like I said. Why? Have you heard something?" asked Girard.

"Not really, but the DEA has been sniffing around the office and the pier. I was wondering if they had been out your way."

"We haven't seen anyone."

"Diego wants you to put on more patrols. He thinks they're working up to something. His receptionist was taken away by DEA agents and hasn't returned to work. Diego is worried. Keep your eyes open and be prepared for trouble. We think there is a war coming."

"My guys are always ready, but I'll pass the word to them. I really hate to start shooting feds. That always brings more trouble." Girard had been in charge of security for a long time and eliminated many intruders, but the only law enforcement officer he had ever done in was a deputy sheriff looking for a bribe and had it coming.

"Tell your men to keep an eye open. We will try to move the operation for security reasons after the next shipment comes in. In the meantime, be careful. I'll be talking with you. Keep me informed if there are any suspicious folks running around out there." Finn trusted his man to keep the locations from public scrutiny.

After hanging up the telephone Finn leaned back in his desk chair and scratched his head. "I wonder what Diego knows he isn't telling me?" Finn asked himself.

Chapter 25

Things had been quiet for the past two days and Mitch DeLong was worried. Today he would be sending Lucy, by commercial airlines, back to her family home in Minnesota. The female agent sitting with her had called to tell Mitch how excited the witness was getting about going home.

"She should be safe once she is back with her family. It will be our job to see to it the people down the street never find out where she went." DeLong was speaking with the agent guarding Lucy. "What time is she scheduled to fly out?"

"Noon, but I'll have her in the VIP lounge by eleven. She won't have to go through the regular security lines. I like her, Mitch. She's just a country girl trying to make it in the big city. She's educated and ambitious. She wants to be on her own and succeed and it's too bad she got mixed up with this group."

"I know how you feel, but the best we are able to do for her is to send her home to her family. If she's as bright as you say she'll find something back in Minnesota."

"I suppose, but I remember when I left home and how lonely I felt. I just feel sorry for her." The lady agent remembered her first years after college and how uncertain life was before she was accepted by the feds and sent to the academy for special training.

"Come back to the warehouse when you get her on the plane. I need you here," ordered Mitch.

Gene Blake had been catnapping at the console in the command vehicle when Mitch stepped up into the big van. "You need to get some rest, Gene. Someone else can take over here for a while. If anything happens here I'll call you, I promise." Mitch worried about the aging technician. His old injuries and advancing age were beginning take a toll.

"Yeah, you're right, Mitch. I can't work three day stretches any longer. I must be getting old. Bring in Kinsman. He can run this bus as well as me. Sorry man, I do have to get some rest. There's a lot of traffic down the street, but no action. Also, if I were you I'd rotate the man in the loft every two hours. It's too small a platform and the officers get cramped up. The discomfort distracts their attention. I'm going home for a few hours' sleep and a shower."

Mitch spoke into his hand-held radio, calling Kinsman into the warehouse to take over for Blake. He also called another officer to relieve the man in the loft. When Kinsman arrived he was briefed by Blake. As the new lookout man took the post and the other came down DeLong walked back into the office to confer with Spasky.

"Art, I want you to begin a two-hour rotation of the officers in the lookout post. Gene says they are getting too cramped and tired with the present schedule. Once something breaks and the action starts it won't be necessary, but for now I think he's right."

"Will do, Mitch," said Spasky. "I just had a call from one of the teams out on the swamps. He said there are more patrols out today. There are nearly twice as many motor bikes patrolling the trails. It sounds like we are beginning to make them worry."

"I hope so, Art. I think they must be getting low on merchandise and I'm hoping they make a move very soon. I have NOAA watching for a shipment coming in. If they spot one, we can follow it to the distribution point. The waiting is the hard part. Doing nothing makes all of us tired and edgy. So, here we sit, all dressed up and nowhere to go." Mitch had become accustomed to the routine, hours and hours of boredom punctuated by instances of insane terror. The adrenaline was what most agents lived for.

The routine continued for three more days until Mitch DeLong received a phone call from Glen Messer. It happened at six o'clock in the morning. "We think we spotted your shipment coming to the fishing fleet," Messer informed DeLong. "We have high resolution photos of the transfer. I am sending them to you by fax. I have the names and numbers of the boats headed your way." Messer quoted the information. "We intend to stop the delivery boats this afternoon for a search. We're waiting to allow time for your delivery boats to get back into U.S. waters so you can follow them. Be careful, these crews are very cautious and wary. They had lookouts posted on the boats the entire time the transfer was being made. Luckily our plane was at an altitude that didn't alarm them. Good luck on your end, Mitch."

"Thanks Glen. I'll get everyone ready. How long before they get back into Florida waters?"

"It's only a guess, but I would say six or seven hours. The two boats are traveling together and moving at the top of their cruise speed. The weather is good and the sea is calm in the area giving them a fast run home."

"Thanks again, Glen. Good luck with stopping the cartel boats. Don't get anyone shot." Mitch was anxious to get the trap ready. He looked at his watch. It would be around noon when the boats came back to deliver the cargo.

Lyle Gunnison was a longtime agent and the supervisor in charge of the search in the swamps. He and his men had done this kind of search many times. The sun was up and Lyle was in his command vehicle, a Jeep Wrangler, when Mitch called with the news.

"Good news, Lyle. The shipment is on the way. My NOAA contact thinks they will be in your neighborhood by noon or soon after. I have the boat names and registration numbers for you." DeLong gave Gunnison the information.

"That is good news, Mitch. I'll have my spotter plane ready by noon. We thought it might be coming because of all the added activity we see out here."

"This will be a big shipment, Lyle. We have to stop it. The men on shore will be on alert for you. Try to keep from being killed, will you?" Mitch indulged in some morbid cop humor.

"My ex-wife's lawyer would be really mad if I did. He might chase me to the grave for the alimony payments." Gunnison had never been married, but went along with the humor. "I have to get ready, Mitch. I'll get back to you later."

Lyle Gunnison had more than twenty men working for him on this detail. It was his task to organize and coordinate the search. The search would be difficult because of the terrain, swamp, canals, mangroves and thick undergrowth. Further, it would be impossible to look everywhere. Gunnison posted his men in groups near every trail and road in the area. The small aircraft patrolling the shoreline would have to inform him of the two boats he was told were headed his way. He suspected there was to be a meeting of the two large fishing boats and some sort of smaller craft from the backwater.

The pilot of the Aviat Husky had been flying large circles watching for any sign of boats coming out of the many canals in the area. He had just turned back toward the seacoast when he spotted two sizable vessels moving toward shore. The spotter in the back seat had his binoculars trained on the boats. It was the Bluefin and the Billfish, the names of the boats suspected by NOAA of being the transport vessels. The pilot paralleled the coast for a few minutes before turning inland again. Suddenly from out of the main canal came four open boats. All were fiberglass boats of roughly twenty feet in length and all with very large engines. The Husky flew inland until he was behind the little armada. The spotter in the back seat picked up his hand held radio to report to Gunnison.

Don't risk being spotted. Give them a chance to load the cargo into the small boats. We can intercept the large boats at the cannery when they dock. Stay well back from the inshore boats and give us reports on which channels they take. Our men on the shore will take over when they land. Good job guys." Lyle Gunnison was excited now.

The pilot climbed to a higher altitude to get a broader view of the many canals and channels in the vicinity. When the four smaller boats parted at high speed from the fishing vessels they travelled together for a short distance up a small river before separating. Two of the boats continued up the river while the first two raced up a large canal into the swamp. The pilot followed the boats in the canal and reported the direction of the two boats on the river. They were headed toward an area where five agents were waiting. The two boats in the canal were now slowing as the canal narrowed with reeds growing tall on either side. Ahead of the boats the pilot saw a large barn on the bank of the waterway. As he drew nearer he saw what had once been a house on the property but it had burned to the ground leaving only the large barn. There were tire tracks leading into the barn. The pilot circled the property once and flew on while the spotter reported the location to Gunnison.

Lyle had large aircraft sectional maps pinned together on the wall and was able to pinpoint the location. He called the nearest team leader to move to the old farm.

As the boats neared the barn the spotter noticed movement in the trees. It was a small band of armed men on motorcycles, dirt bikes actually. Immediately he reported to Gunnison who warned his team. He also dispatched another six man team to the area to assist the first.

The pilot widened his circle and climbed even higher to prevent the army in the woods from becoming suspicious of the plane. As he climbed he saw two SUV's moving down an overgrown dirt track toward the old farm. "The boats are pulling onto the bank at the old barn," reported the spotter.

Gunnison passed the word to the lead team. Then the waiting began.

Phil Dicks was a twenty year veteran of the drug wars and the team leader on this assault. A mile from the barn the team stopped on the wooded lane. He met with the second team and instructed them to wait here while the first team walked closer to the barn and the waiting band of armed men on motorcycles. It was dangerous work. The five-man team made the trek to the edge of the field where the barn stood. They could see several men with small four wheel vehicles and trailers loading large yellow-covered packages that looked like large boxes onto the small trailers. The team made its way through the underbrush to where the bikers were waiting. When the team was in place Dicks stepped out of the palmettos with his badge in hand.

"Drop your weapons, boys," he ordered.

One of the bikers spun around to meet the voice and upon seeing the badge raised a 12 gauge shotgun to fire. He was cut down by one of the team members. Two others raised weapons and dived for cover in the vegetation while three more started the engines on their small but powerful bikes to make a run for it toward the barn. There was a brief spate of gunfire, but no one was hit. The foliage was too thick for either side to see the other. Dicks motioned to his team to begin moving toward the hidden men. At the sound of motors and gunfire the second team moved in the SUV toward the barn. They saw the three motorbikes racing toward the barn as well as the men at the boats began to panic. The small green tractors sped as fast as they could toward the barn while the two boats, with some of their cargo still on board, backed away from shore and turned back toward the river.

The spotter in the Husky reported the action to Gunnison as the pilot turned to follow the two boats.

The men on the little tractors abandoned the four wheelers to run inside the barn through a small man-door in the side of the barn. The SUV stopped a good distance from the barn. Two agents stepped out and made their way to the back of the large wooden structure to cut off any escape. There was no way to tell how many men were inside. The team had seen the six men on the tractors run inside. There was no cover for the team to use while approaching the barn.

The second team leader motioned for the last three men to follow him. He climbed into the SUV while the others walked behind using the vehicle as cover. The team leader parked about thirty yards from the front of the barn. There was no sign of movement from inside. The team waited.

Chapter 26

The spotter in the Aviat Husky spoke to Gunnison by radio. "The two delivery boats are headed downstream, back toward the main river system. They still have some of their cargo on the boats. Is there a Coast Guard patrol on the river?"

There was a short pause on the radio before Gunnison replied. "Not on the river, but near the mouth. I'll have them wait there for the boats to come to them. They have a small Panga style craft and are very fast. Stay with the boats until they are met by the Coast Guard. I don't want to lose them in one of the side canals and I don't want to lose sight of the cargo they have on board. If they dump it, mark it with a GPS for us to pick up when the firefight is over upriver."

From their altitude the pilot could see the mouth of the small river and the orange stripe on the side of the open boat. The view for the two fleeing boats was blocked by the vegetation on the river banks. There were four men aboard the Panga waiting behind a stand of trees on the bank just south of the river mouth. The DEA pilot spoke to his spotter via the intercom. "I'm going to drop down and come up behind the boats. When they see us it may cause enough of a distraction they won't notice the Coast Guard boat waiting for them."

The spotter reached from the back seat, over the pilot's shoulder to give him a 'thumbs up' signal.

The pilot pulled back on the throttle and nosed the small plane downward. He leveled at about one hundred feet to avoid the trees and numerous birds nesting there. As he closed the distance on the two boats speeding toward the mouth of the river he saw one of the men in the lead boat pointing in his direction. He said something into a small walkie-talkie and the men in the second boat turned to see the plane. Both boats added the last inch of throttle, but outrunning the airplane was futile. The pilot slowed the Husky and followed the boats at a distance they were not likely to be hit by any gunfire from the speeding watercraft.

As the boats approached the mouth of the river and sped out onto the shallow blue salt water, their attention was still focused on the small blue and white airplane following them down the river and had not seen the Coast Guard patrol boat as it engaged its two huge Mercury engines to cut off the escape of the two river boats.

The DEA pilot could not hear the sirens but saw the red flashing lights and the armed officers on the government boat. The men on the smaller boats began to throw the cargo overboard to no purpose, because the big yellow packages were floating in the seawater. The airplane followed the chase for another two minutes until the lead boat slowed and the men aboard raised their hands. The second boat slowed and did the same. The pilot circled once and waved to the Coast Guard crew before departing back upstream toward the barn on the canal.

Back at the old barn where the workers had taken refuge, the men inside had quickly discussed the situation and decided it was time to fight. The six men who had been moving the cargo from the boats to the barn and the seven motorbike riders, armed with shotguns and assault rifles, posted lookouts near the two small windows and the man door. The remainder prepared their weapons and started the motorcycles. Two of the cargo handlers were ready to open the big barn door upon a signal from the senior guard who was now reporting the situation to Bud Girard.

"DEA has us pinned down in the barn," he said. "My guys are ready and we're going out on our bikes. If we stay in here we're done. We can't get out. We have to attack. Only half of the cargo is unloaded, and it's sitting out front in the open. The other half is still on the boats. They went downstream and I don't know where they are. You should be hearing from them soon if they were able to escape. I just wanted you to know we're going out of the barn now."

"How the hell did this happen?" asked Girard. "How did they find us?"

"I don't know, but we're going down fighting. If we win I'll call you in a while. If not, you'll know the shipment is lost." The lead guard put the phone in his pocket and revved the motor. He motioned to the two men at the doors to open them.

Three of the riders carried AK-47 assault rifles; the other two had shotguns. The instant the gap in the doors was wide enough the riders raced outside toward the SUV parked a few yards away. The three riders with the assault rifles were in the lead circling the SUV and firing in the direction of muzzle flashes. Attacking the well trained DEA agents turned out to be a bad idea.

They were ready and waiting when the barn doors parted. With the first shots fired by the riders the agents began to cut down the assailants. Two riders went down immediately. Both were shotgun men. The three riders with assault rifles sped toward the SUV shooting rapidly. The DEA agents were in safe positions behind the vehicle with semiautomatic rifles. When the riders came into view on the back side of the SUV they began to fire. Using the doors and the rear of the vehicle as cover the agents were able to cut down the riders.

The lead rider had not stopped to fire his weapon, but had held the rifle he carried at arms-length and fired as he rode by. He kept on a straight course for the wooded area where he and the others had been hiding earlier. At the edge of the clearing he threw the motorcycle to the ground and fled on foot.

Back at the vehicle there was a moment of sporadic gunfire. One officer was hit in the shoulder, but the wound was superficial. Of the seven riders one had escaped into the woods, five were dead and one badly wounded.

The two officers who were at the back of the barn now moved cautiously to the front to approach the open barn door. One agent behind the SUV reached inside and grasped the microphone, switching the radio to Haler mode, he called for the men inside the barn to come out with no weapons and their hands raised above their heads. At first there was no response, but moments later the six cargo handlers began to exit the barn.

The lead agent on the raid, Phil Dicks, called Gene Blake, who had now returned to the command post van, to report the outcome. Two agents were dispatched to search for the person who fled on the motorcycle. The mop-up and evidence gathering would take the rest of the day.

The escaped motorbike rider lay in the woods, frightened and shaken. He whispered into his cell phone while talking to Girard. He reported the outcome and capture of the local crew. Girard was furious, knowing the men he worked for were going to hold him responsible for the loss of both men and merchandise.

Girard reluctantly called Thomas Finn. It was not a call he was in a hurry to make. The two boat captains had sent word they were under attack by a NOAA enforcement boat and were unable to outrun it. Girard had attempted to call them back, but there was no answer from either of them. He had to assume the NOAA boat had apprehended them. He and his men had lost the entire shipment, an event that could well cost Girard his life as well as his job.

"Thomas, I have bad news. We lost the shipment," reported Girard.

"You what!" shouted Finn.

"I had a call from the security team at the barn. The entire security team is dead except for the lead man. The cargo handlers at the barn are all under arrest. They only unloaded half the shipment and the DEA has it. The rest was still on the boats when the attack came and they went down river with it. I can't get them on the phone or the radio. I think they were busted, too."

"Get down to the main office as soon as you can. Diego will want to hear this directly from you. I'll be there. How long will it take you to come to the office?" asked Finn.

"At least two hours if I leave here right now." Girard didn't want to drive all the way to the office for what was going to be a very unpleasant meeting.

"Good, I plan to wait here for the two fishing boats to come back to port. They reported on the radio they would be here in an hour. I need to find out what they know. We just lost two and a half million dollars, wholesale, and it will be tough to convince Diego we could have prevented the loss."

Finn was not looking forward to this meeting. Diego Garcia was not a man who tolerated failure. He had made special arrangements with the cartel for the shipment to come here prior to payment and it had been intercepted. With no cash to pay for the lost shipment there would be life threatening consequences from the cartel. Thomas Finn sat in his office awaiting the arrival of the two boats, the Bluefin and the Billfish.

Mitch DeLong waited in the command vehicle with Gene Blake. The two men made notes as they followed the action on the radios and telephones. It was a confusing batch of mixed messages, but DeLong sorted it all out by addressing each report separately. He placed headings on several yellow pads and took information and noted times of each report on its own sheet. Later he would build a combined scenario using the timetable as the key to the reports.

As things came to an end at each scene—arrests made and contraband seized—Mitch realized he needed to have a large contingent of DEA agents available when the fishing boats came back to the processing plant. He called Ed Lewis.

"It's going down, Ed. I have at least three scenes to cover and I need a lot of men this afternoon."

"How many men?" asked Lewis.

"I have two fishing vessels about to arrive at the cannery. Each will have a crew of eight or so. They will be at the Bluefin Seafood pier, which means they'll have a lot of friends if there is a confrontation. At the same time I will need several agents to move on the Bluefin Seafood, Inc. main office at the other end of the pier. We have to arrest the boss before he can run. I think Garcia and Finn will take off for Columbia if we don't take them into custody." DeLong was attempting to cover all his bases and there seemed to be a number of contingencies to consider.

"What about the men out at the swamp location?" inquired Ed Lewis.

"They are busy with the arrests and seizing evidence, but would never be able to return to town in time to back us up anyway. It would be more than a two-hour trip for them."

"OK, Mitch. I'm pulling a twenty-two man team from another project and will have them at your location within an hour. Get as many men as you can back to the warehouse from the swamp to relieve my other crew as quickly as possible. You're a priority right now, but I'll need them back as soon as possible."

"Thanks, Ed. Time is the governing factor here. I don't want the two main men to take off before we can arrest them. We have to strike now. We have the evidence and we're ordering warrants. It's time to put everything in place and do the raid. Thanks for the man-power. I'll be getting back to you shortly." Mitch breathed a sigh of relief. Game on.

Chapter 27

Mitch DeLong paced the warehouse floor awaiting the arrival of the force he was to command in the upcoming raid. He did his best to consider all possible circumstances they might encounter. It was a daunting task. Every raid had its risks. This one was especially hazardous for several reasons: He commanded an unfamiliar contingent of men, the pier location was guarded by desperate and ruthless men, it was unknown how many men were inside the huge packing facility and he had no idea how much firepower the men inside would have available to them. Mitch had commanded many raids in the past, but this one was, by far, the most dangerous. He was concerned for the safety of the men he commanded.

The arrival of the two drug smuggling boats, Bluefin and Billfish, dictated the timetable for the raid. It was imperative the agents reach the two fishing vessels before the crew could destroy any evidence on board. A simple water hose could erase microscopic evidence on deck.

Mitch called a quick meeting with the team leaders. The plan was to start with two groups: Two raiding parties for the initial raid with half of the agents to go to the pier to take possession of the two fishing boats and send the other half to the offices of Bluefin Seafood Inc. to arrest Diego Garcia and confiscate his files and computers. After the initial raids were complete the teams would be split again to take control of the two fish processing plants and check the identifications of the men working at each plant. DeLong estimated the total number of working crews would be around one hundred men and women. He wanted to command the raid on the Bluefin Seafood office personally, but he was needed at the command vehicle to direct the operation.

Once the team leaders were briefed he sent them to gather their respective teams and attack the fish packing plant. Mitch was inside the van with Gene Blake. There was some, but minimal, video feed from the invading teams.

Team one was to attack the two boats at the pier and arrest the crews on drug trafficking charges. With surprise on their side and the crews aboard the fishing vessels weary from the long fishing trip, the raid was quick and decisive. Once the crews were in custody, the team split to enter the processing plant.

Team two led by Art Spasky entered the offices at the opposite end of the pier. The desk of the receptionist was empty. Agents posted two men in the outer office while the others pushed open the door to the inner office where Diego Garcia was seated behind his desk, chewing on a stub of cigar and studying a ledger. Garcia, shocked by the intrusion, reached to open a drawer on the right side of his large wooden desk. Spasky held out his badge.

"Ah, Ah," said Spasky. "You shouldn't do that. Stand up and put your hands behind your head."

Garcia complied and asked, "What are you doing here?"

"My name is Agent Spasky. You are under arrest for drug trafficking. I'm holding a search warrant to search and seize all records and computers in the offices of Bluefin Seafood, Inc. There will be other charges, of course, which will be read to you once they are filed with the court. Now, step out from behind the desk and put your hands behind your back."

Facing the guns of the armed federal agents Garcia had no choice but to comply. "I want to call my lawyer," said Garcia, spitting his cigar to the floor of the office.

Once again, with the immediate problem under control the team split to begin the task of identifying the laborers working in the fish freezing facility. Thomas Finn had been out of the office at the time of the raid and no one would admit knowing where he had gone. One by one the ID's were checked. Most were released, but several had warrants and were arrested. Those arrested were taken to the jail for processing. The evidence gathering took the rest of the day and late into the evening.

With Garcia in custody and the workers processed, Mitch breathed a sigh of relief. The entire raid was done without anyone, on either side, firing a shot or being injured. It was a success. Late in the evening, as the agents checked in with their final reports, Mitch DeLong released them back to their regular duties. He was now back to his original contingent of agents tasked with reviewing all the evidence gathered today. This task would take several days. The one loose end to deal with was the whereabouts of Thomas Finn and the two Lopez brothers.

It was very late when Gene Blake drove the command truck from the warehouse to return it to the government vehicle barn. Mitch was weary and totally exhausted when he returned to his own apartment. It had been several days since he had been inside his home. He stopped in the kitchen for a glass and some ice. He filled the glass with single malt scotch, carried it to the living room and collapsed into his recliner.

Early the following morning he was in the office with Ed Lewis. He carried a thick folder with all the documentation from the raid. Lewis had already studied the versions he had received on the computer.

Lewis stood to take the hand of his agent. "Great job, Mitch, you handled it perfectly. Only one man was injured and we have enough evidence to file an order to seize all the assets owned by Bluefin Seafood, Inc. The officer shot in the gun-battle in the swamp is going to be alright. The bullet sort of skidded off his body armor and grazed his shoulder; no bones broken and no muscle torn. He was very lucky." Lewis was chuckling, saying, "We filled the federal intake facility. I think they worked all night to finish booking all the prisoners. The court will be facing the same challenge by the end of the week."

"A couple of Bluefin men got away, but we're looking for them. One was the boss of the fishing fleet, Thomas Finn. The others were the Lopez brothers. We haven't been able to track any of them. They may have gone back to Mexico or Columbia. All three were cartel men." Mitch ran his fingers through his hair and blew out a long breath, "When all the paperwork is finished I'm going to take a day off."

"You certainly deserve it Mitch." Lewis understood the stress generated by these raids. He had been in DeLong's shoes many times. "What about the accountant? Have you notified him of the raid and the arrests?"

"Not yet. I've been too busy. I'll call him as soon as I get back to my office. He deserves to know."

It had rained in Homer for the past three days. Dan had been in the office every day since his return. Donna Stanton had done an excellent job of organizing the responses to their business trip before he went to Florida. Dan had told her to hire an assistant for the office and she had interviewed dozens of applicants. One applicant was far more qualified than the others, but Donna hesitated to hire the young woman. It was her appearance. She was a very nice looking blond with a master's degree in economics. When she came to the interview she wore tight leather pants, boots and a leather vest with no shirt under it. The vest was covered with motorcycle patches and had a Harley Davidson logo both front and back.

Donna had eliminated all the other applicants and, after a long discussion about office attire, hired Dierdra Sykes. Di, as she liked to be called, agreed to dress in a less controversial style.

One of the first items on Dan's agenda when he returned to the office was to interview the new employee. He was pleasantly impressed. Upon reviewing the work she had accomplished since her acceptance Dan accepted her as one of the team. A very nice member of the team, thought Dan.

After that first day the three had been engrossed in making the new business work. Dan was an expert in investing and money management. Donna was the organizer and Di began organizing the business tactics department. She answered all correspondence relating to business practices by customers. Dan learned in a matter of days she was as skilled as he when it related this side of the business. Dan was pleased and impressed by the way these two ladies had handled the business while he was absent.

It was a little before ten o'clock in Homer when Donna forwarded a call to his office. It was Mitch DeLong, Florida DEA agent.

"Good morning, Dan," he greeted the accountant.

"Good morning to you, too, Mitch. How are things in Florida?"

"I have some good news for you, Dan. You can cancel your vacation to Miami. We raided the Bluefin Seafood offices yesterday. Thanks to you and the file you gave me we were able to follow a huge drug shipment and arrest the people on both ends of the deal. NOAA arrested the men delivering the shipment from South America and my team was able to track the shipment to the delivery point here in our swamps. We followed the two boats carrying the drugs from the fishing grounds and seized them and arrested the men at the pier. We followed the smaller boats up the canals to the delivery point and, after a short gun battle, arrested the workers and seized the drugs. We also arrested Diego Garcia, the boss at Bluefin Seafood. Our only failure was the boss from the other end of the pier. Thomas Finn and two of his henchmen were out of the plant when we raided it. We didn't get them, but we will."

"You mean you shut down the entire operation?" asked Dan.

"That's what I'm saying. We have you to thank for all of it, Dan. You gave us the information we lacked to track and seize the evidence."

Dan breathed a sigh of relief. "Thanks for the call, Mitch. I am really happy I don't have to return to Florida."

"I just wanted to call with the good news." Mitch, too, was glad he was no longer in an adversarial position with Dan Hanson. "How is the fishing up there?" he asked.

"Come up to Alaska and I'll show you a fishing trip you will never forget. Salmon, halibut, cod, shrimp and crab, you name it and we'll catch it."

"After this case is finished I'm going to need a vacation. I may just take you up on the offer. Thanks again, Dan."

"Thank you for taking me seriously, Mitch. And, tell Starsky he can come here fishing with you." Dan laughed into the phone with DeLong.

Dan walked to the front office to speak with his two office girls, "Ladies, I have just had the best news I've had in weeks. Let's close the office and I'll take you both to Duncan House for lunch. If we leave now we will beat the crowd."

Duncan House is a very old building on the main street through the uptown business district. It is an uphill climb from the parking lot to the entry of the restaurant, but it is downhill all the way back to your car when you finish. The help is friendly and the food is good. The owner will take your order and your money. A nice family atmosphere

"Good morning, Brad," Dan greeted Brad Gamble as he entered the café. Brad and his wife were owners and operators serving good food and local color.

"'Mornin'," said Brad. "Good to see you back in town." Homer is small and everyone knows everyone else's business.

"My professional staff has worked hard and I owe them a lunch," said Dan.

"Did Di ride her Harley up here?" asked Brad.

"No, she's on duty today." Both men laughed.

After lunch the trio returned to the office. In mid-afternoon Owen came to visit with Dan and to invite him to dinner. Once in the small back office he began to tell Dan what he had done with the large sum of cash he was to donate to the city.

"Homer is about to have the best small boat harbor in the state, thanks to you. I wanted them to build a DAN HANSON statue at the launching ramp, but the mayor said he was afraid the seagulls would desecrate it." Both men chuckled about that. "Honestly, Dan, there is no way my family or I can thank you enough for what you've done for us. You are a part of our family."

"No thanks necessary, Owen. I wouldn't be here if it weren't for you. I'm truly sorry I involved you. I didn't know if I would be back, but I am and I hope we can go on being friends. I love your family." Dan spoke quietly and sincerely thinking his past was now resolved.

Chapter 28

The following two weeks were filled with meetings and long hours in the office. Dan had flown to Anchorage twice and to Palmer once for meetings with new clients. The response to his initial client search was far greater than expected and the number of registered clients grew every day. Dierdra had proved to be a godsend. Dan had been extremely busy with the investments side of the new business and delegated the large part of business management practices portion of his business plan to the lady he now lovingly referred to as the 'biker chick.'

The atmosphere in the office was one of relaxed cooperation without any of the usual competition. Each member of the team had an area of expertise over which they ruled without question. It had become a happy place to be and work, a place where visitors came in to enjoy a cup of coffee and the jovial banter. Clients who had come to Homer for a fishing trip stopped in the office to say hello and pass the time of day with the friendly group. The main benefit was that the small company was now in the black and making money for their clients. For Dan, the cordiality and success meant he was at peace for the first time in a very long time.

Dan was in his office this afternoon when officer, now sergeant, Fritz stopped in to see him. Donna provided him a cold soda before leaving the two men alone in Dan's office.

"How have you been, Gary?"

Fritz chuckled, "The town has been quiet since you left. I'm glad you're back. I need some excitement."

Now Dan was laughing, "I hope I don't cause any more excitement for you, Gary."

"Actually that was the reason I came to see you today." Fritz handed a sheet of paper to Dan. "This is from the DEA office in Florida. When I got it

I called down there to clarify the information. That sheet is a notice for us to be on the lookout for three men who could be headed our way. I had never heard of the men and called to find out what the notice was about. The DEA office referred me to an agent who claimed he knew you. It was an Agent DeLong."

"Yes, Mitch DeLong. We met when I was in Florida this last time. He's a nice guy and did a great job of cleaning up a big drug gang."

"He spoke highly of you, too, Dan. He asked me to come down and personally tell you about the three men on this list. One is a Columbian drug cartel boss, Thomas Finn. The other two are Mexican Nationals, Fernando and Phillipe Lopez. They're brothers and hitmen for the cartel. They disappeared after that drug bust you mentioned, but have come back to the U.S." Gary Fritz seemed reluctant to continue.

"Yeah, I know them from my trip to Florida. Finn sent the Lopez brothers after me while I was there, but Owen and I got away from them." Dan didn't want to expound on the details of his story.

"That's why your friend Mitch talked with me. Those three men are back in the states and the word is that they're here to find you. Mitch seems to think they could track you back here to Homer." Gary had dropped the other shoe.

Dan leaned back in his big leather office chair and closed his eyes a moment. "Not again," he uttered. "I don't want to go through this again."

"I understand, Dan, but I have concerns, too. You remember the last time. Those other killers found you, which means, it can be done again. It doesn't only involve you it could be a danger to other Homer residents. I don't want to see anyone in this town hurt, in particular you or your two employees. You lost a secretary last time. I don't want that to happen again. I'm going to have my patrols keep an eye on you and your office. We have descriptions of the three men. It's a small town. If they show up we stand a good chance of spotting them. I came here to give you a warning about the danger. Don't take any unnecessary chances, Dan, people in Homer like you for some reason."

"I appreciate the warning, Gary, thank you. I'll be cautious. Have you spoken to Owen?" asked Dan.

"Not yet, but he is my next stop."

"When you talk with him, ask him to stop by and see me here at the office, would you please?"

When Gary Fritz left, Dan called Di and Donna into his office for a conference. "I have a story to tell the two of you. When I finish you will have to decide if you still want to work here."

Di smiled and joked, "The Hells Angels are after you?"

"No, worse," said Dan with no humor in his voice. He began to tell the entire story about his former bosses and what they did. The only thing he left out was the cash he had taken from the bank in the Bahamas and how much he had given Owen. "So you see the same people are after me again. The police are watching the office, but these are dangerous men. It was different men, but the same organization that murdered Alma Petersen and attacked Owen and me at the hangar. These men are killers. I don't want to see either of you hurt, so if you decide to leave, I understand."

"It seems to me you could use our eyes in the front office to warn you if they come. I don't know about Di, but I'm staying. I'm willing to take the chance you will win them over. Besides, it sounds exciting." Donna Stanton had made up her mind.

"Me too, Mr. Hanson," said Di. "You probably didn't know, but I have to be honest with you, I pack an automatic with me all the time. I can take care of myself. We're both staying. I like working here with you and Donna. I've seen trouble before, and I can deal with it again."

"Thank you, Ladies. I don't know what I would do without either one of you. The good news, I think, is Owen Sutton is on his way down here to see me. He stood by me at the hangar in a gun fight and I trust him. With him on our side we can't lose." Dan relaxed a little knowing he wasn't alone. "OK, gals, we have a lot of work to do. Please be cautious. Let's go back to work."

An hour later Owen Sutton came into the office to see Dan. Gary Fritz had briefed him on the warning from Mitch DeLong. As he entered the back office where Dan was seated he opened his windbreaker to reveal a Colt Commander in his shoulder holster. "I'm ready, Dan. I think you should start dressing in this conservative style as soon as possible."

"Thanks, Owen. I plan to do just that when I get to the hangar tonight. I guess Gary filled you in. Have a seat I'm going to call Mitch. Close the door and I'll put him on speaker phone." Dan dialed the private number for Mitch listed on the business card Mitch had given him.

"DeLong," was the short answer on the other end.

"Hello, Mitch, Dan Hanson here. I just had a visit from my favorite police sergeant telling me he had called you."

"Yes," said DeLong, "I talked with him earlier today. I guess he explained the situation to you?"

"Yes, he did. I thought you had this case all wrapped up and everyone in jail. Now I learn the three most dangerous men at Bluefin Seafood are on the loose. What happened?" asked Dan.

"We thought we had them all, too. As luck would have it the three men, Finn and the Lopez brothers, were out of the office when the raid went down. We didn't see them leave before the raid, but we missed them. I believe someone at the pier must have called to warn them not to come back to the offices. In any case we weren't able to locate them. We heard they went to

Columbia on a private jet. Now they're back and one of our informants said they are here to look for you. I think they're mad at you for some reason."

Dan chuckled at his small joke, "I don't make friends easily. You should know that by now. Ask Starsky, he's a good example."

"Spasky has learned to love you, though, I don't think the three cartel goons have come that far. The point is, Dan, you need to be careful. They'll find you and when they do it will mean another war."

"I know, but I have my bodyguard here in the office and he has vowed to protect me. Since you and your outfit didn't live up to the advertising we may have to, once again, take the bull by the horns." Dan wanted to be light about the threat, but he knew he and Owen had been lucky the last time and didn't want to tempt fate a second time.

"We have men in Anchorage and I'll try to get a couple of them sent to Homer to look after you. The problem is we don't know where the three of them are, and the bosses don't like to send agents to a nice vacation spot without positive evidence there is a threat."

"I know," said Dan, "we went through that before. Do what you can and we'll do our part to prepare for the worst. Let me know if they show up somewhere."

"I'll do that, Dan. Sorry I can't do more. I'll call if we hear anything at all. Stay in touch."

Once he had hung up the telephone Dan turned to Owen, "Now you know as much as I do. Are you still in?"

"Of course," said Owen. "Last time we were able to win because we picked the location and we were prepared. This time I don't think they will attack at the hangar. I think the motivation is different this time. Last time they just wanted to get you out of the picture, this time they want revenge. We don't know if all three will be here attacking or just the two hitmen. I believe they'll attack soon and the attack will be here in this office."

"I hope you're wrong, Owen. It would mean the two girls would be trapped inside during a firefight. There's no back door to this office, so there's no escape route for them."

Owen glanced around the office. "The only warning we'll get is from Donna at the front desk. If she can see it coming she can get back into the hallway before the shooting starts. You and I can make this back office area better fortified and more defensible, at least until they start using mortars and hand grenades. We can build a Lexan polycarbonate barrier on the front walls of your office and do the same in Di's office across the hall. We can install security cameras in the front office to give us an idea where they are and what they're doing. They may cut the phone wires, but we can call Gary Fritz on the cell phone. The building is concrete block construction and mostly fire-proof. We could install an electric fire door at the end of the hall for Donna to close and secure once she is behind it."

"All that sounds good, but where will we find bulletproof Lexan and a locking fire door on such short notice?" Dan was skeptical of the plan. "And what if you're not here when the attack comes?"

"The Lexan is not a problem. I have a whole stack of inch thick panels at my place. They came out of the hockey rink. We can screw them to the inside of the front walls. Unless they use armor piercing rounds the Lexan walls will stop their bullets. The same goes for the door at the end of the hallway. We can cut a piece the size of the door and fasten it to the inside of the door. Once Donna is inside the hallway, it will be her job to slam it shut and lock it." Owen's plan was beginning to take shape and sound good. "What do you think, Dan?"

"It sounds as if we'll be protected from gunfire, but how will we fight back to stop them?"

"You can leave that up to Gary and me. We talked about it and decided with Gary's police officers and my firefighters we could mount a small army to take on the intruders. We can use the fire equipment to box in the front of the office and to protect our men. The police can use it for protection when dealing with the intruders, whether there are two or three of them. In any case your only concern will be to get your staff behind the Lexan walls in time to avoid the gunfire. You won't have much advanced warning to get that accomplished."

Dan Hanson was concerned for his office assistants. "If we knew when these men would attack I could just keep Di and Donna out of the office, but there is so much work here in the office we need to be here to get it finished in a timely manner for the sake of the clients. That fact puts the women in jeopardy. I don't like that idea."

"If we knew when they were coming it would be easy, but we don't. It will be imperative you go with business as usual in order to make the office the best place to attack. Remember, we have to pick the place even if we can't pick the time."

"OK, Owen, let's get started. I'll call Anatoly Rivkin to let him know we are modifying the office. I would appreciate it if you could talk with Gary and have him increase the patrols around the office. I'll brief Di and Donna on the plan." Dan was confident Owen could handle the remodel plan and coordinate the police and fire department tactics. "I can never thank you enough, Owen."

Chapter 29

It took Dan and Owen two full days to remodel the office. The thick Lexan panels were attached to the front walls of both offices. The door was replaced by one the two men had made from an old fire door and screwed the Lexan to the inside of it. They painted the outside of the door to match the trim in the outer office. Five security video cameras were placed in the corners of the office and one outside the front entry. The cameras were fed by Wi-Fi to the computers in both offices. Two steel bars were ready to reinforce the hallway entry door after the receptionist retreated into the hallway.

Di had stashed an extra .45 Colt in her desk with several boxes of cartridges. Dan was now carrying his .45 in a shoulder holster and he, too, had extra ammo in his office.

It was the hope of Dan and Owen to lock themselves inside the fortified back offices and to let the police subdue and arrest the attackers. During the construction period Donna and Di maintained a business as usual schedule hoping to distract attention from the work being done in the back offices. All the office phones were programmed with the speed dial to ring 911 and at the same time dial Owen Sutton's home phone. Late the second day they tested the phone system and it worked perfectly. Now if the attack occurred, help could be summoned by pushing a button on any phone in the offices. Owen planned to stay away from the office, but be ready to respond if a call came in. He was, after all, still a fire captain and worked for a living. He planned to spend nights at home with his family and could respond to any emergency call quickly.

Dan had called a meeting in his office with his office crew, Owen Sutton and Gary Fritz. Procedures were outlined so that Donna and Di each knew what they were expected to do if the intruders came into the office. Fritz supplied pictures of the suspects for her to use in identifying the intruders before they could do any harm. If she saw them enter the office she was to retreat to the back hallway and close the door. Dan would help her install the two heavy locking bars to keep the door hardware from being broken. Di and Donna were to secure themselves in Di's office. Donna was to push the emergency phone signal when she left her desk. This would get the police on the way and alert Owen whether he was at work or home. The success of the plan depended on Donna recognizing the culprits and escaping to the back hallway before she was captured by them. The plan was simple, but effective—they hoped.

Dan was happy with the preparations in the office. Everyone had worked hard to complete the fortification. As a reward he ordered Donna to call Captain David and schedule a fishing trip for everyone in the office and including Owen and his wife as well as Gary Fritz. Halibut fishing is usually labor intensive hard work, but it is fun and rewarded by the amount of fish caught during the day out.

Captain David was booked for tomorrow, but the next day was open for them. Dan was happy to have a day in the office to catch up on several portfolios he had neglected during the past few days.

Donna was in Dan's office delivering the news about the fishing charter. "David had a short charter on Thursday and moved that trip to Friday in order to fit your group into the schedule. I thought it was very nice of him to do that."

Dan nodded in agreement. "I really like the young man. He has been extremely accommodating for us and we always have a good time when we fish with him. Since we will be in the office tomorrow let's try to bring all the Palmer files up to speed. If we can complete all of them today or tomorrow you can call and try to set up a group meeting in Palmer on Friday. Di can watch the office while you and I fly up to the valley for the meeting. I think we will have four files to review with clients, if they all agree to a Friday meeting. We should finish right after noon. So we will have lunch in Palmer and fly home in the afternoon. I'll need to let Gary Fritz know in order for him to have his patrol keep an eye on the office on Friday."

"You're really worried about this threat, aren't you Mr. Hanson?" asked Donna in a motherly tone.

Dan leaned back in his big office chair, "Yes, I am, Donna. I was out of the office when they attacked last time and terrorized and killed Alma Petersen. I should have been here to protect her. She was a super nice person and she died because of me. I can't ever forget that."

"I know you feel guilty about her death, but those men caused her death, not you," commented Donna.

"I know all that, but they came looking for me and I can't help believe I caused her death."

"Well, the situation is different now. Di and I are here because we care for you. We know the risks, and accept them willingly. On Friday Di will be here alone, but she is no pansy. She knows how to take care of herself. Don't let the mini skirt and high heels fool you. Under all that she's still a biker chick with a .45 Colt and she makes a good watchdog."

"Just the same, I don't want to see anyone else hurt because of me." The look on Dan's face confirmed his concern. "Now, what about those files?" he asked his assistant.

By late afternoon the following day the meeting schedule was set. Donna had finalized and made client copies of each file to be taken on the trip to Palmer. Each folder contained an investment proposal as well as a management doctrine for each client and the various businesses they represented. Dan reviewed each file carefully to be sure each one was complete and accurate. It was late when he left the office, which would be closed on Thursday to allow everyone to be out on Cook Inlet, fishing for halibut with Captain David.

The six met for an early breakfast before driving to the Homer Spit. They had come to the Spit in two cars to simplify parking. David had a private parking area behind some business buildings where the two vehicles were parked for the day. The group walked to the boat slip where David's boat was tied. Owen and Gary carried a large cooler containing sodas and water along with some sandwiches for lunch. The sun was high in the sky even at this early hour. Captain David and his deck hand were waiting when they arrived.

"Welcome aboard," he called to the group as they stepped onto the deck of the cruiser.

"Mornin," David," greeted Owen as he stepped aboard and shook hands with the captain and his deck hand, Mark.

Once aboard and the gear stored in the forward cabin, David gave his safety speech, directing his passengers to the fire extinguishers and life rafts as well as the emergency locator beacons, flares and floatation devices. That done, he asked the deck hand to untie the boat from the dock. The engines had been running and warming up. Everyone took seats in the cabin and watched out the cabin windows as the boat moved out of the harbor. Captain David had said it was 26 miles to the fishing spot and it would take a little over an hour to arrive. The day was warm and the sea calm.

Once the boat was anchored and the lines baited, Mark, the deck hand, instructed the fishermen on techniques for catching the big flatfish. Di was the first to have a bite and it was a good one. The two fishermen on her side of the boat reeled up to give her space to fight the big fish. It took several minutes to bring the halibut to the surface. Phones popped out and pictures snapped as they brought the fish over the rail. Captain David estimated the fish at roughly 75 pounds.

"Nice fish, Di," David complimented the fisherperson. "You can have one more, but it will have to be a small one. It's a regulation put in place a couple of years ago."

Di kneeled down beside her fish lying on the deck, white side up, for a photo taking event. This picture would go on her office wall.

The day was filled with excitement and laughter. Irish lords were caught and thrown back. Two small sand sharks were taken and returned to the salt water. Gary Fritz caught an octopus and Owen caught a huge Alaska skate. By mid-afternoon the limits were filled and the fishermen were tired. Muscles ached from reeling up the fish from a depth of one hundred thirty five feet. They had marveled at the different coloration of the halibut as the boat swung in the tide and the bottom changed from gravel to sand to big rocks. There had been puffins near the boat as well as sea otters swimming nearby. Captain David was able to identify most of the seabirds when asked.

The fishermen were mostly quiet on the return trip. Dan and Owen drank coffee from a thermos bottle. It had been a carefree day, one that was sorely needed by the entire group. Once back at the Homer Small Boat Harbor Dan instructed David to have the fish filleted and frozen. He would pick them up at a later time. Dan paid the captain and added a nice tip for both him and his deck hand. A carefree and relaxing day was what this entire group needed and Captain David had helped them meet that goal.

Dan bought them all dinner before calling it a night and returning to the hangar. He needed to check his Cessna for the morning flight to Palmer. The long Alaska days made him forget the time of day and to enjoy his chores. It was nearly midnight when he finally climbed to the loft in his hangar for a short night's sleep.

He was in the dingy little airport restaurant having breakfast by five thirty in the morning. He was joined by Donna who brought a large banker box full of files to be used at today's meetings. Conversation at the breakfast table mostly consisted of a rehash of the fishing trip and the silly things done by each of the fishermen. By six thirty a.m. the Cessna was outside and pre-flight completed. Donna sat in the right seat in the cockpit with a headset over her ears tuned to the intercom. The headset cancelled the engine noise and enabled them to speak quietly to each other during the flight.

Donna had a rental car waiting at the Palmer airport when they arrived. She had also scheduled a small conference room at a downtown hotel where the meetings were to be held. Individual meetings were to be held in order to review each client's portfolio. She had allowed one hour for each client, which, as it turned out, was perfect. They had just finished the last meeting when Dan's cell phone rang. It was Dierdra Sykes.

"Mr. Hanson, I think a man who just came in may be one of the men you warned us about. He didn't resemble the men in the picture, but he asked a lot of questions about you. He gave me a card with the name of Jim Sullivan, but I don't think that was his real name."

"What did he look like, Di?"

"He was pretty tall, dark skin, swarthy looking, if you know what I mean. Spanish looking, I guess."

"Was he well dressed and wearing a big diamond on his right hand?" asked Dan.

"As a matter of fact he was. Do you know him, Mr. Hanson?"

"Yes, I'm afraid so. Call Gary and let him know. Tell him I think the man is Thomas Finn. The DEA is looking for him. You be careful, Di. This man is dangerous. The two men in the pictures won't be far behind him. I'll be home in a couple of hours. Donna and I are leaving Palmer now. Call Gary and keep your eyes open. Don't take any chances. I'm on my way."

Chapter 30

Upon arriving in Homer Dan didn't bother putting the Cessna inside the hangar. Instead, he locked the cabin door and left the airplane parked outside the closed hangar. He and Donna had taken the files from the aircraft and placed them in the back of the Jeep. Within minutes of landing they were in the office where Gary Fritz was waiting with Di.

When he entered the office he could tell Di was shaken by the encounter. "Are you OK, Di?" he inquired.

"Yes, I'm fine. It didn't bother me at all until I learned what kind of man had come into the office. I guess I'm not as tough as I thought."

"I meant what I said before, Di," said Dan. "If you want out I understand. This is dangerous business."

"Oh no, I'm staying. If I ran out now I would have to turn in my leathers. I'm here for the duration. Gary came right away when I called. He called the patrol car and they were here in about one minute. They kept a good eye on me and the office while you were gone."

Gary now joined the conversation, "She was really calm when she called me. She didn't begin to worry until I told her about this Finn guy. I have a printout from DEA and he's a bad dude. DEA is sending two agents from Anchorage. They should be arriving any time now. On the phone I told them I would have an officer pick them up at the airport."

"Have you sighted the other two?" asked Dan.

"No, but according to DEA, Finn is their boss. They said if we saw Finn the Lopez brothers were not far behind. That's why I came to sit in the office with Di. The DEA chief in Anchorage said your friend, Agent DeLong, in Florida had called him and asked him to send a couple of agents down here, but with no evidence there was no justification. Now, with the sighting of Finn, they have a reason to be here. With them on the job and my patrol car in the area the office should be safe."

"Donna and I are back now and we have our escape plan in place, so we're ready if they come. Thanks for looking out for Di, I appreciate it, Gary."

"Happy to do it, Dan, don't hesitate to call the office if anyone suspicious comes around. Owen said he was stopping by later." Gary gave a short wave of his hand and stepped out of the office to speak with his patrolman parked in front.

"Well girls, we should get back to work. I'll get the box from the Jeep and we can start on the new files. Thanks to the two of you my little consulting business is beginning to pay off. I'll buy dinner this evening. The two of you can pick the restaurant. I plan to work until around seven if you want to stick around."

"I'll stick around and watch the front door for you, Mr. Hanson," said Donna.

"Me, too," said Di. "I have quite a bit of work to catch up on. I didn't get much done today."

The three were finishing for the day when Owen Sutton came into the office. Donna greeted him when he entered. "Hello Owen, have you come to join us for dinner?"

"No, but thanks anyway. I have to go home and broil burgers for the family tonight. Is the boss in?"

"He's in his office. You can go back there. He's just finishing for the day."

Owen strolled back to the little office on the left side of the hallway. He poked his head around the corner of the doorway.

"Howdy Dan," he said.

"Hello, come on in. I was just locking my files and quitting for the day. I'm taking the staff to dinner tonight; would you like to come along?"

"Thanks, but I can't tonight. I just came by to see how the three of you were holding up under the stress." Owen had genuine concerns for his friend.

"Gary was here this afternoon and has had a patrol car close by all day. Finn hasn't come back and no one has seen the Lopez brothers. DEA has two men in town looking for them. I don't know how much more we can do to protect ourselves," Dan said matter-of-factly.

"OK then, I'm going home to barbeque for the family. You three enjoy your dinner." It had been a welfare check by Owen and he was satisfied everything was OK for now.

Dan and his two assistants rode to the end of the Homer Spit where the hotel had a very nice restaurant. Each ordered a cocktail before dinner. The table talk was light and cheerful. All three ordered the halibut dinner and a dinner salad. While waiting, Di asked Dan about his Cessna. By the time he finished his cocktail and the description of his airplane their dinner had arrived. It was a pleasant evening during which Dan offered to take Di on his next flight and teach her the basics of flying. She seemed excited and accepted the offer.

After dinner he returned them to the office where Donna's car and Dierdra's Harley were parked. Dan drove to the hangar to tend to his airplane and put it inside the hangar. It was still light when he finished the chore and was standing outside in the sunshine when a strange vehicle pulled to the front of the hangar and stopped. Two casually dressed men stepped out.

"Are you Dan Hanson?" asked the one on the passenger side.

"Yes, who wants to know?"

"Sorry, Mr. Hanson, but we're with the DEA. Sergeant Gary Fritz asked us to check on you. We understand you're acquainted with the three cartel men on our wanted list. Is there anything we can do for you?"

"Yes, you can help me put the Cessna back into the hangar, if you have the time."

The two agents helped maneuver the large plane into the hangar, all the time asking questions about the three fugitives they were pursuing. Dan told them what he knew about the men and what they had done in Florida. Once the big hangar door was closed the two agents excused themselves to get back to the search. The population of Homer increases by nearly fifty times during the summer tourist season making the search very difficult. The long daylight hours make it possible for tourists toting cameras to stay busy far into the nighttime hours.

Dan spent an uneasy night waking up each time the large metal hangar snapped and creaked as it cooled from the setting of the sun. He arose early to shower and shave, stepping outside the hangar once to check the weather and take a breath of fresh salty sea air. Returning to the hanger, he strapped on his shoulder holster and fill it with one of his Colt Commanders. He drove his Jeep through the electronic gate and down the short distance to the grubby little restaurant at the end of the row hangars and offices of the airport. Inside he said hello to the cook/waitress and picked up a newspaper. Moments later the door opened again and two men entered to seat themselves next to Dan.

"Good morning, Mr. Hanson," said one of the DEA agents.

"Good morning to you fellas," replied Dan. "You didn't get much sleep."

Both agents chuckled, "You know how we tourists are: we never sleep while on vacation. We do that when we get back to the job."

Now it was Dan who snickered, "How about some breakfast, boys?" The place isn't much, but the food is good."

"Sounds good." The cook/waitress brought a short menu to the agents.

"Did you boys see anyone you knew last night?" asked Dan.

"No," said the agent on his left, "but we didn't realize how many people are in this little town in the summertime. We can't figure out where they all stay."

"The entire economy of Homer is based on the summer tourist business. My business is consulting with businesses on ways to improve profits. The businessmen in Homer have it figured out pretty well." Dan pointed his thumb over his shoulder toward the Homer Spit. "Those businesses do ninety percent of their business in the summer, May through September. They work long hours in the summer and take the winter off, closing up shop in October. These businessmen never get to enjoy Homer at its best."

"We were out in the town nearly all night and it bustles all night long. It's impressive," stated the agent on his right.

"They sell a bumper sticker here which states, "Homer, a quaint little drinking town with a fishing problem.""

Both agents laughed. "We will have to get one of them to take back to the office."

The cook/waitress brought Dan's order and he dug right in, eating without speaking. Shortly thereafter the agents' plates were set in front of them and all conversation ceased. When Dan finished his meal he paid for all three breakfasts and waved to the agents. "I'll be at the office all day," he said.

The office was open and Donna was seated at her desk when he arrived. "Good morning, Mr. Hanson," she greeted him, cheerfully.

"Good morning, Donna. Is Di in her office?"

"Not yet, but she's never late."

Just then the two were startled by the revving of a loud Harley Davidson motorcycle engine and signature pipes.

"She's here," quipped Donna.

Moments later Di entered the office wearing tight black pants, a black short sleeve shirt and black leather vest. She had on tall leather boots. The entire black ensemble was offset by the long blond hair and beaming smile. "Good morning everyone, it's a beautiful morning, isn't it?" she said cheerfully.

Dan was shaking his head and grinning, "I like your outfit," he said. "Where do you hide the .45?"

Again she smiled that smile and lifted the bottom of the leather vest. Under it was a new concealed carry holster fitted tightly to her shapely body. "Right here, Big Boy," she said, laughing.

"It's a good thing you have the back office," Dan teased. "Those two DEA agents were at the hangar last night and I saw them this morning. It makes me feel a little easier knowing they're here." Dan made his comments as he walked back to his office.

Donna followed him with two new files in her hands. She handed him the files and stepped out to get him a cup of fresh, hot coffee. She was about to say something when she heard the front door open and close. She returned to her desk to greet the newcomer. She recognized Phillipe Lopez. Through the window she could see the other brother, Fernando, sitting behind the wheel of the rental car parked near the front door.

"May I help you, sir?" she asked.

"Possibly. Is Mr. Dan Hanson in today?"

"Yes, sir, may I tell him who is asking?"

"We're old friends. I would like to surprise him," said Lopez.

"He's very busy this morning, sir. Is it possible for you to come back after lunch?"

"My brother and I are leaving town today and I really would like to see him right now," Lopez insisted.

"Of course, sir; let me check to see if he can make time for you." Donna stood and stepped toward the hall door. "They're here," she called out as she turned to close and drop the bars on the hallway door.

Without hesitation Di punched the emergency speed dial to call 911 and Owen. Dan jumped from his chair to assist Donna with the locking bars on the door. "Good job, Donna."

Dan's desk phone was ringing. Owen was calling his private line.

"What's happening, Dan?" he asked.

"The Lopez brothers are out front. Donna, Di and I are locked in the back, safe and secure for the moment. I can't see what's going on out front, but Phillipe is still standing at the desk. It looks like he's trying to decide what to do. I don't think he's seen the cameras. Oh, oh! He just motioned for Fernando to come inside. Gary had better get here pretty quick."

"I'm on my way," said an excited Owen.

Another line was ringing as he hung up from the first call. It was Gary Fritz. "I'm on the way. ETA two minutes. Are you safely locked in?"

"Yes, Donna recognized one of the brothers and came back to close the door. I have them on the security cameras and they are talking to each other in the outer office. It looks like they are planning an attack. Hurry, Gary."

Chapter 31

Both Dan and Donna were in Dan's office watching the security monitor screen while Di remained in her own office across the hallway. On the small television screen the two men spoke to each other, but there was no sound available for Dan or Donna to hear what was being said. As they watched the two men the sound of sirens could now be heard. The two men in the front office heard them too and ran from the office. They hastily entered the car in front of the office and backed away from the building. When they put it into Drive, the rear wheels threw rocks and dirt across the parking lot and sped away.

The monitors picked up the speeding police car chasing the car leaving the parking spot in front of the office. Another police car stopped in front of the outer office door and Sergeant Fritz and another officer came inside. Fritz called out to Dan.

"Dan, are you back there?"

"Yes, Di, Donna and myself. Give me a minute to open the door."

Dan and Donna stepped out of the office and into the hallway to take the metal bars from the door. The system had worked perfectly. Sergeant Fritz was standing in front of the door when it opened. The other officer stood near the front entry door.

"Are the three of you OK?" asked Gary as they came into the front office.

Dan nodded and said, "Yes, we're fine. Thanks for getting here so quickly."

"If you are all OK I'm going to back up my other officer. They're headed up Baycrest Hill. The trooper is in Anchor Point and headed this way. I gotta go. I'll be back later." Fritz motioned for his officer to go to the car with him following. The patrol car flew out of the parking area with red lights glowing and siren howling.

From the office window the three watched the policemen depart. Once they were gone Dan became contemplative. Finally he turned to the two employees, "I hate to mention this, but, even if they catch the Lopez brothers, we still have Thomas Finn to worry about. We can't let our guard down just yet. Now," he said, "let's try to get some work done. By the way, the two of you did an excellent job here today. Thank you for being brave."

Di took a step toward her office, turned toward Dan and said, "Aw shucks, Boss," then continued toward her office and desk. Dan smiled and Donna shook her head, laughing, and sat at her own desk to continue working on the files she had abandoned before the ruckus started.

At this same time a shiny Gulf Stream III was landing at the Homer Airport. One man stepped from small jetliner. It was Mitch DeLong. The two DEA agents in Homer had been waiting in their car in front of the small terminal building. Mitch made his way through the small building to the front where he was met by one of the agents. "Are you Special Agent DeLong?" he asked.

"Yes," said Mitch, displaying his ID.

"The greeter reached out to shake hands, "I'm Agent Lisco and that's Agent Cody driving the car."

"Pleased to meet you, Lisco. Is there any news of the fugitives?"

"Homer PD is out on a call right now. They spotted the Lopez brothers in the offices of Dan Hanson. Dan and his staff had secured the back offices prior to the sighting and escaped to the rear offices. By the time they figured out what to do about it the Homer Police were one the way, and intruders fled by car. HPD is chasing them north right now and an Alaska State Trooper is traveling south to intercept them. Do you want to join the chase?"

"No, but I would like to go to Hanson's offices to chat with him."

Mitch sat in the front seat of the car with Cody driving and Lisco seated in the rear. It was only a short drive from the airport terminal to the little office building where Dan had set up office. "You fellas can come inside with me, but I want to see Dan alone."

The three men entered the office to be greeted by Donna. "How may I help you gentlemen?" she asked.

"Please tell Mr. Hanson Mitch DeLong is here to see him."

"Yes sir," she said as she stood to deliver the message in person. Dan appeared pleased with the visitor and asked her to show him in.

Dan stood to shake hands with the DEA agent when he entered. "Good to see you Mitch," he said in a cheerful voice.

Mitch returned the handshake and smiled, "Good to see you, too, Dan. I see you cause trouble wherever you go. I thought you only did it in my bailiwick."

"Yes, you missed the fun by about a half hour. Come in and sit down."

Mitch took a seat across the desk from his friend.

"Are you here on business or pleasure?" asked Dan.

"A little of both, I borrowed the government's Gulf Stream to get here. I am sending it to Anchorage. If we can arrest the Lopez brothers and Thomas Finn I'll be able to take a couple of days to go fishing. That is if you can find the time to go fishing with me."

"My assistants and I were just talking about Finn. The police are chasing the Lopez brothers as we speak, but I haven't heard if they caught them. As for Finn, I think he was in the office a few days ago. Di, my second office assistant, spoke with him when he came in. When she described the man to me I was sure it was Finn. I haven't seen him though. I think he was waiting for the Lopez brothers to get the job done and he's laying low."

"I was just noticing the front wall of your office. I can see you took some precautions prior to the attacks. I like your armor plating. Is that Lexan?"

"Yes, Owen had a stack of it from the hockey rink. I hope it does the trick if we have a shootout in the office. I lost one good secretary and don't want to lose another."

"Let me get you some coffee, Mitch, and we can talk while we wait to hear from the police."

At this very instant, eight miles north of Homer, the Alaska State trooper car had placed his car across the narrow Sterling Highway forcing Fernando Lopez to stop. Before he could turn his car around and escape he was blocked from the rear by a Homer police vehicle. Half a minute later another Homer PD car joined the blockade; it was Sergeant Fritz.

The fugitives sat in their car trying to decide what action to take. As other traffic was forced to stop behind the police some of the drivers began to exit their vehicles to see what was causing the traffic stop. The trooper blocking the north side of the incident was out of his car shouting for everyone to return to their vehicles. A Homer police officer was doing the same on the south side. Fritz kept his eyes on the Lopez vehicle.

When the crowd was dispersed from the scene Fritz picked up the microphone in his car to call a warning to the Lopez brothers. "Get out of the car with your hands where I can see them. Leave your weapons inside your vehicle. Do it now!" declared the loud speaker voice under the hood of the Homer police car.

Fritz could see the trooper poised behind the open door of his patrol car. The officers from the other HPD car were behind their vehicle. Fritz was shielded by the door of his own patrol car with his partner standing beside him.

The Lopez brothers seemed to ignore the order. There was a long tense moment when suddenly the passenger door of the trapped vehicle opened and Phillipe stepped out, holding a large handgun. He reached to the rear of the car to open the rear door for protection. He fired two shots in the direction of the patrol car parked crosswise behind his car. When he fired the driver door opened and Fernando Lopez stepped out to open his rear car door. Fernando, too, was armed but with an AK-47 assault rifle.

Once again Fritz spoke into the microphone, "Drop the weapons and raise your hands."

The order was met with several shots in his direction from the assault rifle. At the same time Phillipe fired at the other patrol car. Without a clear target the Homer officers did not return fire, but remained behind the protection of the cars.

The Alaska State trooper took advantage of the gunfire in the opposite direction to get into his car and speed to the driver's side of Lopez vehicle. With his left front fender he struck the driver side door of the rental car pinning Fernando and causing him to drop his AK-47.

The commotion caused Phillipe to spin around to fire at the trooper. When he did an officer behind the HPD car was able to get a clear target and fired two shots striking Phillipe in the center of his lower neck and right shoulder, killing him instantly.

Fernando was screaming profanity at the officers. The trooper approached the fugitive vehicle to remove the weapons from the reach of either of the Lopez brothers.

Fritz and his partner ran to the trooper's aid to handcuff Fernando, but had to wait until the trooper moved his car to cuff the second hand behind the back of the remaining Lopez brother.

With the situation under control the trooper let Fritz and his men take control of the crime scene, moved his vehicle and opened one lane of the Sterling Highway to traffic.

Fritz asked his men if anyone had been injured in the fight, none had. He then called dispatch to have a state investigator join him at the scene and document the event. Fernando was removed to the Homer Jail while the body of Phillipe remained at the scene until the investigator arrived. Once the crowd was dispersed and the scene under control he used his cell phone to call Dan Hanson.

"We got 'em," he reported to Dan. "One is dead and the other under arrest."

"Are you and your men OK?" asked Dan.

"Yes, we have an investigator coming and I sent two men with Fernando Lopez to the Homer Jail. He's probably going to want some medical attention, but the jail personnel can take care of that. I just wanted you to know we got them."

"Thanks, Gary. I appreciate it. I'll see you later."

After finishing with Fritz, Dan turned to Mitch DeLong. "That was Sergeant Fritz reporting they got the two Lopez brothers. One is dead and the other is on his way to jail here in Homer."

"That's good news," replied DeLong. "Can we get some lunch now?"

"Good idea. I'll take the ladies, too. Lunch is on me," said Dan, relieved by the fact two of the three killers were now off the streets.

Dan officially introduced Donna and Dierdra to Mitch DeLong. "These are my amazing assistants. Donna, the brains of the outfit and Di, the muscle; as you can see from her attire, she's a 'biker babe.'"

"A very beautiful biker babe, I might add. How do you do? I'm Mitch DeLong."

"I'm taking us all to lunch, Ladies, Duncan House or somewhere else?"

Donna and Di looked at each other and nodded, "Duncan House," said Di with Donna nodding in agreement.

Lunch was pleasant and conversation was light. There was no mention of the day's activities during the public lunch break. Once back at the office things changed and Mitch became an officer again. He was making phone calls to advise his boss, Ed Lewis, of the arrest of Fernando Lopez and the demise of Phillipe. He had finished his call when Gary Fritz came into the office followed by Owen Sutton. Once again the activities of the day were reviewed to everyone's relief.

DeLong had called to book a room at a local motel where he intended to spend the night. Owen invited all of them to a barbeque at his home this evening. It was, indeed, a good day to celebrate.

Dan was glad the Lopez brothers had been put out of business, but was still uneasy about Thomas Finn. Finn was the brains of the criminal organization with the Lopez brothers, the enforcers. Dan thought it was likely Finn would find another hit man, but was fully capable of doing the job himself. It was too early for him to let down his guard.

Chapter 32

Fernando Lopez had been taken to the Homer Jail for booking, but he was in such pain he was transported to the hospital before the booking was completed. It was discovered his left arm was broken and he had a cut on his back requiring several stitches. The doctors treated his injuries and gave him a shot for the pain, but he refused to take any other pain medications to be administered later at the jail. It was late in the afternoon when his booking process was completed. He was placed in one of the small cells where he immediately fell asleep.

It was late when he awoke to begin screaming for a jailer. The officer on duty came near the cell to ask what he wanted. When he was close enough Lopez reached with his good arm to grab the unarmed officer. Mark, the jail officer, was not unfamiliar with hard-case prisoners and maneuvered the arm up and behind Lopez. Fernando attempted to strike Mark, the jailer, with his new plastic cast on his left arm. Mark was able to avoid the strike and spin the prisoner around, sending him to the floor in pain.

The jail officer called an on-duty police officer to officially arrest Fernando for assault. As the police officer and Mark departed from the small cell area they heard Lopez call after them.

"You may keep me in here, but I'm going to kill you before I leave."

"Be sure that remark is in your report when you write it, Mark," said the Homer police officer.

It took Mark several hours to make out the witness forms and write his statement. He checked the cell area every half hour because of the injuries to the prisoner. It was three in the morning when he made another check. The prisoner was on the floor, bleeding. Mark keyed his radio to ask for an officer assist in the jail before opening the cell door. When Mark opened the door and bent down to check on the unconscious prisoner Lopez hit him in the head hard enough to disable him for several minutes. This gave Lopez time to take the keys from Mark's belt and lock the cell door with the officer inside. Lopez had heard Mark call for assistance and waited in the booking area for the officer to arrive. There were no weapons in the booking room, but Fernando had broken a metal leg from a chair as a weapon. When the police officer entered, looking for Mark, he was struck from behind with the chair leg.

As the officer staggered and dropped to his knees Lopez hit him again several times. He then stripped off the officer's duty belt with his keys, including the ones to his patrol car, pepper spray, duty weapon and portable radio. He then made his way to the rear door of the jail and let himself out. There were two patrol cars parked behind the jail, but the keys fit the first one he tried.

Thomas Finn had rented a small cabin near town and Lopez knew the place. He had stayed in another of the cabins with his brother. It wasn't dark but dusky when he arrived at the cabin to bang on the door to wake Finn.

Finn was groggy when he answered the door, "What do you want Fernando?" he asked in Spanish.

"You have to follow me, Thomas. I have a police car and they will be looking for it. I'm going down this road to the beach and dump the car. Come pick me up when you get your pants on." This message also was delivered in Spanish.

Minutes later Finn stopped to allow Lopez inside his rental car. "How bad is the arm, Fernando?"

"Useless, it's broken and I have a bad cut and stitches on my back, but this has gone on long enough. I want to finish it and get away from Alaska. All these years and I've never been hurt bad. Now I come here and lose my brother and get a broken arm. I'm gonna kill that bookkeeper tomorrow and we can leave."

"Are you sure you can do this job with a broken arm?" asked Thomas.

"I'll get it done. I just want to go back to Columbia and heal up. I want to take my brother back with me and have him buried in Bogota with my father and my other brother. Mama will want it that way." Fernando hung his head, "She is old now and Phillipe was her favorite son. I am now the last of the family, except for three sisters, but there are no more boys. Mama will want him home."

"I will see to it he is sent home, Fernando. You two have been with me a long time. He deserves to be home with his family. I am truly sorry about Phillipe. I will send your mother his pay and I will pay for his funeral."

Fernando went with Thomas back to the little cabin to get some sleep. Thomas let him use the bed while he turned on the television and watched the morning news. It was now daylight and another delightful day in Homer.

Dan opened his office at seven in the morning, having had a small breakfast at the airport café. He wished he could be out on the Inlet fishing halibut,

but he had been out of the office so much lately he was far behind with his work. He felt guilty because his clients had hired him to take care of their investments and to advise them of improvements to make that would increase sales and profits. Di had done an excellent job of keeping up with the business advice for each client, but the investments had lacked attention because of his absence. It was time to put his shoulder to the wheel and do what he had promised.

At eight thirty Di came into the office singing a country song. She sounded happy. She stopped to put her head in the doorway of Dan's office before taking off her sweater and beginning her day.

"Good morning, Mr. Hanson," she said cheerfully.

"Good morning, Di. You sound cheery this morning."

"I've been out riding this morning. Riding the Harley always makes me feel good. You should try it."

"No thanks, I have an airplane that does the same thing for me."

"I'd like to go for a ride sometime. Maybe you could teach me some basics of flying. If I liked it I could study and get a license." She didn't mean to be patronizing she really meant the quest.

"I'll be happy to take you some time, Di." He paused a moment. "How are you coming on those Palmer and Wasilla business files?"

"I have one more to do. I came in a little early today to get it finished. The clients really like the package you have put together. I think this little business is destined for big things."

"You are a big part of it, Dierdra. You have done an outstanding job in that department. I don't think it would have been this successful had I done it all myself. Now I won't be able to get by without you. If I were you I would ask for a raise right now." Dan had been honest with her. He did appreciate her efforts and skills and was contemplating a raise for each of the staff.

"If I got a raise I might buy a bigger Harley," she said as she returned to her office to begin her day.

They were both engrossed in their tasks when the front door opened. Dan looked at the monitor to see a dark skinned man with a cast on his left arm. The man walked past Donna's empty desk to the hallway. Dan reached for his .45 in the top drawer of his desk, but the man, Fernando Lopez stepped into the center of the doorway with a semi-automatic in his hand.

"OK, bookkeeper, keep your hands on the desk." Dan complied. "You have caused me a lot of trouble, Mason. You caused my brother to be killed and got my arm broke. I think I killed a cop last night breaking out of jail. I'm ending this chase right now." He raised the gun to fire, but a small voice behind him made him stop.

"You might want to reconsider," said the voice.

Lopez took a step back and turned to see who was behind him. He was surprised to see a petite young blonde with a Colt .45 in her hands. He grinned at her and moved his gun in her direction. Before he could fire Di pulled the trigger hitting him center mass, driving him two steps backward before he fell.

"You OK, Boss?" she shouted.

"Yes, thanks to you. Is he dead?" he asked.

"I'm pretty sure," was the reply.

"If you're sure, go put your gun on your desk and come in here. I'm calling Gary at Homer PD."

She did as he requested, knowing she would be questioned about the shooting and it wasn't wise to be holding a firearm when the police came to the office.

Gary Fritz and two other officers had arrived at the office just as Donna parked at the front door. She was perplexed by all the activity at her desk in the front office. A police officer stopped her when she entered, but let her inside when she explained she was the receptionist and should be at the front desk. Inside she took off her light jacket and hung it with her purse on the coat rack in front of her desk. When done, she stepped into the hall where Di was standing next to a body on the floor.

"Oh my word, Di, what happened?" asked Donna.

"I shot the guy. I'll tell you about it later. The cops are asking me a lot of questions right now. Go out front and take all the calls. The phone is driving me nuts."

Gary Fritz saw her in the hallway. "Donna, I would appreciate it if you could keep everyone out of the office for a while until we finish our investigation. Can you do that for us?"

"Of course, Gary, I'll be at my desk in the front office," she said, still staring at the body on the floor, her senses overwhelmed by the odors emitting from the body and the smell of burned gunpowder in the air. Onlookers were now gathering outside the office. Each time one of them opened the door to inquire about the shooting she would ask them to leave until the police finished their investigation.

Thomas Finn had been parked in front of the office waiting for Fernando, but sped away when police cars approached. He now waited in his car a block down and across the street watching the activity at the little office complex. Police officers came and went and two hours after the shooting an ambulance came to remove a body from the office. He saw Dan step out of the office to speak with a police officer and return to the office. Now the task was up to him. It would be impossible to attempt it now with all the police activity.

Finn continued to wait in his car and watch the office until late afternoon. He saw the secretary from the front office leave the office. He started his car and checked the Glock on the seat beside him. He saw Dan through the front window of the office approaching the office door. Putting his rental car in gear he began to ease out of his observation place. There was light traffic and he was able to angle toward the turn lane in the center of the main street. As Dan approached the doorway Finn sped into the parking lot in front of the office. He timed it well and stopped just as Dan exited the office. His side window was down. He picked up his Glock with his right hand and pointed it out the window of the car. He was about to pull the trigger when a blond figure rushed from behind Dan to push him out of the way of the shooter. She lifted her shirt to draw the Colt Commander in the hideaway holster.

Finn saw the gun and mashed the gas pedal on his car, at the same time pointing his Glock in the direction of Dan Hanson. He fired twice, missing with both shots. Di fired two shots at the speeding car striking the rear door and window. The car raced from the parking lot while Di held Dan's arm and pulled him back inside the office.

"Are you hit?" she asked.

"No, just scared, that's twice you saved my life today. It's like having a guardian angel looking out for me. Thank you, again."

"I think we should get away from these windows and call Gary." She was being cautious, but with good reason.

Chapter 33

Gary Fritz arrived at the office with a passenger in his car. It was Mitch DeLong. The first question Fritz asked was, "Are you two alright?"

"We were leaving the office and when we opened the door I stepped outside. I was talking with Di and didn't see the car idling in front. He had his window rolled down and when I stepped outside he poked a gun out the window. Di saw the gun and pushed me out of the way. She took out her .45 and fired at the car as it sped away. You probably saw the bullet holes in the front of the building when you came in. He had fired twice at me. I don't think she hit the guy, but he made a run for it. It was Thomas Finn. We have to eliminate him. He's not going to quit until he gets me." Dan recited the report in an excited tone.

"Which way did he go?" asked Fritz.

"He went out the left end of the parking area and turned right, toward the north," reported Di.

Fritz dispatched his other two cruisers to look for Finn's car. The description of the vehicle was on the earlier report. Gary made notes in his little book and asked a few more questions. At that time Mitch joined the conversation.

"This guy Finn is a slippery cuss, Gary. He managed to slip out of the big raid in Miami when we took down the entire drug ring. We seized a fish processing plant, two boats, a truckload of drugs—coke, heroine, meth and marijuana. We also arrested seventy-one people including the big boss in Miami, Diego Garcia. Somehow Finn and the Lopez brothers slipped through. We still don't know if they knew we were coming or if they were just lucky and out of the plant when we raided. He's the main reason I came to Alaska. If your men spot his car they will have to move fast or he'll be gone again. I'm going to call my two agents and have them join in the search. If it's OK with you I'll stay with you Sergeant."

Dan was still shaken, but commented, "I think we should all take Owen's barbeque offer. That way we will all be together for protection and I don't think he knows where Owen lives. That way Gary and his men will have some time to locate Finn."

"That sounds like a good idea, Dan," said Gary Fritz. "Why don't you go with Dan, Mitch? And I'll go help the rest of my men look for Finn."

Mitch agreed to ride with Dan to the home of Owen Sutton with Dierdra following on her Harley Davidson motorcycle. Dan called Owen to let him know they were on the way and to ask if he could bring anything for the cookout.

When they arrived at Owen's home his wife greeted them at the front door. She put an arm around Dan's neck and kissed his cheek. "I heard what happened, Dan. Are all of you alright?"

"Yes, we're fine. There will be one more of us. Donna had an errand to run, but will be here shortly. Are the kids home?"

"Yes, in the back yard with their dad, cooking the salmon and burgers."

The little entourage walked single file following Sutton's wife through the house to the back door and large yard where Owen was sipping a beer and cooking on the grill.

He waved to the group as they emerged from the house. He had not yet heard about the second attack at the office. "Come on down, folks. Have a beer. Mitch DeLong, how are you? Have you met my wife?" Owen handed Mitch a cold beer.

"Yes, we met at the front door. Thanks for the beer."

"We had another shootout at the office this afternoon, Owen," Dan said softly.

Owen was surprised, "Oh, no, was anyone hurt?"

"No, but Di saved me again. She saw the gun and pushed me out of the way and took a couple of shots at him. It was Thomas Finn."

"Dan, you need to marry this gun-totin' woman. You keep drawing gunfire and she keeps saving your hide. It sounds like a match made in heaven. After all, she carries a .45, rides a Harley and wears leather. What more would you want in a woman. She sounds perfect for you." Owen was teasing the both of them.

Mitch laughed, "I agree, Dan. You have needed a bodyguard since the first time I met you in Miami."

"OK, Guys, I admit I've been preoccupied since I came to Homer, but once Finn is out of circulation I may be able to think of romance," Dan admitted.

"Perhaps you could settle for lust over love for a while," commented Owen.

Owen's wife ended the debate. "That's enough," she said. "The children don't need to hear this conversation, for heaven sakes."

"You're right, Ma," said Owen, turning to Di. "Tell me Dierdra, they say every biker names his bike. What's the name of yours?"

"What you heard is true. We love our bikes. Mine is Pegasus, the winged horse. And she can fly." Di spoke with a huge grin and great pride in her Harley.

Now Mitch joined in, "You could do a lot worse than old Dan, here. He flies an airplane, but you can't hold that against him. He can still learn a new trick, like riding a motorcycle."

Dan and Di both laughed.

"I think you have picked on Di and me long enough," said Dan. "I like Di and she saved my life twice today. I owe her more than lust, Owen. In fact I'm going to take her flying soon. Maybe I should take her today to get her away from you two jokers."

Everyone laughed.

Owen checked the grill and said the salmon and burgers were done. "Everyone grab a plate. Salmon, burger or both, and there's corn on the cob on the grill. Salad is on the table along with buns and condiments. Don't be bashful, dig in."

There were three folding tables set with chairs and napkins. Donna found a seat next to Mitch with Di and Dan across from them. Owen and his family occupied the next table.

It turned out to be a pleasant evening, the choice of drinks changed from beer to coffee and sodas. No mention was made of the ongoing search for Thomas Finn. It was later noted that Donna was clinging to the arm of Mitch DeLong while he spoke with Owen and his wife.

Di was carrying two cups of steaming coffee when she came to sit with Dan. "It looks like the boys are matching you and me up," she commented.

"They like to joke, but the truth is I really do like you, Di. Right now it's pretty difficult for me to think about anything but staying alive. I can't thank you enough for staying with me," said Dan. "When this is all over I would like to see you, away from work. We could take the Cessna and go somewhere for dinner, if you're interested."

"I think I would like that, Dan. I'm not as hard as the person I project around the office. I like you very much, too, and I would like to see if we are compatible. You are a special man, Dan." Dan had never seen this soft side of Dierdra, but he liked it very much.

He had a huge grin on his face, "We had better join the others before we really give them a reason to harass us."

It was late and the dinner party ready to break up when Gary Fritz called Owen. "We haven't been able to find him," Gary admitted. "We found his car abandoned on the beach. It looked like Di had hit it twice when he drove away, once in the rear door and once in the rear door window.

Good shooting. We're still looking, but it looks like he got rid of the car and walked back to wherever he is staying. We checked all the hotels and motels, but he isn't registered and no one recognized his description. I think he must have rented a cabin somewhere. Tell Dan I'll have a patrol keep an eye on the hangar tonight."

"I'll tell him, Gary. They're just leaving. I'll see you tomorrow." Owen hung up the phone and relayed the message to his guests.

"Thanks Owen," Dan said as he stepped out onto the front porch. We had a great evening. I'm going to the hangar tonight. I don't think Finn will try anything until tomorrow. Heck, he may have given up and left town." Dan didn't believe that and neither did Owen.

As soon as the office opened the following morning Donna called a carpet cleaning company to rid the office of blood and debris left by the events of the previous day. Dan was in his office working on the last of the Palmer and Wasilla files while Di completed her assessments of the same files. He had asked Donna to set up a meeting schedule for the following week, and he had decided to take both assistants with him on the next trip.

By Friday Mitch had stopped at the office several times "to check on you and speak with Donna." He had taken her to dinner the night before and was asking her to go to lunch with him today. It seemed, to Di and Dan, the couple was getting very cozy.

Dan called to the front office for Mitch to come to his little space. "I was just thinking, Mitch, how would it be if I took you and Donna along with Di and me, to Kenai for lunch? It only takes a few minutes to fly up there and we could spend a relaxing afternoon."

"You fly, I'll buy," Mitch said.

"Good. Tell Donna to close the office for the day. I'll tell Di. You can help me get the plane ready to go. On the way back from Kenai I'll swing over to Chinitna Bay to see how many bears are in the flats near the river."

The air was smooth and the weather good for the flight. The group found a cab in front of the Kenai Airport Terminal for the ride of less than a mile to Louie's Restaurant. The food was excellent and the company was even better. Cathy, the little waitress with the long braid hanging down her back had waited on them and called a cab when they had finished their lunch.

Dan departed Kenai in a westerly direction, crossing Cook Inlet at its narrowest point, nine miles of open water, to fly along the beach viewing seals, whales and bears as they went. He took many side trips to view the volcano, Mt. Redoubt, and look at bears catching fish in the many streams along the way. In Chinitna Bay he slowed the craft and dropped his altitude to a few hundred feet in order to see the bears, bears, and more bears, over 40 in number along the river and beaches. The turbine engine of the Caravan is quiet and the wildlife paid little attention to the red over white Cessna passing overhead.

Commercial salmon fishing boats were in the bay where the fishermen were setting nets for silver salmon, also known as cohoe salmon. Dan made several passes over the bay and grassy flats to allow his passengers to see a sight seldom seen by outsiders. It is this spectacle that makes Alaska the destination of a lifetime for tourists and visitors from all over the world. It also allowed them to forget the events of the past several days that caused so much tension, fear and stress for the group on board this flying carpet.

After the sightseeing portion of the flight Dan flew directly to Homer, a very long, over water flight. The Inlet was full of commercial fishermen, charter fishermen, whales, otters and sea birds. It was a scenic flight enjoyed by all, especially Mitch DeLong who was experiencing it for the first time.

Back on the ground in Homer Donna and Mitch drove away together to visit the Homer Spit and the gift shops lining the roadway. Dan and Di waited together for the fuel truck to come before putting the Cessna back inside the hangar.

Di leaned against the airplane while Dan checked the oil and looked at the engine. "I didn't think there was anything that could compare with riding my motorcycle, but flying with you comes darn close."

"Maybe you can take me for a ride on your bike sometime," Dan commented.

"Any time," she said. Her expression and voice turned sad, "Do you think this Finn guy will try again?"

Dan paused a second before answering, "I'm sorry to say, but yes. He can't quit. He works for the Columbian drug cartel and they won't allow me to live. They were the ones who came after me the first time and killed Alma Petersen. Owen and I caught them by surprise and killed them, but the cartel sent more men. The managers of the Miami operation were killed and the cartel sent more men. The raid DeLong headed arrested and killed the entire operation, and now they are here for me again. I just want it to end." He looked into her sad eyes, "And when it does end I want you to think about building a relationship. I mean a personal relationship, away from the office and other people. I like you a lot, Di, but I can't endanger you any more than I already have. I can't see you getting hurt. I certainly don't want to be the cause. You are too precious to me for that."

"I hope they catch Finn today because I feel the same way. Although, I don't blame you for all that has happened. I think a personal relationship would be nice. I like you very much, too."

The fuel truck arrived, and after refueling, the plane was pushed into the hangar.

Chapter 34

After ditching his car Thomas Finn had gone to the Kachemak Gear Shed to purchase clothing more in keeping with the fisherman look seen around Homer. He bought a flannel shirt, blue jeans, running shoes and a knit cap. It wasn't really a disguise, but changed his look enough he could venture out without being as easily recognized as Thomas Finn. He had been inside his little cabin residence since the confrontation at the office but needed to get out and find Hanson. This had to end and it had to end today.

To take the 'new' off his new wardrobe he took the clothing out to the parking pad in front of the cabin and rubbed them in the dirt. When they were sufficiently soiled and rumpled he returned to the cabin and changed into the grubby attire. Satisfied with the change in appearance he left the small cabin with his handgun stashed under his new flannel shirt. He walked the few blocks to the office building, but it was locked and no one was around. It was nearly a mile to the Duncan House Restaurant where he chose to eat some breakfast. The walk took almost a half hour. He was happy he had not met anyone on the walk and he sat alone in the café without being noticed.

When he finished he decided he should go back to the office to see if Dan had returned. He paid the man at the cash register. He was a pleasant man with a large mustache and wore a baseball type hat. "Have a good day," said Brad the cashier. Finn waved a reply and began his walk back to the office building. During the walk a Homer City patrolman passed him, looked him over and kept on driving. The change of clothing had worked.

When he approached the office there were two women inside as well as a carpet cleaning company truck parked in front. He could hear the large vacuum in the back of the truck running and see the large hose stretched to the inside of the office. Hanson's Jeep was nowhere to be seen. Finn decided to cross the street to a roadside bench on the other side where he could sit and watch the office without attracting attention.

Nearly an hour later Dan drove up in front of the office and parked in front of the carpet cleaner's truck. There was another man with him. It was Mitch DeLong. The two stepped inside the office, out of sight. Finn knew this was a poor place to make his move, but was running out of options since the police were out looking for him.

He reached under his shirt to pull his semi-automatic from the shoulder holster he wore. There were two new loaded clips for the weapon in his pants pocket. Pulling the slide, he checked to be sure there was a cartridge in the chamber. He reached into his pants pocket to retrieve one of the new clips in case he needed to reload in a hurry. He decided to use Dan Hanson's Jeep as his mode of escape and would need to retrieve the key fob from Dan's body when he finished his work.

Finn took a deep breath and crossed the street to the office, keeping the handgun out of sight until he was entering the office. The noise of the vacuum truck prevented anyone in the office from hearing him enter.

Donna was behind her desk, wiping it down with a disinfectant wipe when he entered. She noticed him come inside but didn't recognize him. "I'm sorry, but the office is closed for some cleaning and remodeling." She spoke to the newcomer without getting up from her chair.

Finn didn't answer, but pulled the automatic from under his arm and aimed it at Donna. She was about to scream when he pulled the trigger, the bullet striking her in the upper chest and killing her instantly.

Dan and Mitch were in Dan's little office when they heard the shot over the sound of the cleaners. Both men instantly ripped their own weapons from the holsters and moved toward the doorway. Dierdra, too, heard the shot and, reaching for her own weapon, raced toward her office door.

Finn had stopped to check the condition of his first victim giving Di time to attempt to close the hall door. The hoses from the vacuum truck blocked the door and prevented her from closing the armored passage. She immediately motioned for the two men cleaning the hall to get into the small coffee room to their left. Dan was now in the hall pointing his gun at the gunman in the outer office. Finn was now turning his attention to the people he could see in the hall. He fired two shots, the first striking Dan in the lower part of his left arm. The second shot missing as Dan fell to the floor. Di had jumped back into her own office and Mitch was now standing over Dan firing rapidly at the man near the desk in the front office.

Finn went down, being struck twice by the hail of bullets from Mitch DeLong's weapon. The wounds, however, didn't stop him from firing. He pointed the gun toward the hallway, unable to sight a target properly because of his wounds, but fired his weapon three more times before being struck in the head by a bullet from Dan's weapon which he had fired from a prone position on the hallway floor.

Di was in her office dialing 911 while Mitch was checking the condition of the attacker. He was dead. He returned to the hall to check on Dan and his wound, but Dan was now on his feet, holding his left arm. The wound was bleeding severely, but the bullet had not done serious injury to his arm.

The two carpet cleaning men ran from the office to shut down the noisy vacuum and get away from the gunfire. With the truck vacuum turned off, sirens could be heard as the police approached the scene. Gary Fritz was the first to arrive. He entered with his weapon drawn. Mitch told him the scene was now secure.

Gary returned his weapon to its holster as two more officers arrived. Fritz asked one of the officers to call the troopers for an investigator to assist at the scene.

Di had also called an ambulance for Dan and was in his office at his side, attending to the wound. "Oh, Dan, I was so frightened when I saw you go down. I was afraid you were killed."

"I'll be OK, Di. Thanks for your quick thinking."

Mitch and Gary were now at the door of Dan's office. "How are you, Pal?" asked Mitch.

"It hurts like the devil, but I don't think it's too bad. Did we get Finn?"

"Good shooting, Dan," commented Mitch. "He's dead."

Gary was now attempting to take charge of the crime scene. "OK, I want everyone out of the office. The investigator will be here soon and I don't want the scene contaminated. Dan, the ambulance is coming to take you to the hospital to have your arm looked at. I'm guessing Di will want to go with you. Mitch and I can stay here and wait for the trooper. I'm sorry about Donna, Dan. Finn killed her, too."

Dan's shoulders drooped and he hung his head attempting to hold back tears of grief. "First Alma and now Donna, none of this should have ever happened. They were both innocent bystanders in all this. I'm so sorry."

"Finn and the cartel are responsible for their deaths, Dan, not you. Don't accept their guilt. You did nothing wrong and there was no way you could have done any more to prevent their deaths," said Mitch, "now go get in the ambulance. I'll come see you later."

The ambulance had just pulled into the parking area near the vacuum truck. Dan and Di went outside to meet with the EMTs.

It was mid-afternoon when the scene was cleared by the trooper and Mitch was able to get away to the hospital to learn his friend's condition. Dan was in the process of being discharged from the emergency care unit when he arrived.

"Come on, you two. I'll give you a ride back to the office and you can take your own Jeep. I think Di should drive you, though. The drugs they gave you while they sewed you up are enough to keep you out of the driver's seat. Besides she makes a good nurse."

"If she's my nurse, I'm going to need a lot of care," Dan joked.

Dan was on his bed in the hangar, sleeping off the drugs when Mitch came late that evening to visit. Di was in the small kitchen fixing some soup and crackers for his dinner and about to wake him when Mitch entered the hangar.

"Want some soup, Mitch?" she asked.

"No thanks, I just came to see the cripple. Is he awake?"

"I'm just going up to awaken him. He needs to get up and eat some dinner."

Mitch was sitting at the little table in the small kitchen when the two of them came down from the loft. "How do you feel, Dan?"

"Not too bad, I guess. Thanks for being there for me today, Mitch. I owe you, big time."

"You owe me nothing, Dan. You gave me what I needed to shut down one of the largest drug importing businesses on the east coast. I owe you."

"Yeah, Mitch, about Miami, there's something I need to tell you. I have to get it off my chest in order for me to get on with my life on a clean slate."

"Oh, yes, Dan, there was one thing I wanted to tell you. Do you remember when the first two bosses at Bluefin Seafood shot each other?" asked Mitch.

"Yes, that's one of the things I needed to talk with you about."

"It was a funny thing about that shooting. The Miami police said the two men shot each other. I didn't like that conclusion at the time, but the more I think about it the more I think it happened just that way. Those two bad guys had a disagreement and shot each other. A lot of people do that, you know, get mad and charge into the other person's office with the intent of getting even. Sometime it works out and sometime it doesn't. It looks like this time it worked out and the right people got even.